TAKING MEGHAN

DISCIPLES 5

IZZY SWEET

SEAN MORIARTY

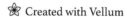 Created with Vellum

ABOUT THIS BOOK

Alexei Rastov is the most vile, evil, despicable man in the world...

And my father tried to force me to marry him.

Dragged down the aisle, I prayed to God, to anyone, to save me from a lifetime of cruelty and abuse.

Then he came... a force of nature...

Disrupting the ceremony with a storm of gunfire and death.

Massive, powerful, and handsome, the enemy of my enemy has promised me his protection if I agree to give myself to him.

But sometimes the devil you know is safer than the dark angel who wants you in his bed...

PROLOGUE

Meghan

One month ago
Bethlehem

"I TAKE it you called me here because everything went off as planned?" a smooth Russian voice drifts into the hallway outside my father's office.

My father is so confident, so fucking brazen, he didn't even bother to close the door. No, it sits wide open, allowing anyone and everyone walking by to overhear. He either has supreme faith in our household's devotion and loyalty, or he's grown stupider and stupider over the years.

I'm inclined to believe the latter.

"Yes. The target, Lucky Tails, is..." My father pauses. There's a metallic clink followed by the unmistakable sound of a lighter being sparked. "No more."

"Good... good." The Russian chuckles and then the old, stiff leather of my father's chair creaks. Someone inhales and exhales. "Any notable causalities?"

A wispy white cloud of smoke floats out of the room.

The lighter clinks shut and my father seems to hesitate before reluctantly admitting, "Only our inside contact."

"I trust you're taking care of that?"

Again, my father hesitates, and it gives me great joy to know it pains him to admit his failures.

"My men are on it. Her house is being dealt with as we speak."

Her?

"Very good," the Russian says, sounding pleased, and then there's a long moment of silence.

I shift uncomfortably on my feet and glance down the hallway, my ears straining. If any of my father's staff catches me eavesdropping on him, I'll be beaten and locked inside my room for the next twenty years.

But I need to know why my father called me home from school. I need to know why he's locked me up in this house. Why he won't let me leave or contact anyone. Why all my IDs, credit cards, cash, computers, and phones have been confiscated...

And I have this awful, dreadful feeling that the answer is enjoying a cigar with him in that room.

"Alexei?" my father finally says, breaking the tense silence.

"Yes?" the Russian drawls out.

"I've fulfilled my side of the bargain..."

"You have," Alexei answers simply, and it's obvious even to me that he's playing my father like a fiddle.

How my father retains his control over the Callahan family is a mystery even to me. I suppose most of it is due to a great deal of luck and opportunity. Most of the other Irish families in this part of the country have been wiped out by the Italians, causalities in a senseless turf war.

There simply aren't enough powerful men left to overthrow him.

"I believe it's time to take the next step and solidify our alliance."

An alliance between the Irish and Russians... Just the thought makes me sick to my stomach.

What is this world coming to?

Hasn't there been enough death? Enough bloodshed?

"Indeed," Alexei says, sounding strangely pleased. "Is she here?"

She, as in *me*? Fuck. I'm currently the only 'she' in residence. My beloved mother passed away in a car bombing a year ago. My father blamed it on the Italians, but I know deep in my heart it was the Irish, this family, that killed her. The Italians may have set the bomb, but she would have never been in any danger if it wasn't for this damn family.

"Yes. I called her home two weeks ago."

Double fuck. I wish for once in my life that my gut was wrong. Why they need me to solidify their alliance though still doesn't make any sense.

Unless... but no... that's too old school and beyond archaic.

My father is a bastard of the highest degree, but I still refuse to believe he'd force me to marry a man I don't want to marry. There's still a touch of decency inside him. Still a touch of compassion for the only blood he has left...

"I trust she's been prepared and knows what will be expected of her? I'd hate to have to break her in..."

Even as the blood drains from my face, I can picture my father's face flushing bright red as he sputters with indignation. "My Meghan is a fine, upstanding young lass, and would make any man proud."

God, what the fuck? Have I time-travelled back to the eighteenth century? This can't be real.

Alexei chuckles as if he finds my father's statement amusing, and then says, "You mean *my* Meghan."

The way he says it, at first it comes off almost casual, but there's a firmness there. Beneath the left-over amusement of his chuckle lurks something dangerous. Something that causes all the little hairs on my body to stand on end and my skin to prickle with apprehension.

To be married to that man... to be owned by him...

It's simply unthinkable. I'm not a fucking object to be bargained off. I'm a person, goddammit.

Even my father is thrown off guard by Alexei's declaration. "Y—yes," he stammers and clears his throat. "Of course. Your Meghan."

Someone inhales, then another cloud of smoke drifts into the hallway, giving this whole scene playing out in front of me a hazy, almost dream-like quality.

Maybe I'm dreaming and this is all a nightmare.

"That's relieving to hear," Alexei says after a moment. "Because my sources tell me you allowed her to move across the country to attend university in California. Unchaperoned. Left to her own devices. Her young mind vulnerable to the corruption of the liberal agenda."

There's this sad, almost desperate quality to my father's voice as he rushes to explain. "It isn't safe here. With the Italian bastards growing bolder and bolder with Lucifer's backing, I let her go. I couldn't risk losing her..."

"Still, who knows what kind of thoughts have already tainted her pretty little head? I require complete and utter obedience. Anything less is simply... unacceptable."

"You will have it," my father declares with entirely too much confidence.

He's either lying through his teeth or he truly believes it. And if he truly believes it, I don't know what parallel universe he's living in. I wasn't raised to be a dutiful, submissive wife. I was raised like any other normal American child. Brought up to believe I can be anyone or anything I put my mind to if I work hard enough. My mother saw to that, God rest her soul.

"If she gives me any trouble, any trouble at all... You understand, I'll have to take certain unpleasant measures to ensure her complete and utter obedience and cooperation?"

"She will not give you any trouble. She wants vengeance for her mother as much as I do."

So that's what this is about? That's why my father is willing to trade me off like I'm chattel? Vengeance?

I hear my father huff in a deep, ragged breath before he adds defeatedly, "And she knows it's only a matter of time before those damned Italians get me and her too..."

The blood chills in my veins. I've known my father

long enough to know he truly believes what he just said.

Yet he's never let on that I was in any danger. He let me believe he was indulging me when he approved my move to California.

"Ah... well..." Alexei says like he's bored and could care less. "Once I walk out of this room, that will no longer be a worry, yes? She, and by extension, you, will be under my protection."

"Yes... yes, yes," my father mumbles distractedly in agreement.

"Good. Now, where is this bride-to-be of mine? I'd like to meet her in the flesh before I depart."

And that's my cue to leave. I need to find some way to get out of this house. Some way to escape before my father can force me to do this. Force me to sell myself to save us both.

I start to slowly, quietly back away from the door before my father calls out for me, freezing me in place. "Meghan?"

Fuck. Fuck. Fuck.

He's not the stupid one, I am. He left that door open because he *wanted* me to hear. He wants me to know.

"Meghan?" he calls out again while I hesitate, unsure what the fuck I should do. "Please come here."

Run... I should run. But where to?

Every door is guarded. Every car locked. I have no

money, no ID, no one I'm willing to risk putting in danger to call.

I'm trapped like a fucking rat. Maybe earlier I could have gotten away... but not now.

"Meghan," my father says, growing impatient.

There's no doubt in my mind that he knows I'm standing right here. I'm so fucking predictable, he anticipated it.

Dammit. I'm my own worst enemy.

My mind races, trying to think up a way to get out of this.

I could throw a fit. I could barge in there and declare that there's no way, no fucking way, I'm marrying that Russian.

But what good will that do me? My father? Anyone?

It certainly won't do me any favors. They'll probably beat me or worse to get me to go along with their plan.

The way I see it, I only have two choices. I can balk, resist, and fight—and suffer the consequences, whatever they may be.

Or I can go along with this entire sham for the time being.

"Meghan," my father says more firmly, and I hear the leather of his chair creaking.

No doubt he's getting up to come get me.

Mind racing, I come up with the perfect plan.

I can let them believe I'm docile, compliant.

Even obedient.

Gag.

I can be the perfect little daughter, the perfect little fiancé.

And as soon as they're not looking, as soon as their heads are turned the other way...

I'll run and never fucking look back.

1

GABRIEL

Staring through the windshield of Simon's SUV, I can't help but think that things couldn't be looking up for me any more than they are right now. I was in prison for ten years, only to get kicked out like a fucking roach in the kitchen...

All so I can cause some bedlam and mayhem.

Fuck, maybe my life isn't over just yet.

The hum of the wheels on the asphalt feels almost like a dream, and it's cold as fuck outside when I open the window a bit to let some fresh air in, but damn does it feel good on my face.

"You've got this car as hot as my nutsack, Simon. You roasting your little balls for the holidays?" I ask, turning toward him.

"It's never too late to let you walk to the truck stop,"

he snarls as he leans toward his door. "Though the fresh air does help with your offending smell."

Asshole thinks he'd be able to get away with leaving me in his dust...

That's fucking doubtful. I'll fucking kill him before he gets the chance to leave my ass to rot anywhere again.

Lucifer asked me to take the fall for what happened ten years ago, but it doesn't mean I'll ever go back. Fuck that shit. I've had enough cramped spaces and isolation to last me a lifetime.

"The smell's from living in a six by eight cell with nothing but time. Fuck your delicate sensibilities," I say as I spot the sign for the truck stop we'll be stopping at.

"Delicate..." Simon chuckles as he hits the blinker for us to merge off the interstate.

"Why'd the Devil bring me out, Simon?" I ask him quietly.

I was the sacrificial lamb. The one to take the fall for the carnage Lucifer needed.

Lucifer said he'd get me out before I went in, but I think we both knew that wasn't going to happen. And if that fucker, Simon, had his way, I'd still be in prison. After a couple of years, I figured Lucifer felt the same way. I mean, I'm the one who wiped out the rest of the family when he took over. Even his uncle.

"Like I said, he wants Garden City to be brought

back under his control. We've been hit too many times from forces outside his sphere of influence."

"What forces?" I ask, trying to remember exactly who the powerholders were ten years ago.

"Like I told you earlier, the Yakuza, Russians, and Saudis, just to name a few," Simon says with obvious annoyance as we pull into the parking lot.

"The Saudis?" I ask with a snort, remembering he did mention them. "How the hell did Lucifer manage to piss those sand-fuckers off?"

"He didn't. My wife did," Simon says as I hop out of the car.

Looking back to the SUV, I watch as he sits there, waving me on. I guess he can't risk contracting a cold from the truck stop.

Fucking pussy.

Stepping into the store, I look around and finally feel something akin to freedom. I can buy any drink I want. I can eat anything I feel like, and I don't have to worry about some fucking guard coming in to slap his wooden baton up against my head for the hell of it.

I slip my hand down into the bag Simon handed me when I got in his car and fish around for a wallet. Pulling it out, I open it to see what John gave me. Knowing that fucker, it probably has some chick's driver's license in it.

Flipping through the wallet, though, I'm pleasantly surprised. There's an updated driver's license for me and a couple of brand new credit cards. That, and the thousand or so in cash, help me feel like I won't have to be too reliant on Simon.

CLIMBING BACK INTO THE SUV, I smirk as Simon looks at me in revulsion.

"I thought you were going to shave the beard completely off, at least. You know, try to advance past the Neanderthal stage of your life," he sneers at me as I close the door.

"Nah, I think I'll keep this scruff on a bit longer. Bugs the fuck out you, doesn't it?" I ask with a smirk.

"Infantile ass," Simon mutters as he opens up his glove compartment and hands me a little black plastic thing with a glass top.

"The fuck is this?" I ask as I look down at the screen.

"A phone. Technology has come a long way since you went in," he says as he pulls out of the parking lot.

Heading back to the highway, he motions to the phone.

"Push the button at the bottom, that pulls it out of rest. Once it's up, the icons should be self-explanatory," he says with a laugh, and I'm pretty damn sure it's because of my lack of knowledge when it comes to technology.

Pushing the button on the phone, I watch as the screen comes to life and feel as if I really am a caveman coming into the twenty-first century. I swipe where the screen says swipe and reveal what looks like a computer desktop.

Fuck me. I guess things have come a lot further than I thought.

"Interesting," I say as I shove the phone into my pocket. "Where we headed?"

"Matthew is having a little get-together to welcome you home. It should be right up your alley, if you haven't turned into a rat while you were in prison."

"Yeah, yeah. Suck a dick," I grumble and lean my head against the glass of the car door.

Motherfucker knows I didn't turn rat.

Folding my arms across my chest, I slip into a slow doze as I think of the things that could be waiting for me once I get out of this car. I highly doubt it's going to be a balloons-and-cake kind of event.

I can feel my eyelids growing heavier as I shift enough to feel the comfortable presence of the forty-caliber pistol snuggled into my hip holster. It's been a long time since I've had my little mistress at my side, and I ain't going to lie, it's giving me a sense of peace that helps me feel better about falling asleep.

Violence gives me purpose, something beyond sitting in a cell block waiting for death to come.

Violence gives me the power to take control of the world.

MY DREAMS ARE FUCKED UP. In my mind's eye, I can see everything floating around me in a crimson lake of fire. There are bodies bloated from the gases built-up after death. Charred planks of wood surround them, encased in frames.

Snapping awake, I go from frozen, unable to move, to instantly putting my hand on the gun nestled at my hip.

Old habits die hard.

Even back in prison, I'd go reaching for my gun when the guards would start in on me. Not having it is the only reason they're still breathing.

I just need to get the fuck out of this SUV. I've been confined for too long, and sitting in this car for hours is starting to get to me.

Too much surrounds me. Seats, heat, windows, and another human are just too fucking much to deal with right now.

Just before I start putting fucking holes in every-thing around me, Simon pulls up to our destination.

Lucifer's favorite little hidey-hole of torture.

Getting quickly out of the car, I slam the door behind me and take in my old killing grounds.

The old sheet metal warehouse looks exactly the same as it always has—like it's about to fall down around its concrete footers. I have no doubt Lucifer has spent money to keep it this way. When I look closer at the 'rusted' beams keeping things in place, I can tell he's had them painted to look that way.

I guess this place will stay up and looking this way as long as he has a use for it. A use for violence and answers.

"What's the situation we're heading into?" I ask as I walk beside Simon.

His gimpy ass tries to take the lead and walk in front of me, but he doesn't have the sack to take the pain his cracked ribs will cause him. That's his problem, he's never had to endure pain long enough that you come to crave it just a little. Crave how it keeps you sharp.

Crave how it feeds the anger and violence pent up inside you.

"Same as always. We have someone who annoys us, and we need to get all the information we can from him," Simon says as we open the heavy steel door of the building.

Inside, the cold isn't as bracing. The spring winds that rip through Garden City are shut out.

A high-pitched wailing scream suddenly pierces the air, and the sound causes a bit of that old, familiar excitement to pump through my heart.

I missed being on the outside of the cage. Missed being able to hurt people when I needed to, and when I just felt like it.

I'll be the first to admit that there's nothing healthy about my brain. I like to cause people pain, and I don't mind watching the light dim from someone's eyes.

"Sounds like they started without me," I say as I walk past Simon. "No need to show me the way, gimpy. I know it."

"You miserable, suffering cunt," Simon hisses as I leave him behind.

"Yeah, so was your mother," I say over my shoulder.

Walking through the rows of unused machinery, I wonder how much of this shit was used before Lucifer bought the building. Used for different, more legitimate purposes, no doubt.

"Just hold the asshole still, James. Jesus fucks a mule, hold him down!" I hear a loud, gruff voice shouting over what sounds like a gagged-asshole trying to yell his head off.

For the first time in what feels like an eternity, I feel the blood starting to course through my veins.

It's like getting fucking high, but so much better.

Walking into the room, I stop short as I take in the scene unfolding before my eyes. A man strapped into an old metal chair bucks and thrashes as he rages behind a taped-up mouth. He's got that Eastern European look to him, and from the tats on his chest, I can tell he's been inside a Gulag. Long years in a Gulag, if I'm reading those tats right. He's one tough fucker, and I'm betting he's got stars on his knees.

So this is my welcome home present.

Removing my coat, I stand in place for a long moment, just watching the room. Most of the guys are here, and the ones that aren't are most likely dead.

Sucks for them, I guess.

"Gentlemen," I say, and the words annoy me because my throat aches as I talk.

I haven't talked this much in ten fucking years.

Almost as one, Andrew, James, Jude, Johnathan, and Lucifer, all turn to look at me. Each one has a different expression on their face, and it's startling to me that I can read the emotions now when all I ever saw for so long were the cold emotionless faces of the guards.

Everyone's all smiles that reach their eyes, even dear old Lucifer. The man I spent ten long fucking years in a cell for. From what Simon said, I probably would have spent the rest of my life there if they didn't get the governor in their pocket.

They know I didn't rat on them, but the fucker in the chair will mostly likely be my baptism back into the family.

Instead of water, I'll be christened in blood and murder.

John takes three long strides over to me, his arms

opening up as he tries to wrap me up in a hug. He stops short though when he looks into my eyes. He knows better than to touch me right now. He spent enough time in a cell.

Nodding his head, he shoves a hand out to me. "Good having you back, brother."

I force myself to shake his hand then look over to the rest of the guys. After nodding to them all, I focus on Lucifer.

He's perched on the side of a desk and his face is pensive now. He knows I served a long ass time for him, and I'm betting he's trying to figure out where we stand with each other.

I've done time for this man's will and sins. I did ten long fucking years in a cage. Ten long years of beatings. Ten years of my sanity slowly slipping into this dead husk that's now who I am. All that I have left inside me is rage and barely controlled destruction.

My hands clench into fists so tight I can feel my nails threatening to break the skin on my palms.

Ten long fucking years for my crimes, for his crimes. I should have been in the chair, though. I should've fucking fried for all the things I've done in my life.

But I'm out now.

And like I said earlier, I'll fucking kill anyone who ever dreams of putting me through the system again.

I should have killed them for even doing it in the first place.

That thought rips through my mind as I stare at the man. The devil. From this distance I won't miss. He'd be dead in a matter of seconds.

Dead at the hands of his own fucking hellhound.

He holds my stare without flinching or apologizing. He knows what I've done for him. He knows the lengths I went through to keep him on the outside.

I'm not sure how long we stare at each other, but the tension in the room grows so thick I can't fucking stand it. Before I snap and start punching all the shit around me, I decide the unfinished business we have will have to wait until later.

Walking over to him, I pull my gun from its holster and hold it firmly in my hand. "Matt, been a long time."

"It has," Lucifer says to me when I call him by his real name. "That gun for me?"

The corners of my lips quirk up and I hold the gun a little longer than necessary, letting him wonder what I plan on doing with it, before I set it down beside him.

I nod my head and the tension in the room instantly evaporates.

And I feel like I fucking *belong* again.

"You still have my gun as long as you need it," I say, cementing my place back in the family.

Lucifer nods his head and then visibly relaxes. He

even smiles when he stands up from the desk and straightens his jacket. Then he motions to the man that's strapped to the chair.

His eyes light up with amusement as he says, "John was wanting to castrate him, but I said you had better ideas."

Chuckling, I turn to look over at Johnathan, giving Lucifer my back. "Still with the dicks, dude? You remind me of my boyfriend in prison, Doug."

"Oh shit," I hear Lucifer mutter behind me.

"Dude, you went gay in prison?" James asks me.

"No, you jackass. Your dick rot off yet?" I ask him with a grin.

"No glove, no love. My shit's good." He smirks.

Nodding my head, I take in the men surrounding me again. It feels good to be back among my brothers. But at the same time, I can feel the space closing in on me. They're too fucking close. Too fucking happy. Lucifer and his band of merry fucking men.

Too fucking close.

"Can we stop the tomfoolery and actually work?" Simon asks with an annoyed huff.

Well fuck, I never thought I'd be grateful for Simon, but he's giving me a valid reason to move the fuck away and put some space between me and everyone.

I walk over to the restrained Russian, all the while keeping an eye on the guys.

Simon's face flushes as he slowly removes his outer coat. The pain in his ribs must be getting to him.

Shit, if I'm not mistaken John isn't as spry as he normally is, either. He's hunched just enough to show me he's got a wound somewhere.

Fuck. Taking another look around me, I see all the gaps and missing faces. I'm not fully up to date with all that's happened since I was locked up, but if it's as bad as Simon has been saying, we're missing a lot of men.

I know Paul and Peter are dead, but what about the others?

"Where's Thomas and Bart? They out on assignment? What about Thad?" I ask.

The silence around me is instant and deafening.

Searching their faces, hard resignation stares back at me. All except Andrew. Andrew's face tells me all I need to know.

"What the fuck happened?" I ask.

"Bart betrayed us. Thomas took a bullet because of him," Andrew says.

Damn.

Thomas was a good man. Quiet as could be, but solid as a fucking rock.

"Where's Bart?" I ask.

"Dead," Lucifer says with a sigh. "Peter and Paul are both gone. Peter was blown up investigating our recent bombings, and Paul... He died protecting Evelyn and Abigail."

"Who are they?" I ask.

And that question causes another fucking silence.

"Evelyn is my daughter, and Abigail is Andrew's," Lucifer says with a smile.

"Your what?" I ask with surprise.

This has to be a joke, right?

"Dude, me and Jude are the only ones who haven't gotten pussied up. Everyone's married and shit." James motions to the guys around him.

"What?" I ask again and stare at the guys. "And Thad?"

"Thaddeus went back to Ohio to help the Italians. He's trying to help plug a bunch of holes over there," Andrew grunts. "Fucker's been out there living like a playboy while the rest of us are here in the trenches."

"We have a lot to talk about, but first lets get to work," Simon says as he points to the Russian. "We need to know what the fuck is going on."

"Someone blew up our strip club with a shit ton of people inside. Cherry got wasted, and when Peter was searching her house, they took him out with a big ass bomb," Johnathan says as he walks over to stand beside me.

Both of us look down at the guy, and he starts to yell from behind his gag.

"What else?" I ask.

"The Yakuza have been causing us more issues," Simon says.

When I give him a look, he explains, "Awhile back, a drug deal went south in Ohio and a guy got five million off of us."

"Five fucking mil?" I ask, incredulous. "What the fuck? How'd he get that much?"

"It was a mistake that was remedied, but with it came the Yakuza and Russians. This all falls back to that five million loan. Since then, we've been at war with both groups," Lucifer says.

"The Russians are claiming no responsibility for the bombings though, and have offered peace talks through Father Coss. Which doesn't sound right coming from them. The Yakuza have been silent throughout all of this, except for the attempt on mine and Meredith's life," Simon says.

Ah, shit. That old fucker's still around. I thought he was fucking dead.

"I'm not going to see that asshole," I say.

And now comes the laughter, and I've got a feeling I'm the butt of a joke.

"What?" I ask.

"He's asked to see you already," Lucifer says with a smirk.

"Send James," I say as I move over to an empty desk.

Dropping my coat on it, my new phone falls out of the pocket and clatters against the floor.

Squatting down to pick it up, James starts to hand it

to me before snapping it out of my reach.

"Simon gave you this, right?" he asks.

"Yeah, though I have no clue what the fuck I'm supposed to do with it. I mean, phones are for making calls. Why the hell do I have a computer screen on it?" I ask.

Eyes wide, James breaks out in a grin. "I'll set it up for you. Simon's too fucking stupid to do it right."

With a shrug, I say, "Sounds good. But what the hell do you do with 'em?"

"You do remember the internet, right?" he asks.

"Yeah, that's where all the porn is at?" I smirk.

"Something like that. Oh, and no chance. I already did my confessional time back in elementary school," he says as he starts tapping on my phone's screen.

He must be in his own little world now because he looks like some happy kid who just got a Christmas present.

"I want to visit the graves," I say quietly to James.

Looking up from the phone, he stares at me for a moment and then nods. "I made sure they were buried properly. I'll take you over there."

Heading back over to Lucifer, Simon, and the rest of the guys, I motion to our current warehouse resident.

"Don't forget the Saudis, though," James says to us from where he's sitting.

"Yes, but they have been handled for the time being. We'll discuss them later," Lucifer says.

"One of you is going to need to give me the rundown on just what the fuck's been going on since I left," I say.

Shrugging his shoulders, Jude says, "I've been out of the state for almost a year. I just about shit when I came back and found everyone fucking wifed up with kids running around."

"What?" I ask.

"Bullshit! Not this guy," James says, raising his hand over his head while he keeps working on the phone.

"Okay, except James." Jude shrugs.

I can feel a fucking throbbing pulse of pain forming behind my eyes as I try to adjust to everything that's been thrown at me. Bombings, millions of dollars lost, wives and children.

When the fuck did crime become so fucking complicated?

"Let's get this show on the road, gentlemen. Meredith and I have plans for the evening." Simon says.

Motioning to the Russian, I ask, "Does he need to be alive at the end of this? What do we know about him?"

"That fully depends on him. If he gives us the

information we need, then he might be able to go free. But I doubt he'll make this easy," Lucifer says.

This fucker's a corpse already. No way we'd let him go after this.

"His name is Anton Yelchin..." Simon says. "Yes, just like the actor."

"Huh?" I ask.

"Never mind, you were in prison. We found him flying into Bethlehem three days ago, under a different identity of course. I'm willing to bet, though, he's just a testing rat for the Russians. They're seeing where they can get in without our notice. Bethlehem is close, and they've been using it as a staging area. They want easy access to us."

"Bethlehem is another powder keg that's full of rats." Johnathan says.

"When the fuck did Bethlehem go to the fucking rats?" I ask as I look around at everyone.

Spreading his hands out in a what-can-you-do gesture, Lucifer says "We've had our hands full with getting Garden City under our full control. If it wasn't the Russians, it was the Yakuza, or the crack-slinging gangs that are sprouting up here and there."

That doesn't surprise me, although it probably should. I've been gone for ten years. A lot can happen to a place in that long of a stretch.

Time to do something I've had to keep bottled up

for ten long fucking years. Ten years and I finally get to do what I've always done best.

I get to hurt someone.

Squatting down in front of our special guest, I ask, "You speak English?"

The man just stares at me. He was squealing like a stuck pig when I walked in here, but I'm betting he thinks we're just going to give him a good scare and he'll get to go home. He's not too big of a guy, probably fifty or so pounds lighter than me, and at least six or seven inches shorter.

He's trying to act tough to the big man in front of him. He's been in prison though, so he might just make it past the first couple of rounds with me.

"Simon, can I use your black bag?" I ask without looking away from Anton.

"Of course," Simon says, and I hear him shuffle behind me.

There's a loud plop as he drops his bag down beside me.

Anton's eyes barely shift from my face, but they do. Just a brief flutter of movement.

"Now Anton, I know you're gagged, but you need to nod your head if you can speak English," I say quietly.

Nothing comes from him. He's trying to act hard, like the interrogation isn't going to break him down.

That's fine, I've got all night if need be.

Reaching up, I push his sweaty hair out of his eyes. He needs to see the mistake he just made.

"Alright, man. That was your only chance to answer me without pain. I'm going to start causing you some now. I won't be asking any questions during it, though. But don't worry, you'll have a chance to talk after I'm done," I say as I pull the black bag from my side.

Inside, I find all kinds of toys. Most of the metal instruments were originally meant to heal. No longer, though, Not here in this place of hell.

"Jude, I'm going to need his right leg secured from the knee to the foot," I say as I pull out a scalpel.

Jude moves instantly to grab ratchet straps to help me secure the leg.

That gets Anton's attention. He starts trying to buck up in his chair.

John moves to my side, preparing to calm Anton down with his fists, but I wave him off.

Looking down at the scalpel, I examine its razor-sharp edge.

"Ah fuck, I'm out." John grimaces and walks away to sit with Lucifer.

Jude looks up from Anton and shrugs his shoulder at the work of the ratchet straps. "This tight enough?"

"Yeah, I don't want to push all his blood down there. Don't want him bleeding out," I say.

Anton has calmed a bit now. His eyes are practically bulging out of his skull, but he's trying to play the hard-ass who isn't scared.

"Anton, I'm going to give your leg a skin avulsion from the knee to the foot," I say as I cut into the jeans covering his leg. "This shit's going to hurt, not gonna lie about that. You'll probably pass out from this, but we'll wait until you're awake to ask another question."

He's got a couple of tats on his leg that look like they're straight out of the jailhouse, but they're well done.

That's a shame.

"I'm going to ruin your ink, man."

Lifting the pant leg up and over his knee, I look at the stars tattooed there. "Your boy here's a made man with the Russians."

"Then he should have plenty to talk about," Simon says.

"Sure, looks like it," I say, and then look Anton in the eyes.

He may have given a bunch of oaths over in Russia about how loyal he is, but I doubt they'll hold true here.

Pushing the scalpel into his shin bone, I work slowly around his calf.

His screams reach past his gag and fill the room with the sounds of pain.

Blood spills out of the wound. As the life sustaining

fluid runs over my hands, I almost feel like I'm washing my hands clean of ten years of restraint.

"Jude, push down on his shoulders. James, I'm—" I start to say, but James immediately shoots me down.

"Nope. I did a face peel with Simon recently. I've filled my quota," James says, and I can tell he won't be budged from that.

Just what the fuck did I miss? Simon's been doing face peels without me? Well fuck, looks like big brother has grown up without me around. I used to be the one who did shit like that for Lucifer. Now it's like everyone has been doing my fucking job.

"Looks like it's just you, me, and Jude," I say to Anton.

Digging my fingers into the wound, I push past the hypodermis until I hit bone.

Pulling down isn't exactly an easy job, given all the blood. Makes things a bit slippery.

Midway down, I stop and look up at Anton. He's screaming and his eyes are almost rolled completely back. He's about to go under.

"Remember, Anton, I told you I wouldn't ask you anything until I'm done with this," I say, and then yank as hard as I can down his leg.

It's like skinning a deer. I feel the fat and hypodermis ripping away from what's beneath it. Then I push the flesh down until it folds up like a pair of pants when a guy's sitting on the shitter.

"And... he's out for the count, ref," Jude says with a laugh.

"He lasted longer than I thought he would," I say as I stand up from where I've been kneeling.

Anton screamed until I reached the bottom of his ankle.

"I would have told you my mom's social by mid-calf. Then again, that crack-headed bitch would have given me to you for a twenty spot," Jude says with a shrug.

He's right, that bitch was one careless whore.

Looking through Simon's bag, I spot a small bag of vials with fresh needles. "You got anything to wake him up with?"

"Yes. I stumbled across a cocktail mix a few years ago from a CIA dossier. It wakes them up pretty quickly, but it plays hell on the heart and respiratory system after too many uses," Simon says.

"Eh, not like this fucker's going to need either of those in a couple of hours," I say and hand the bag back to Simon.

Simon quickly pulls a vial and syringe from the bag.

Handing both of them to me, he says, "Into the neck artery is the quickest method of getting him to come around."

"Got it," I say.

Ripping the tape off Anton's mouth, I yank the dirty

gag out as well.

"Jude, wake this fucker up," I say as I hand him the needle.

Like a Christmas fucking miracle, the asshole wakes up from his stupor and lets out a low moan of pain.

Slapping his face twice brings his eyes back into focus.

"Let's get started with the questioning. I ask, you answer. If you need clarification, tell me so. That's it, got it?" I ask.

"Fuck you—" he starts to say, but I slam my fist into his balls.

His moans like a little bitch.

"Uh-uh. We've already established the routine, and that wasn't part of it," I say as I slap him across his sweaty face.

When he finally quits whimpering and moaning, I ask, "Do you understand the rules that I've given you?"

"Yes," he says quietly.

"That's fucking grand. Is your name really Anton Yelchin?" I ask and lean over so that my eyes are looking directly into his own deep brown eyes.

"Yes," he answers quickly.

"Are you a made man? You've got the stars."

He hesitates. I know why he doesn't want to admit it, but that hesitation is going to cost him.

"Yes," he finally says.

"Jude, remove his right big toe," I say without looking away from Anton.

Eyes wide, the man starts to struggle while sputtering, "I'm telling you the truth!"

"I know that, Anton, but you hesitated. You didn't want to tell me something, and I can't allow that," I say.

Jude lines up the snips with Anton's toe and the stupid fuck's sputtering turns into screams of rage. "You can't do this!"

Snip.

The sound is clearly heard over his protests before he starts screaming in pain.

I don't move away from, Anton. I keep my eyes directly on his while he screams and spits in my face. He needs to see me, he needs to know I'm the fucker whose causing the pain.

I'm the man that's become god in his shitty little world.

When his head finally drops forward, I decide to take a breather. I head over to a wall and wipe my hands on Anton's ripped shirt. My hands look big and bloody still, but I figure it's only going to get bloodier.

Walking back over, I poke around again in Simon's bag and pull out a small spray bottle of bleach.

Aiming it at his leg, I give five direct squirts.

It takes his body a couple of seconds to realize that the cold liquid isn't a soothing balm before he starts to howl so loud I swear he's going to burst my eardrums.

I've gotta admit to myself, that screaming sounds pretty fucking good.

"Damn dude, that looks like it hurts," James says with a laugh, coming up to stand behind me.

"I bet it does," I say chuckling.

"You fucking bastard!" Anton roars out at me as he tries to wrestle his way from the chair he's strapped into.

"I am." I shrug my shoulders then punch his nose.

Punch it hard enough that I feel it breaking.

"Why are you fucking around in Bethlehem?" I ask.

"You ran us out of Garden City. We want somewhere to work," he slurs from the blood draining down his throat.

"Who else is working with you guys?" I ask.

"What do you mean?" he asks.

Lashing out, I catch him in the stomach. The air inside of him explodes out in a rush and I watch his eyes go round.

Knocked the air right out of him.

Standing up from Anton, I look to James and Jude. "Cut off the big and baby toe on his uninjured leg."

"You going to work your way up his body?" Andrew asks.

"Yeah. He needs to understand I don't give a fuck. He answers me or he hurts. I don't care if he's gonna be legless by the time this is done," I say.

James and Jude get to work on Anton, and I have to

raise my voice so I can be heard over his screams. "Lucifer, Simon. What specifics do you need?"

"We need to know who's funding their operation. The Yakuza theoretically have the means, but it's not feeling right," Andrew says as he looks to Lucifer.

"Agreed. They recently took a chance trying to take me out at a church," Simon says after him. "They shouldn't have been able to find me that easily. We've patched up any security leaks since then, but I'm not entirely sure who's fucking with us."

"The bar and Cherry's home were very expertly done," Lucifer adds.

"What do you mean?" I ask.

"They blew up a bar with almost fifty people in it, or someone did. The men they used were out of Eastern Europe. What we can tell from the bomb forensics is that they weren't random men. These men had military explosive experience. They made sure to do exactly what they needed with precision."

Fuck me. I'm not surprised Lucifer has taken over so much space, but international fucking warfare is definitely above what I was expecting.

"Let's get to it then," I say as my hand slams into Anton's testicles.

The whimper he lets out isn't loud enough for me, though. His leg, and everything else he's been through, has worn on him pretty heavily.

And I *need* louder. I *need* more.

"Time to up my game," I mutter to Anton. "You guys still have any of those rivet guns they used to use here for the sheet metal?"

"Oh fuck," James groans as he points to Jude. "I'm not holding any more bloody stumps tonight. I've touched too much gore lately."

"For shit's sake, man." John laughs. "You need to get your ass out from behind your sniper scope. You ain't been doing any of the hard shit for too long."

"Dude, I did a face peel with Simon. That's earned me some get out of jail free cards." James laughs.

"It's going to take a couple of minutes to get it set up. Air compressor still good, Simon?" Jude asks.

"It should be," Simon says from where he's perched beside Lucifer.

Walking over to the toolbox, I pull out a bucket of metal rivets. They're almost like nails, except these go into sheet metal. I should be able to use them pretty well with our dickhead.

Anton is fidgeting nervously when I walk back over to him.

Holding a rivet to his shoulder, I smirk at him. "This is about to get real painful, man. Painful, and I'm going to completely ruin all your fucking ink. That's the one thing I feel bad about. All that ink work getting fucked up beyond repair."

A bloody wad of spit lands on my chest and Anton

tries to stare at me with defiance. It's not really defiance, though. There's too much fear behind it.

This motherfucker has something in him.

He hasn't spilled all the magical beans yet... but he's going to.

Jude walks by me with the rivet gun in his hand. His eyes are bright with an almost maniacal glee.

Holding the gun out for me to take, he asks, "Where ya starting first?"

"I'm gonna go with the hand first," I say as I look to Anton's hand.

"You must stop," Anton garbles out from his bloody mouth and nose.

Spittle flies everywhere as he shakes his head at us.

"Get his pants off completely for me," I say as I hold the rivet gun in one hand and grab Anton's hand with the other.

I hold his hand firmly down.

"What are we going to do below the waist?" Jude asks.

"Shin bones, kneecaps, and I'll probably rivet the ballsack to the table," I say with a grin then squeeze the trigger of the gun.

There's a loud popping sound right before Anton screams.

The rivet hit right through one of his hand bones, and I bet that hurt like a motherfucker.

RUSSIANS, Yakuza, and out of all the fucking things I didn't think would be included, the fucking Irish.

Anton spilled the beans once we shaved off all the toes on his left foot and two from his right. Not sure why the fuck he waited so damn long. We kept going though. I wanted to know his sister's middle name and when she lost her fucking cherry to his uncle.

From what we got out of him, the Irish were paid to blow up the bar and Cherry's house. They used some former Polish military to do it. The hit on Simon definitely was the Yakuza from everything Simon got off the guys, but Anton and his boys weren't a part of that and they're not cozying up with the Yakuza.

Seems there's a bunch of bad blood there we could take advantage of.

Lucifer and Simon say that the Russians have been trying to call a ceasefire and even denied the bombings, but we just found out why. They did it through the Irish for plausible deniability. The Irish are working with them for a reason we haven't figured out yet.

But one thing we do know, there's going to be a wedding tomorrow afternoon and we're going to be attending. Some guy named Alexei is marrying the Irish boss's daughter.

I've got a headache that feels like it's going to

fucking split my fucking skull in half. I'm not entirely sure what the fuck I stepped on, but I'm willing to bet it's a fucking landmine.

Walking toward the exit of the building, I ask the guys, "Any of ya'll got a light?"

"Thought you would have quit smoking in the pen," John says to me as he digs into his pocket.

Taking the zippo from his hand, I say, "I did. But I still gotta roast that Russian fuck's body."

"Ah." He points to a black pickup truck out in the parking lot. "That's your new ride, picked her out myself."

Looking at the big, hefty black pickup truck with tinted windows, I grin. "Good, I wasn't looking forward to having Simon taxi my ass everywhere."

"I'd rather slit your throat," Simon says from behind me.

Shouldering the corpse we wrapped inside a plastic sheet, I smile at Johnathan. "I appreciate it."

"You gonna need any help with the body?" he asks as he moves too slowly beside me.

I heard a little about the stomach wound he took from some battle on a landing strip, and I can tell he isn't up to helping me even if he wants to.

"Nah, brother, I got it," I say to him.

"Gentlemen," Lucifer says. "Let's get together tomorrow night at seven. Bring the family. Lily is planning a large dinner for us all. With the wedding in the early afternoon, we should have plenty of time to clean up and deal with any issues that might arise."

Fuck me, that doesn't sound like my scene at all. I'm guessing Lily is the big man's wife.

Andrew nudges me with his elbow. "That means you, asshole."

What the fuck?

"Yeah, I saw you looking for a way to get out of it. Doesn't work like that. Lily would skin you alive for missing one of her dinners," he says with a grin.

"She would more than likely have me do it," Lucifer says as he opens the door ahead of us.

The guys all split off as they head to their vehicles, but Lucifer sticks by my side.

"We need to talk tomorrow evening, Gabriel," he says calmly.

Walking up to the back of the truck, I wait as he opens up the cover over the bed for me.

Flopping the corpse into it, I listen to the heavy thump of the lifeless body. I'm going to dump this pile of shit right on the doorstep of the Russian Orthodox Church and see what rats come scurrying out. Might even be able to toss some gasoline onto the fire it's going to start.

"Yeah, when and where?" I ask as I push the hardtop back down to cover the bed of the truck.

"At the compound, and how about six?" he asks.

Nodding, I point over to James. "I'll have James

bring me out there. Gonna try to see Thomas after the wedding. I need to say goodbye."

"I see. I'll see you tomorrow then, and Gabriel?"

"Yeah?" I ask as I turn back from watching the rest of the men leave.

He pulls me into a tight hug with a rough pat on my back before I have a chance to stop him. I'm pretty sure my stiff posture doesn't bother him though, nothing ever does.

Pulling back from me, he looks me straight in the eyes as he says, "I'm glad you're home, and thank you for doing it for me."

I just stare at him. Those are the fucking last words I expected or needed to hear.

I'd tear his throat out if I wasn't sure I'd be bored shitless not working for him. Fuck, even now, after ten long years in the fucking pen, I'm still tempted to do it.

Pulling the phone from my pocket, I press the open button on it. Seems pretty easy, I guess.

"Everything on here I need to get started? Numbers and such?" I ask.

When I went in a fucking decade ago, I was just starting to see these phones out in the public. I had a flip phone, not a personal computer in my pocket.

"Simon has everything set up and encrypted. Everything should be good to go."

Looking back up at Lucifer, I ask, "What the hell's Tinder, Plenty of Fish, and Grindr?"

2

MEGHAN

Staring at my reflection in the mirror, awareness and horror slowly begin to creep in.

If the reflection staring back at me is true, I've been gowned in a snow-white wedding dress, and I can't remember how it happened.

Have I been drugged? Or is this another nightmare to torment me?

Even now the edges of my vision is hazy and my movements are slow. Too slow. My thoughts struggle to surface, to breathe, as if I've been held underwater for too long.

Blinking my eyes, I reach out and touch the mirror in front of me, hoping my reflection will change. That I've somehow become Alice and fallen down the rabbit hole. But everything remains the same. Only the expression on my painted face changes. Shifting from a look of confusion to one resembling anger.

I push at the mirror, half-expecting my fingers to go through it, but it's solid.

"Those... bastards..." I softly mutter, my words coming out slightly slurred.

Someone must have spiked me with something this morning... Someone who wanted my compliance guaranteed.

I strain my brain, trying in vain to pull up the moment it happened, but it's a wasted effort. It doesn't matter when it happened, just that it happened period.

Reaching down, I tug at the bodice of my dress. It's uncomfortably tight and constricting. Vaguely, I can remember women speaking in Russian as they prodded, poked, and pulled on me, treating me like their doll.

My dark hair has been curled, swept up, and pinned. My makeup artfully done. Jewels glitter around my throat and dangle from ears. My arms are covered up to my elbows in silky gloves.

I've been molded into a beautiful bride.

And yet, I can only faintly remember bits and pieces of this being done.

Giving up on the tight bodice, I drop my hand and shake my head, trying to clear it. The sharp, sudden movement though only causes a wave of intense dizziness to sweep over me.

Jesus, whatever they gave me is strong.

Looking to the mirror again, I focus on my reflection as I wait for the dizziness to pass. When it finally does, I decide it's time to get the hell out of here while I still can.

Turning away from the mirror takes more effort than it should. Another wave of dizziness threatens to overwhelm me, so I take it very slow. Like I'm outside, watching my body struggling without me, I carefully put one foot in front of the other and make my way to the door.

Hand reaching out, my fingers brush across the knob when it suddenly turns. My reactions still delayed, my hand lingers in the air as the door swings open.

"Ah, there you are," Alexei says as he suddenly appears in front of me.

An apparition from my deepest, darkest nightmares.

Like a trapped bird, my heart flutters behind my ribs, and my feet itch with the need to escape his presence. To run and run and run.

The things I've learned about this man have haunted and tormented me since the announcement of our engagement.

I discovered he's not your typical Russian kingpin. No, he's so much worse than that. He's a monster, even in the eyes of the criminal underworld.

His deeds go far beyond kidnapping, extortion, and even murder. Go far beyond what's considered beyond the pale even in our circles.

He deals in the selling and exploitation of young women and children.

Most of his empire has been built on the success of his human trafficking operation. Built on the success of selling little boys and little girls to the highest bidder.

It makes me sick. So fucking sick and scared.

He has no soul. No heart. I doubt he's even human.

Standing in the doorway, Alexei's black eyes sweep slowly over me, appraising me with keen interest. My eyes are much slower to move over him, and when they do, when I finally see what he's wearing, I feel like I'm going to puke.

He's dressed in a sharp black tux that's been tailored to fit his body perfectly.

Oh god, maybe we're already married…

Hand finally dropping, it bounces against my skirt in defeat.

He takes a step into the room, and I nearly fall on my ass as I take a stumbling step back.

Closing the door behind him, his body blocks off the exit.

"Going somewhere?" he asks, his eyes hardening.

If he wasn't so damn big, and if I wasn't so damn clumsy and slow from being drugged, I might be able to get around him. But as it is, I'm fucking trapped.

I briefly consider trying my luck anyway, but the last thing I need right now is to force a physical confrontation with him. He's got at least six inches on me, and probably a hundred pounds of pure muscle. No, it would be better if I wait for a better opportunity... like when the drugs wear off and I actually stand a chance.

What I really need right now is to know if we're married. Because if we are... fuck...

I might as well be a dead woman walking.

Going out on a limb, I manage to slur out, "Isn't it bad luck for the groom to see the bride before the wedding?"

His lips curve into a sharp smirk and I find myself holding my breath as I await his answer.

"You know this ceremony is merely a formality. A show for the families," he says dismissively, taking another step toward me. "I already own you, Meghan."

Any relief I might have felt to learn that we're not already married is immediately crushed beneath the weight of his statement.

At first, I want to balk, to protest. He doesn't *own* me. I'm not a fucking object, I'm a person. I can't be bought, sold, or traded.

But isn't that exactly what my father did? He traded me to Alexei in exchange for the Russian's protection.

I've been reduced to a fucking bargaining chip.

"What did you drug me with?" I ask as he

continues to approach me, eating up the distance between us.

I'm hoping my question will trip him up, or at least stall him. If he touches me or even breathes on me, I don't think I could take it.

Despite his handsome face, everything about him repulses and unnerves me. When I look at him, my skin crawls and my stomach clenches. I don't see his perfect bone structure or his soft, pouty lips.

All I see is the cold, dead space inside his eyes that's utterly inhuman.

My little ploy seems to work because he pauses for a moment, as if he's thinking, before saying, "We were forced to administer a mild sedative when you became hysterical."

"Hysterical?" I repeat, my voice thick with disbelief.

When have I ever been hysterical? I don't think I've ever been hysterical at any point in my life. In fact, I believe I've held up pretty fucking well given all the shit that's happened to me lately.

"Yes... hysterical..." he drawls out, as if he wants those two words to really sink in. Then his eyes suddenly gleam with a strange light as he continues. "You were quite distraught over poor Callum."

Poor Callum?

"Why would I be distraught..."

My brain jumps in to answer the question for me before I even finish the sentence.

Flashes of blood and gore flood my mind as the memory comes pouring back in. The smoking gun in Alexei's hand. Callum sprawled on the floor with half of his skull blown out. His once beautiful hazel eyes that sparkled with life, empty of light and staring up at me accusingly.

Callum is... was... my father's youngest enforcer. He was so eager to please, and as loyal as a damn puppy. I always knew he harbored feelings for me. I even messed around with him for a bit before I went off to find myself at university.

Fuck. I tried to use Callum to help me get away and Alexei killed him.

"Oh god," I mumble, and sway on my feet, my white skirt swishing around me.

This nightmare is too damn real.

"Meghan," Alexei says, sounding a little bit alarmed.

Before I can fall to the floor, his arms are around me, catching me and pulling me close.

His touch, his hold only increases my distress. I try to push him away, but I just don't have the strength to do it.

His arms tighten. "Don't fret, my dear. It's all done and over with."

Don't fret? Don't fret?! A man is dead because I tried to use him. A man I was friends with is dead because Alexei killed him.

Leaning as far back in Alexei's hold as I possibly can, I glare up at him accusingly. "You... you didn't have to kill him!"

Alexei's face hardens as he stares down at me. His eyes are so dark, so cold, they're practically glinting like black glass.

"Of course I had to kill him. He tried to take what's *mine*."

Any normal girl would probably be cowed by the look on his face, or at least have the sense not to push a murderer when he's holding her trapped in his arms.

But I'm obviously not a normal girl. I'm not a very smart girl, either, for that matter.

Because I open my mouth and tell him, "But it wasn't his fault... I tricked him into helping me. He didn't deserve to die, Alexei. If anyone deserves to die for betraying you, it's me."

Alexei just stares at me. He stares at me for so damn long, it goes beyond creepy. The air seems to chill around us, his cold expression sucking all the warmth out of the room, and I have plenty of time to wonder if I just played my last hand.

He could kill me right now and no one would stop him. I have no protection. No one to help. No one to come to my rescue. Now, I don't even have my father. I've been abandoned for *the good of the family*. We haven't even spoken any vows yet, but I'm completely and utterly at Alexei's mercy.

He can do anything and everything he wants to do to me.

But maybe it would be a mercy if he killed me right now, before we walk down the aisle. Then I wouldn't have to endure our wedding night. I wouldn't have to endure him forcing me to consummate this marriage.

But I don't want to die, dammit. I want to live. As stupid as I am, I'm not ready to give up yet.

"Meghan," Alexei finally says after what feels like an eternity. "I think you're still suffering from some hysteria. Perhaps another sedative is in order?"

What the fuck? Seriously? He's giving me an out instead of punishing me for my admission?

What's up with this guy? And why is he showing me, of all people, mercy? Sure, I'm his bride-to-be, but this is an arranged political marriage. He's not necessarily marrying me because he actually wants to marry *me*. He's marrying me for the benefits. He could easily use this as an opportunity to get rid of me and still have his alliance with the Irish.

So why isn't he?

I just stare at him in confusion, unable to make sense of him. Then he releases one hand from me and reaches into his tux pocket.

"No!" I blurt out and grab his wrist, fearing he's reaching for that sedative.

If he drugs me again there's no way I'm going to

have the mental capacity to escape if the opportunity presents itself.

When he arches a brow at me, I realize my mistake.

Softening my voice, I immediately release his hand and hope my impulsive reaction doesn't cost me my life. "I'm sorry, I mean no more sedative. I'm fine, really. Any more and I might fall asleep. Any more and I'll be too groggy to say my vows…"

"Are you sure?" he asks, his eyes narrowing with what could be suspicion, but what could also be taken as skepticism.

"I'm sure." I bob my head maybe a little too enthusiastically. "The moment has passed. It won't happen again."

I swear at first he looks like he doesn't believe me, and I don't blame him. I wouldn't believe me either.

But something, I don't know what, must change his mind because his expression softens. "Very well."

I'm still so out of whack, I almost say *whew* out loud. Seriously, I feel like I literally just dodged a bullet.

Then he grabs my hand, the one that grabbed his wrist, and wraps his fingers around me. His grip isn't harsh, but it might as well be given how much I loathe his touch. I have to stop myself from yanking my hand back as he pulls it up, close to his mouth.

At first, I'm afraid he's going to maul me, or do

something else awful, like bite my fingers off one by one.

But then his lips brush gently, slowly, almost tenderly, across my knuckles, and my skin wants to crawl right off my bones.

Eyes locking on mine, his grip suddenly tightens painfully around my hand as he keeps it poised close to his mouth.

I have to bite my lip to keep from crying out as he says, "If you feel it coming on again, *zaika*, you must let me know. Because nothing in this world, and I mean n*othing*, will stop me from protecting you and keeping you safe."

Grip suddenly loosening, his head dips and his lips brush once more across my knuckles as if he's trying to soothe the pain he created.

Then he looks up and flashes a smile so chilling my blood runs cold. "Even if I have to protect you from yourself."

Alexei's words sink into me with the pain, filling me with apprehension and dread.

What the hell is going on here? And what the hell does he mean by that? He's sounding more and more like a possessive groom instead of a man who looks at me simply as an object or obligation.

Does he want this marriage for more than political reasons?

A knock on the door pulls Alexei's attention away from me.

"Yes?" he calls out, a look of annoyance passing over his sharp features as he lowers my hand and keeps it trapped in his.

Every frantic beat of my heart seems to purge the lingering effects of his sedative out of my system. I'm almost completely sober now, and I don't know what's worse, being drugged against my will or having to face all this shit fully aware of what's happening.

"It's almost time, sir," an unfamiliar Russian voice answers on the other side of the door. "The priest would like you to take your place now."

"Ah, very good," Alexei says, the corners of his lips pulling up as his attention returns to me.

His eyes gleam with smug pleasure, and I have the sudden, almost irresistible urge to yank my hand out of his grip. I want to yank it out and slap that smug look right off his pretty face.

But before I can, his grip tightens, and he uses my hand to pull me into him.

Breasts meet chest and hips meet hips.

I start to push away, unable to bear being so close to him, when his lips fall upon mine.

His kiss is cold, so damn cold.

I freeze in place, chilled to the bone.

I endure his touch, the sensation of his cold, dead

lips moving over mine, and try my best not to throw up in my mouth.

Is this what I must endure for the rest of my life?

I don't kiss him back. I don't try to reciprocate in any way, but Alexei doesn't seem to mind. He just takes and takes.

His mouth pulls and pulls.

The kiss stretches on and on, trapping me in my own personal hell.

When he finally breaks away, his hand comes up, cupping my cheek tenderly as he breathes hard.

"We'll finish this after the ceremony," he says ominously.

I'd rather light myself on fire.

Alexei stares at me for another moment as if he expects me to say something.

I just stare back at him, trying to come to terms with the dawning horror that my earlier suspicion was correct.

He wants me, and not only for the alliance.

3

MEGHAN

Alexei forces another kiss on me before leaving the room.

Once the lock clicks in place behind him, my hands go to the bodice of my dress, tugging and tearing in desperation to free myself from it. As if shedding it could change my fate or what I am.

Only the sound of the lock turning again stops me from trying to gnaw the damn thing off with my teeth.

I freeze in place as the door swings open, fearing it's Alexei returning to torment me some more.

My father appears in the doorway, a grim shadow of the man I've known all my life. I swear, in the past two weeks, ever since he informed me of the arrangement, he's aged twenty years.

I almost feel a pang of sympathy for him. Almost.

Then he informs me, "It's time, Meghan."

Any sympathy I was feeling for him immediately evaporates in a cloud of anger.

"No," I say firmly while straightening to my full height and throwing my shoulders back.

Alexei may scare the bejesus out of me, but my father is an entirely different matter. He doesn't frighten me in the least, and standing up to him might be my ticket out of this mess.

"Meghan..." my father sighs, and instantly a dozen more wrinkles that weren't there a moment ago line his face.

"No," I repeat, my hands clenching into fists. "I won't marry him. You have to call this off. I won't fucking do it."

Before I even get a chance to finish my refusal, my father makes a motion with his hand, frowning like he expected this.

A big, beefy thug suited up in all black steps around him and begins to approach me. The thug is no one I recognize, so he must be Russian.

Another Russian to deal with me. What the fuck happened to my fellow Irish?

"Don't make me do this, Meghan, love," my father says as I back away from the thug, throwing my hands up. "Come along nice and peaceful now, and let's have us a lovely wedding."

"If you want the wedding so bad, why don't you marry him?" I spit back as my spine hits the wall.

"Would if I could," my father mutters under his breath just as the thug grabs me roughly by the arm.

I try to shake the thug off, and his fingers bite down, digging into bone.

A whimper of pain and anger escapes my mouth, and I lash out, kicking the thug hard in the shin.

The kick doesn't faze him one bit.

"Now, now, Igor, gentle now. She's my daughter," my father says with reproach.

Igor's grip immediately loosens.

Igor... of course the thug's name is Igor. *Fucker looks like an Igor*, I think as I try to yank my arm back.

"Sorry, boss," Igor says, his Russian accent grating on me.

I've heard enough Russian accents today to last me a lifetime. I swear the Russian accent must be the ugliest sound in the universe.

Like nails dragging across a chalkboard.

I give another hard yank on my arm, trying to take advantage of Igor's loosened grip, but like the annoying bottom feeder he is, he remains latched on.

"Meghan, lass, if you don't calm down and cooperate, I'll have to give you something to calm you."

My eyes snap to my father in disbelief. Is he threatening to drug me, just like that monster Alexei?

"You wouldn't..." I challenge, but as soon as the words leave my mouth, I know deep in my heart that he would and he will.

I no longer expect him to treat me with any sort of respect or dignity. No, he's shown how much he truly cares about me by trading me away and forcing me to do this.

Igor looks at my father expectantly, and with another sigh my father nods his head in agreement of something.

"I don't want to. Believe me, I don't want to resort to this, but you give me no choice, lass…"

No choice? I give him no choice? Oh that's rich, coming from him.

One beefy hand still locked around my arm, Igor reaches into his pocket and pulls a syringe out.

"No!" I cry out as Igor lifts the syringe up to his mouth and bites the plastic tip off with his teeth.

I start to throw my weight forward, trying anything and everything to get the brute off my arm.

Igor spits the plastic tip out and orders me to, "Stay still."

Ignoring him, I slam my heel down on his foot and watch with satisfaction as he lets out a yelp of pain.

My satisfaction is short-lived though when his grip tightens. No matter how hard I fight him, he has no trouble straightening my arm out against my will.

I slap at him and even make a grab for the syringe. As soon as I do, he lifts it high out of my reach and gives my trapped arm a twist.

The resulting pain causes my knees to buckle beneath me.

I drop to the floor.

Igor looms above me, and I watch in horror as he pushes the syringe toward my arm.

Reaching up, I try once more to slap the syringe away.

He gives my arm another twist and yanks the syringe out of my reach.

The pain is unbearable. My arm feels like it's ripping away from my shoulder.

Looking to my father once more, I finally resort to pleading.

"Daddy, please," I beg with tears swimming in front of my eyes. "What would mother think?"

My father reacts as if I punched him in the gut. The color drains from his face and he seems to shrink in on himself.

I wasn't afraid of my father, wasn't afraid to stand my ground on this, because he's always been my safe place. With my mother gone, he was the one person I could always turn to. The one person I could always count on to at least take care of me...

But not anymore.

And it hurts. It fucking hurts beyond words. I'm powerless now, utterly helpless, with no one in this dark, fucked-up world.

"Igor, stop," my father orders just as I feel the needle prick my skin.

Hope swells inside me. Perhaps I've finally gotten through to him...

Igor looks to my father with a frown of confusion. My father takes a deep breath, regaining his composure.

Then he looks at me, his eyes filled with both love and sadness.

"Your mother would want me to do anything in my power to protect you, Meghan. And that's what I'm doing."

I shake my head in denial, the word, "No," spilling from my lips.

How can he possibly believe giving me to Alexei protects me?

"But she would also want me to give you another chance," my father goes on. "So I'm going to give you one more chance, lass, to come with me calmly."

So that's it then? Once again, I'm being given the choice to do this clear-headed or drugged out of my mind.

Perhaps you should take the escape, a little voice whispers inside my head.

Maybe I'll wake up tomorrow and this will all feel like a bad dream.

Or maybe I'll wake up with Alexei grunting and thrusting on top of me.

Staring at my father through the blur of my tears, his betrayal boils inside me like hot acid, eating away at the love I once felt.

The choice he is giving me is really no choice at all.

"So Meghan, what will it be?" my father presses for my answer when I remain silent.

To be drugged or not to be drugged...

That is the fucking question of the day.

To stay in control or say fuck it...

"Fine. I'll come calmly," I mutter bitterly.

THE DOUBLE DOORS leading into the Cathedral are thrown open wide. The pews are sparsely filled with men in black suits and a couple of women dressed in pastels that wilt against all the dark. As soon as my father and I come into view, the first chords of 'Here Comes The Bride' blare from the organ. So loud, I can feel every note vibrating in my bones.

The entire left side of my body aches as I walk down the aisle, the pain radiating from my arm. Reminding me with each step that I chose to do this sober.

I chose not to take the out.

"Don't forget to smile," my father hisses through his own flashing teeth.

I attempt to stretch my lips into something resembling a smile and fail.

There is absolutely no joy left inside me, no hope. I can't even muster up a happy memory or two to help me fake it.

'Here Comes The Bride' might as well be my funeral march. There's no way, no way in hell I'm going to let Alexei violate me tonight, or any other night of my life.

My gaze falls upon Alexei standing at the end of the aisle. Tall, dark, and as handsome as a fucking prince. He watches me with black, glittering eyes as if he finds my misery amusing.

Tonight, one of us is going to die. I know it deep in my soul.

God, please don't let it be, I pray.

Unable to look upon him for a second longer, I tear my gaze away, taking in those who've come to witness this farce.

My side of the church contains only a few high-ranking Irish. Men who helped raise me. Men who I looked upon as second fathers and uncles. Their wives and daughters however are suspiciously absent. I recognize a couple of mistresses, but no women of worth. No women I can trust to help me.

A small, tight group of big men in dark suits stand in the pews on Alexei's side of the church. The men study me with sharp eyes that size me up. Every inch of me, from the top of my head down to the bottom of my toes, is being judged.

At this moment, I can't help but feel like I'm the pretty young sacrifice being led to the edge of the volcano. My father willing to give me the push to appease the savage gods.

With that depressing thought, I return my gaze to the end of the aisle.

Only a couple of pews remain between me and the rest of my miserable life.

My father's arm tightens around mine, sensing my desire before it even registers in my brain. The need to run, to flee, courses through my limbs.

Would they stop me? Would someone tackle me and drag me up to the altar?

"Don't even think about it," my father hisses. "You agreed to be calm."

His steps quicken, and with my arm trapped in his, I have no choice but to speed up too.

Well, I guess that answers my earlier question. They will indeed drag me up to the aisle against my will.

I finally look to the priest, hoping to find an ally in a man of God, but the bastard is avoiding my eyes.

I stare long and hard, willing him to look at me. To fucking *see* me. To step up and call this off.

Color begins to creep up his neck, staining his droopy jowls.

He knows I'm looking to him for salvation, he has to know...

The priest clears his throat nervously and asks, "Who gives this bride in marriage?"

Coward.

Impatient, or simply aware that I'm about to make a scene, Alexei takes a step forward as my father answers, "I do."

Silence falls across the church as my father's arm slips from mine and Alexei grabs my hands.

With a little tug, he forces me to turn, facing him.

Fingers squeezing around mine, he holds me tight as the priest tries to lead everyone into prayer.

"Remember, I already own you, *zaika*," Alexei whispers softly as the priest's wheezy, old voice drones on and on. "This is merely a formality."

My gaze jerks up to peer at his smirking face.

"Nothing you do or say during this ceremony will change the outcome. It's already been predetermined."

I know he's trying to scare me into not embarrassing him, but it's actually having the opposite effect. If everything is already predetermined, if nothing I say or do will change the outcome, then there's really no reason to hope for the best and bite my tongue.

My lips curving to mirror his own smirk, I ask softly, "What kind of loser forces a woman to marry him against her will?"

Alexei's hands suddenly squeeze painfully around

mine and I let out a little yelp just as the priest finishes his prayer.

The priest glances at me in alarm and a few angry murmurs and grumbles from my side of the church reach my ears.

"Carry on," Alexei growls.

Glancing down at our hands, for a moment the priest looks like he's going to protest. Then Alexei shoots him a dark look.

"Yes... yes... where was I?" the priest nervously stammers and looks away.

He begins to start up the same prayer again only to stop abruptly.

With a look of frustration, Alexei snaps, "Just get to the vows."

"Of course," the priest grumbles and begins to flip through his book.

Returning his attention to me, Alexei stares into my tear-filled eyes.

Thumbs stroking against my hands, he says, "My patience is limited. The next time you insult me, I won't be so gentle. Do you understand?"

Fearing he might hurt me again, I have no choice but to nod my head.

Pleased by my answer, Alexei smiles and gives my hands another squeeze. "Good."

Pain suddenly shoots straight up my bad arm, and I can't tell if he did it intentionally or unintentionally.

"This marriage can be quite pleasant for you, if you allow it. Or you can be completely miserable. The choice is yours..."

Before I can even think of how to respond to that, the priest begins to recite our vows.

"Alexei Rastov," the priest stammers. "Do you take Meghan Fiona Callahan for your lawful wife, to have and to hold, from this day forward, for better, for worse, for richer, for poorer, in sickness and in health, until death do you part?

Grinning like he's the cat that ate the canary, Alexei stares into my eyes as he says, "I do."

The priest nods and looks back down at his book. I know he's purposely avoiding looking at me.

"Meghan Fiona Callahan, do you take Alexei Rastov for your lawful husband, to have and to hold, from this day forward, for better, for worse, for richer, for poorer, in sickness and in health, until death do you part?"

Alexei squeezes my hands, his grip becoming tighter and tighter until I cry out, "I do."

The priest smiles, a look of relief settling over his wizened face. "What God joins together, let no man—"

A gun shot rings out, echoing off the rafters in the nearly empty church.

At first, I think my ears must be playing tricks on me. But then another one rings out, and another.

Chaos erupts around me, so sudden, so unexpected, I can't help but wonder if this is real.

Seriously, is this shit really happening?

"Meghan!" my father cries out, and I spin to face him. Clutching at his arm, he orders me to, "Get down!"

Before I can act on his order, Alexei gives me a shove toward the nearest pews. "Igor, protect her!"

Igor appears out of nowhere and grabs me roughly by my bad arm, dragging me and shoving me down behind the pews.

More gun shots ring out and shouts go up, a mixture of Russian and English.

I try to pop my head up to see what the hell is going on only to have Igor shove me back down.

"Stay," he grunts as he aims a pistol and fires at the front of the church.

Knowing it's probably in my best interest to follow his command and make myself as small of a target as possible, I twist around and drag my legs in as far as my big fluffy white skirt will allow me.

"Dear Lord, protect me from the evil forces that desecrate this most holy sanctuary," the old priest prays frantically, crawling his way over to me from the altar.

He struggles, partly because of his age, and partly because of his robes getting in the way, and I find myself unable to muster up one ounce of sympathy for him.

"There's too many of them!" one of my father's men cries out.

"Fall back!" my father roars and then grunts as if he's in pain.

My heart immediately lurches inside my chest, my hate for him is momentarily forgotten.

Is he hurt?

Logic fleeing, I try to pop up again to check on my father, only to have Igor shove me back down.

He curses and then shouts something in Russian.

Alexei shouts back.

The priest finally reaches me just as two of my father's men stumble down the aisle. Shooting wildly at the front of the church, they don't even spare me a glance as they run for the doors flanking the altar.

Only one of them makes it. I watch in horror as the smaller of the two, a man I don't know by name, takes a shot to the head and drops to the floor.

"God have mercy," the priest whimpers, and then the smell of something acidic hits the air.

It takes me a second to place the smell, but once I do I scoot away from him in disgust.

He pissed himself in fear.

"Meghan! Meghan!" my father cries out and then he appears, being dragged down the aisle by Alexei.

I note at once that his right arm is hanging limply

at his side and a blossom of blood the size of my fist stains his white shirt.

He's wounded, and the little girl inside me cries out, "Daddy!"

Three Russians shield my father and Alexei, using their huge bodies as a wall as they shoot at the front of the church.

"Bring her, Igor," Alexei orders as he drags my father past me.

Igor glances at him before firing off a few more rounds. Then he reaches down and grabs me by the shoulder a second before he just drops beside me.

It happens so fast, I find myself blinking down at Igor's motionless body in shock.

"Fuck!" Alexei roars and begins to shout frantically in Russian as he continues to drag my father further and further away from me.

One of the three men shielding him moves toward me only to drop dead with a bullet in his head beside Igor.

"Meghan! Meghan!" my father wails desperately, and not knowing what else to do, I begin to crawl toward him.

A stream of bullets suddenly hit the floor in front of me, blocking off my escape. I scramble backward as another of Alexei's guards falls to the ground, dead.

Thrusting my spine into the front of the pew, I look up in time to find Alexei staring at me. His eyes lock on mine, intense and full of something I can't place as he reaches the door beside the altar.

A shot rings out, this one somehow much louder than the last.

The only guard standing in front of Alexei falls to the ground, his body thumping into the floor with a wet crack.

Then another shot rings out, this one hitting the door as it closes behind my father and Alexei.

I just stare at the door as two more bullets splinter the wood.

Then it finally hits me.

"They left me..." I say out loud in cold disbelief.

They fucking left me here to die...

A heavy silence falls over the church.

No more shots ring out.

No more voices pierce the air.

The only thing I can hear is the old priest wheezing beside me.

Seconds pass that drag on like minutes. A million thoughts race through my mind.

Is everyone dead? Are the attackers gone? Maybe now's my chance to get away?

Staring at the bullet-riddled floor in front of me, my heart pounds so hard I fear I might be sick.

The thought of popping up only to drop to the floor like the dead men in front of me keeps me from moving.

So I wait, my ears straining.

The silence stretches on and on.

Then the first heavy footstep falls, echoing throughout the cathedral, and my heart freezes in mid beat.

Oh god, the attackers are still here.

One footstep becomes two, three, then four.

My brain finally processes what I'm hearing. Someone is walking up the aisle.

The footsteps stop.

"Dead," a deep voice says.

Then they start again only to stop.

"Dead," the voice says again.

The footsteps grow louder and louder, coming closer and closer.

Two gunshots suddenly ring out and I nearly jump out of my skin.

"Dead now."

Fuck. I'm dead if I make a run for it, and I'm dead if I stay here.

If I want to live, I'm going to have to find a way to fight.

The footsteps start again, and knowing I only have a few precious seconds to save myself, I make a grab for Igor's gun beside me.

I manage to reach it and get it settled in my hand just as I hear the footsteps approaching closer.

Taking a deep breath, I turn myself around, count to three, and then rise.

The most striking pair of baby blue eyes pierce right through me as I come face-to-face with the owner of the footsteps.

For a heartbeat, I'm frozen, stricken stupid by the handsome giant in front of me.

Then my survival instinct comes roaring back in.

It's kill or be killed.

Adrenaline spiking again, time slows down. I catch the surprise, the confusion, then the acceptance in the bright blue gaze of the man looking down at me.

He's ready to die, his eyes tell me, and I almost hesitate.

Almost.

My hand shakes and I wrap my other hand around the barrel to steady the gun.

Then I close my eyes, ask God for forgiveness, and pull the trigger.

I expect a little recoil and maybe even a warm splash.

What I don't expect is for the gun to click and nothing to happen.

What the fuck?

I open my eyes slowly to see the massive man smirking down at me.

Shit.

4

GABRIEL

Normally when someone puts a gun to my chest with the intention of shutting down my beating heart, I rebel against that very notion and stop them.

But something about the way this girl's deep blue eyes look up into mine stops me from moving.

Feelings that are completely alien hold me in place as I stare into her eyes. I don't even get to give her a grin before she pulls the trigger.

Click, smack.

I'm not sure who's shocked more, me, her, or the guys behind me.

There's a lot of smoke and loud sounds echoing through the church, but that click of an empty chamber resonates through my ears as if it's a big fucking gong.

I can't help but smirk at the little woman standing in front of me when the gun doesn't go off.

"Damn, that bitch was gonna cap your ass," James shouts as he jogs past me, heading toward the back of the church, chasing after the fleeing Russians and Irish.

I just stand in place as the men flow past me. I was the first in and should be the one leading the charge, but I can't seem to move my feet. It feels like I've been fucking cemented to the floor. Like I've been weighed down with cement boots and tossed into the river. I'm floating down, down into the inky blackness.

The trigger is pulled again and panic begins to fill her eyes, her cheeks red and flushed from whatever emotion is flooding through her.

I don't know exactly what the emotion is, but I'd say it isn't exactly murderous rage that I was trying to kill her future husband.

"Thing isn't going to kill me itself, girl. You need to reload it," I say loud enough so that she can hear me over the sudden roar of gunfire coming from the doors behind the cross.

"Fuck," she groans as her fingers go slack around the metal grip of the gun.

"Yep."

Reaching out, I cradle the small, delicate hand holding the pistol with my own and pry it easily from her fingers.

Pocketing the gun into the back of my jeans, I reach out and take her hand again in mine, then I yank her along with me. I guess I got us a prisoner of war or something. Ain't tortured a chick in a long time, though. Not sure if I'm going to be down for that. Not one with a set of balls as big as this blue-eyed girl's got.

"We gotta move. You gonna be a problem I have to take care of?" I ask as we move down the aisle toward the entrance of the building.

It's probably going to get a bit hectic if she's going to be putting up a fight.

"I... I..." she stammers as we come out of the church's entrance.

Cars screech across the cold asphalt of the parking lot, and the gunfire hasn't stopped out back either. Fuck.

"Michael," I say through our comms. "You get the tracker tags on the black Audis?"

"No, too many guards. Simon, do you have visual through the city?" Michael asks.

"Not yet, but I will. How many men are down?"

"I count five inside, four outside. Not sure how many got out, Alexei wasn't one of them."

Fuck. We needed to hit Alexei.

"What about the Irishman?" I ask.

The bride beside me freezes up instantly as I try to get her to the black Tahoe I came in.

Shit, that's right, that's her dad. She was supposed

to marry Alexei. I'm not entirely sure where my head is at right now, it's somewhere between the delicate hand I have clutched in mine and the need to unleash catastrophic violence on the men who we came to kill.

Racing around the corner of the church, two more Audis swerve away from us as they try to escape the havoc that's being unleashed.

Split-second decisions suck at a time like this.

Yanking the chrome .45 from my hip holster, I unleash half a clip into the back tire and window of the last car.

Shattering glass and a swerve send the vehicle slamming into another parked car.

Even now, in the moments of death and smoke, I feel the little dark-haired girl trying to pry my fingers from around her wrist.

"Stop it," I growl to her as I pull her along with me.

"Let me go!" she yells as she slaps at my shoulder.

I gotta admit she's got some fight in her, but she's all mine and she had her chance to get away when she tried to kill me. Sucks for her that the gun was empty.

"I need a situation report for the front of the building, Gabriel," Simon says over the comm piece in my ear.

Tilting my head to the side to activate my controls, I say, "One of two black Audis got away. I've immobilized the one that didn't. Anyone able to come up and give me backup? I need to check who's inside. I've also picked up the bride. Currently making sure she doesn't try to put a bullet in me."

"Oh, how I wish she would," I hear Simon mutter through the comms.

"On my way," Jude's voice says in my ear. "I've got a priest with me in tow. Might be able to get some answers out of him."

"That's fucking funny, a bride and a priest. We just need a groom..." James laughs into the comms channel.

"On my way, as well. All Russian and Irish threats are down," Andrew says.

"Any intel on them?" Simon asks quickly.

"Very little, except some cellphones and a few wallets," Andrew responds.

"James, as good moral strengthening, I need the thumbs of each man there," Lucifer says into the comms.

Aw fuck, poor guy. That's a messy job.

Walking toward the Audi, I tug the girl behind me but keep a tight grip on her wrist.

Ignoring the whining and bitching of James, I say over my shoulder, "You had your shot at getting away, and there might be more bullets flying soon. Don't fucking move from behind me, you hear that?"

"Why?" she stutters.

"Because I'm a shit ton bigger than you and I can take one," I say before I put her hand on my leather belt. "These guys aren't going to be happy you're with me. Keep your hand on my belt and don't fuck about."

"Okay," she says quietly, and I feel her wrap her fingers tightly about my belt.

Releasing her wrist, I pull a new clip from the band on my hip and change them out.

"Oh yeah... You run, you'll most likely die. I'm your only option," I say as I move us toward the car.

Inside I can see a figure slowly turning around in the backseat. A barrel moves into view, but my finger pulls the trigger a microsecond before his. His shot goes wide as my two shots slam through his head. Another head moves in the vehicle and I blow four more shots into the back window, stopping all movement.

"Two down inside. Doesn't look like any movement," I say into the comms.

"Coming up behind you, Gabriel," Jude says loudly from behind me to make sure I don't accidentally shoot him.

"Driver and front passenger aren't moving. Can you check 'em?" I ask.

"Moving into position," Jude says as I pull both me and the lady in white behind a car for protection.

"So..." Lucifer drawls over the comms. "Any sign of Alexei or Brady Callahan?"

"Negative in the back. Both got into the cars," Andrew says. "Heading forward, I'll assist James with the thumbs. We need to get moving."

"Who has the priest?" I ask over the mic as some thought deep in the back of my brain lights up with an awfully interesting idea.

"Left him pissing and quivering inside the front doors," Jude shouts back to me as he puts two bullets through the men in the car's front seat.

"Why?" Simon asks through the radio.

Looking down at the little bride-to-be beside me, I notice the ample cleavage that's been pushed so far up her dress it looks painful. Dragging my gaze back up to her face, her deep blue eyes are almost too intense for me. It's like she's looking so fucking deeply into me she can see all the shit that's wrong inside me. She can see all the horrible things I want to do and will do to people.

She's not backing down though, and I like that. I've got at least a foot on her in height, and I can't even begin to guess what her weight is compared to mine. She's tiny...

Tiny, but her body has curves... like holy fucking stripper curves.

"Seems like a perfectly good day for a wedding, is all," I say, and pull the girl by her hand as I walk toward the front of the church.

"What do you mean by that?" Simon asks over the radio, and I can't help but grin.

"You wanted bedlam and mayhem," I say as I look down at my would-be killer.

I'm not entirely sure what my plan is past the next day, but something about her makes me want to keep her around. She's beautiful, and she took her own destiny in her hands when she tried to put a bullet through my chest.

"Sorry about your wedding being ruined like that," I say as we pass by Michael who's come out of the church carrying a black trash bag, most likely full of cellphones and wallets.

It's only when we walk into the church that I notice how red her exposed shoulders are from being out there in the cold. I have a long-sleeved black shirt on, but this little one had nothing but fucking lace and whatever the hell dresses are made of.

"I wasn't exactly a willing participant in it," she mumbles.

Her hand briefly tries to pull away from me as we pass a dead body, but then she freezes up as if I'm going to hurt her or something.

"I can't let you go, girl..." I say as I bend over a cowering white-shrouded priest.

"Why not?" she asks loudly as I yank the man up by the collar.

"Get the fuck up," I growl at him before I notice the

huge yellow stain on the front of his robes. "Did you fucking piss yourself?"

"He did. Did it right beside me when you guys were shooting," she says beside me and I hear the tiniest of laughs when she says it.

Looking back at her bloody and dirty dress, I don't see an ounce of yellow anywhere on it.

"Looks like you kept your shit together," I grin at her.

"Right up to the point where the gun didn't work," she grins right back at me.

I shrug my shoulders. "So you didn't like the fucker this priest was going to marry you to?"

"I'd rather have slit my fucking wrists. It would have been me or him tonight if we were married," she says.

"Lord help me," the priest moans quietly as I begin to yank him down the aisle with me and the girl.

"What's your name?" I ask, ignoring the little bitch of a priest.

"Meghan, why?" she asks before she stops dead in her tracks.

She's so rooted to the floor, I stop to see what's caught her attention.

James looks up at us with a frown as he snips a guy's thumb off. "I call dibs on the next bride. I'm done with thumb duty for the next couple of lifetimes."

"Quit your bitching," Andrew says with a gruff laugh as he elbows him to continue.

Pulling both the quivering priest and the now pale girl past the thumb show, I say, "Andrew, I'm going to need your help."

"With?" he asks as he tosses the bag of thumbs to James.

"Need a witness, I think. Shit, I don't know. I ain't ever been to a wedding," I say, and look over at Meghan.

"I'm Gabriel, by the way," I add, wondering when she's going to look at me.

She's still staring at James even though she had to turn around almost completely to do it. She's not really staring at him though, it's more like staring at what he's doing.

That's good she isn't staring at him. I'd hate to have to snap his neck.

Pulling her and the priest along, I look up at the large cross hanging behind the alter, then at the surrounding bodies left by the bullets that tore through them. It's an odd feeling that all of these men died and I ended up only taking a ghost round through the chest.

"What are we doing?" Meghan asks as I stand us before the alter and shove the priest in front of us.

"Guaranteeing I piss off your old fiancé as much as

possible. He's going to be wanting you back," I say with a smile.

"By what? Forcing me to marry you?" she squeaks out now that she's figured out my plan.

Her voice hits a high octave at the end, and I'm pretty sure she's not gonna be happy about this.

"Force ain't got nothin to do with it, darlin'. You marry me or you stay our prisoner. You can't go back to the Russians. We can't let you go. My side or yours will be using you as a chess piece," I say and elbow the priest.

"A chess piece?" she growls at me as her nails dig into my hands.

She's trying to get me to let her go.

Yeah, that won't happen.

"There's no fucking way!" James shouts.

All four of us turn to James as he starts cursing loudly.

Oh shit.

Trying to contain my laugh, I watch as James tries to wipe the blood off his face that squirted up from one of the stiffs.

"Oh, dear lord, I'm going to be sick," the priest murmurs before he turns his head and starts to retch.

"Fucking hell," Andrew growls as he grabs the priest by the collar.

"He pissed himself earlier..." Meghan says as she looks at everything going on around her.

Shaking her head, she looks up into my eyes. Her eyes are starting to look a little dazed.

Looking down at her small hands enveloped in mine, I can't believe just how soft they are, how delicate they look compared to my big hands.

"I can't do this!" she moans loudly.

"If you want to live past sunset, you will," I respond.

"How the hell did I end up in an even worse situation?" she asks as she tries to tug her hands from mine.

I don't let go. I'm not going to hurt her, but if she runs now, she'll get hurt just as quickly from my side or hers.

"My boss will use you as a pawn. An unbelievably beautiful pawn, but a pawn all the same. I keep you by my side, you stay safe." The words come from my mouth unbidden, but it's the absolute truth.

I know it deep down.

Meghan stands before me, staring up into my eyes, her eyes full of pain and hurt. She's in a deadly position right now. Whatever union she was going to enter with Alexei and the Russians wasn't to her liking, but this one might be even harder for her.

"You're going to force me to marry you, just like Alexei. You're no better than him!" she shouts.

"You're right," I say with a rising of my shoulders, and she is.

"If you try to touch me, I'll slit your throat when you sleep," she snarls.

"I get it," I say again with another shrug of the shoulders.

And I seriously do get where she's coming from, but it isn't going to change her current situation, or mine. She's going to be fucked no matter what she does. She's in a completely shitty situation. I feel for her, I truly do. I've been there myself, but it ain't going to stop me. I went to prison for ten long years for the crimes of another, she's going to marry me because she's a pawn in a deadly war.

Life fucking hurts and it's murder.

"I'll make you a deal. You don't fight, and I'll make sure no one touches you without my say so," I say to her and stare into those deep blue eyes.

She's beautiful. I know I've noticed this already, but it keeps slapping me in the face every time I look at her.

Little things I haven't discovered keep standing out and grabbing my attention. The way her full lips have this natural pout to them. Her bottom lip sticks out just enough that I want to capture it with a kiss so hard that it bruises. There's a small smattering of freckles splashed across the bridge of her nose, and I can't help but wonder where else she has freckles. I'd like to peel off that damn abomination of a dress she's wearing and search for them.

Long dark eyelashes open and close as she peers up at me. She isn't showing any fear now. No, she's got her backbone straight and she's looking at me with challenge.

Nodding to the priest, I say to Andrew, "Get him started."

"What the fuck is going on right now?" Simon sneers over the comms. "We don't have time for this shit."

"Mayhem and bedlam," I say with a chuckle into the comms. "Get me a marriage certificate fully approved. List our residential address as Cherry's address. If it wasn't these fucks who blew up the house, it wont hurt anything. If it was, it's a message."

"Well thought of, Gabriel," Lucifer says through the comms.

"Dearly beloved," the priest stumbles through the beginning of the ceremony.

A look to Andrew gets the process moving.

Andrew jabs a gun into the priest's side.

"Let's move to the important parts here, Father. We need to be moving," Andrew says quietly.

"Calls are making their way into emergency services. I'm unable to stop them all. We need to get out now," Simon says into the comms.

Pushing the priest away from us, I look into Meghan's eyes and ask, "Do you accept my protection?"

She stares for so long into my eyes that I swear she's gone mute, but she hasn't. She's studying me, reading into those deep, dark recesses inside of me.

"I do," she finally says and then adds, "Do you accept that I'll cut your dick off if you ever touch me without my permission?".

"Oh fuck, that's fucking awesome!" James crows from nearby.

Staring back into the deep abyss of her eyes, I look to make sure I still see her soul. She's putting it out for the world right now. She wants to know what type of man I am.

"I do," I say and pull her small body tightly to mine. Looking at those lips again, I add, "But you're not skipping out on this kiss."

Leaning down, I watch as her eyes go wide with shock before I press my lips tightly against hers and keep her there.

She's going to break before I do, I swear.

Closing my eyes, I slant my mouth slowly over hers. Each time I push deeper for the kiss, she resists, but I can feel her resolve breaking. Before long, she's got her fingers clutching at my t-shirt as a tiny groan comes from her mouth.

Pulling away from her, I watch as she slowly comes back to herself, her beautiful face flushed with excitement. Those wondrous breasts pushed up so high, heave up and down as she looks at me with lust and rage.

Damn, that's a sexy fucking look.

Her hand lashes out as fast as lighting across my cheek before she yells, "Asshole!"

Fuck, that turned me on almost as much as the kiss.

Nodding my head, I can't help but agree. "Yeah, but you married me, so you can't say much."

5

MEGHAN

With my lips still tingling from that kiss, Gabriel tugs me out of the church and leads me up to a black Tahoe parked in the parking lot. Without a word, he pulls open the passenger door, expecting me to get in. When I hesitate, he gives me a little nudge like he expects me to obey him without protest.

Sirens blare in the distance, and I know there's only a few minutes before the authorities show up.

Feet firmly on the ground, I square my shoulders, deciding this is the hill I'll die on.

"What are you doing?" Gabriel frowns at me and gives me another nudge.

Unfortunately, despite my unwillingness to move, I end up taking a stumbling step back before I catch myself.

The fucker is strong. Strong and big. I thought the height difference between Alexei and me was enormous. With Gabriel it's downright ridiculous.

"I'm not getting in the car," I say, squaring my shoulders again to stand my ground.

I have to tip my head back to glare up at him.

"The fuck you're not," he growls and reaches down, grabbing me around the waist.

Hefting me up as if I weight nothing, he begins to stuff me and my enormous fluffy skirt in the car.

"Stop. Put me down! I'm not going with you!" I screech, fighting his hold and pounding my fists against his chest. "Just leave me. I won't tell them anything, I swear on my mother's grave. Just let me go!"

Gabriel exhales loudly through his nose as he struggles to get both me and my skirt inside the car while ignoring my fists.

"Gabriel, please!" I plead, my aching fists slowing.

Pounding on him is like pounding on concrete.

"We're married," he practically snarls before shoving me into the seat.

I manage to get out, "But not legally!" before he slams the door in my face.

Through the glass I watch him smirk and shake his head at me. Immediately I try the door handle, but no matter how hard I pull and yank on the thing the door won't open.

Dammit, he must have some kind of child safety lock enabled.

As he begins to walk around the front of the car, I get the bright idea to find the lock and disable it. Launching myself toward the driver's side of the car, I reach for all the buttons on the armrest only to abruptly come up short.

It takes me a precious second to figure out something is holding me back. Looking over my shoulder, I see that a big chunk of my skirt is stuck in the door.

Dammit!

I'm trapped inside this damn car until he helps me out.

The driver's side door opens and Gabriel slides his gigantic body into the seat.

I recoil immediately, scooting as far away from him as possible.

Without looking over at me, Gabriel starts the car up and says, "Put your seatbelt on."

I refuse to at first in stubborn defiance.

Gabriel shrugs his shoulders. "Suit yourself."

Putting the car into the gear, he hits the gas and we squeal out of the parking spot. Then he takes a very sharp, very unnecessary turn to the left that pushes me into the door.

"Shit," I mutter under my breath.

When the car finally straightens, I hastily do up my seatbelt.

Eyes sliding toward me, he grins and says, "Good girl."

"Fuck you," I sputter back, caught off guard.

Seriously, who does this guy think he is?

His lips twitch and his eyes gleam with amusement at the windshield. "Maybe later... If you promise not to cut my dick off..."

He hits the gas harder.

I could sputter some more, blush, or even wilt into my seat, but I'm starting to get my bearings back. I know I should be afraid of him. I mean, he did burst into my wedding and shoot the place up.

And the thumbs... damn, the thumbs.

But there's just something about him, something about the way he's tried to protect me even though I tried to kill him, that makes me feel like I don't have to worry about him suddenly backhanding me or something.

Flashing him a feral smile that's all teeth, I say, "Did I say cut off? I meant bite off."

Gabriel slowly turns his head toward me then his lips stretch into a feral smile that mirrors my own. "I don't know what kind of pussies you were with before you married me, but I like a little teeth."

What the fuck?

I open my mouth, knowing I should give some witty, snappy retort, but I've got nothing. Absolutely nothing.

Gabriel chuckles and returns his eyes to the road.

Then he decides to add, "For future reference."

Oh god, I know I shouldn't be trying to picture in my head exactly what he means by 'a little teeth' but that's exactly what I'm doing. Does he mean he likes a little teeth because he likes to be bitten in the heat of the moment? Or does he like it when a woman scrapes her teeth against him while giving him head?

Fuck, I so shouldn't be thinking about this right now.

Heat begins to creep down my neck, down my breasts, and I wonder what the hell is wrong with me. I've had a terrible day. I was drugged, abused, almost forced into a marriage, almost killed, and then forced into another unwanted marriage...

Yet here I am, trapped in a car with a stranger who's now my husband, and wondering what it would feel like to have him in my mouth.

Thankfully, the screen on the console starts to ring with an incoming call, pulling me from my perverted and totally inappropriate thoughts.

Gabriel scowls at the lit-up screen and starts jamming all the buttons surrounding it like he doesn't know what the fuck he's doing.

I watch him in silent amusement.

Does he not know how to use the phone?

The screen stops ringing, the call most likely going to voicemail, and he growls out, "Hello?"

"Uh... you didn't answer it," I point out, then smirk when he gives me a frustrated look.

The screen starts ringing again, and once again Gabriel starts to jam buttons in confusion.

And I feel like we've come to a crossroads.

I could spend my time trapped in this car, watching him struggle to answer the phone like some out-of-touch cave man... It would be amusing and would most definitely serve him right after forcing me to marry him.

But maybe it would be better to help him. I could kill two birds with one stone. I could earn a bit of his trust and gather some information in the process.

If I want out of this mess, I need to know what the hell I'm dealing with.

Coming to a decision, I bump his hand out of the way, and say, "Here."

Then I press the big green accept button on the screen.

Gabriel shakes his head in dismay as my eyes laugh at him.

"What the fuck, Gabriel?" an angry voice comes through the speakers.

"Simon," Gabriel mutters.

"Did you really marry the Callahan girl?!"

"Yeah," Gabriel responds. "She's *Whitmore* now."

So that's my new last name, that's good to know. Not that I plan on keeping it long.

"Do you have any fucking clue what you've done? How much you've fucked up?" Simon growls.

I watch Gabriel's face harden with annoyance. "Yeah, I've done exactly what I've been sprung to do..."

The man, I assume Simon, launches into an angry tirade about how much Gabriel fucked up. He goes on and on about how Gabriel ruined the whole operation. How I'm a liability. How my family will now have the motivation to retaliate against Lucifer and 'the Family'.

Gabriel's eyes flash with menace and his hands tighten around the steering wheel so hard I swear it starts to bend under the pressure.

I feel my own anger reaching the boiling point after listening to Simon's long-winded rant. I've had enough of men talking about me like I'm disposable trash for one day, thank you very much.

Then Simon says, "You should have killed her and saved us all the trouble. Now—"

"You're on speakerphone, asshole!" I snap at him, and press the disconnect button, cutting off his call.

Gabriel shoots me a look and I immediately realize what I've done. "Oh, sorry... I know that was rude, but he was starting to get on my nerves."

Gabriel shakes his head and a smile starts to light up his face only to die an instant death when the phone starts ringing again.

"Fucker," he mutters and begins to reach for the screen.

I bat his hand out of the way. "I got this."

Gabriel arches a brow at me but otherwise he doesn't stop me.

Taking his lack of stopping me as permission, I hit the accept button.

"What the fuck, Gabriel? Did you hang up on—"

"New phone, who dis?" I say, and then hit the disconnect button.

There's a moment of silence, and I start to wonder if I seriously overstepped my bounds and fucked up.

Then Gabriel starts to chuckle. "What the fuck does that mean?"

Smiling in relief, I say, "It's hard to explain, but it should royally piss him off."

"Good," Gabriel says with satisfaction, and I feel myself warming under his grin.

Shit.

I totally shouldn't like his approval. And I totally shouldn't be getting myself involved in this crap.

And Gabriel should probably be keeping his eyes on the road, but he keeps staring at me, making me grow warmer and warmer.

If I must be completely honest, I really hate looking at him head-on. Not only is he entirely too good looking for his own good, with his strong, rugged features, and blonde, scruffy beard, but there's also something about his eyes that suck me in, shutting out the rest of the world.

Perhaps it's because unlike Alexei's eyes, his eyes aren't empty and dead. No, they're full of barely constrained emotion and passion, even when he's not provoked.

Suddenly the screen starts to ring again and Gabriel groans, but I'm thankful to be pulled out of another unsettling moment.

"Do you want to answer it?" I ask.

Gabriel snorts. "Fuck no."

I hold out my hand. "Then give me your phone."

Gabriel doesn't even hesitate, foolish man. I watch him lift his ass off his seat and dig around in his pants pocket. Then he pulls out his phone and willingly places it in my hand.

I could do so much fucking damage with this...

But first, I unlock his phone with a swipe. No pin, interesting. Then I immediately disconnect Bluetooth.

The speakers stop ringing.

"How did you do that?" he asks.

He's truly clueless.

"I turned Bluetooth off..."

He grunts as if it makes sense, but I seriously doubt it does. I flip the button on the side of the phone and it falls silent.

"So... how come you don't know how to use a phone?" I ask, hoping to distract him while I poke around on the screen.

He answers casually like we're discussing the weather. "I just did ten years in a supermax."

My head jerks up in surprise and I blink at him. Though, I don't really know why I'm surprised by this information. He did try to murder everyone attending my wedding... and succeeded in taking down most of them.

"Let me guess? For murder?" I ask sarcastically, not expecting him to glance over at me and answer with a, "Yeah."

A little chill courses down my spine.

"Only ten years, though?" I say, poking for more information as I break eye contact and drop my attention back down to the phone. "Sounds like you got off easy."

"I was sentenced to life," he says casually again, as if it's not a big fucking deal.

What the hell? Did he escape?

"How did you get out so soon? Parole?"

I try to keep my fingers from flying across his phone. There are so many ways I could reach out for help, but I don't want to tip him off.

"No. I was pardoned."

"You're shitting me," I blurt out, my head jerking up again in surprise.

A big fat shit-eating grin spreads across his face. "By the governor himself."

Damn. That means his organization must have the

governor in their pocket, and if their ties are that powerful, there's no telling how high or deep they go.

I'm probably well and truly fucked.

My fingers hover over the send button. I managed to type out a short message, planning on blasting it out to my social media, but this new information makes me pause.

What if they have the cops, the FBI, or any other law enforcement agency in their pockets? Would sending a distress signal get me killed?

I hesitate for too long.

Brows pulling together, Gabriel scowls at me. "What are you doing?"

I swipe quickly out of my account without pushing *send*. "Just checking out your apps."

He holds his hand out expectantly.

With a huff, I start to hand over the phone when it starts vibrating.

Glancing down at the screen, I ask, "Who's Lucifer?"

"Answer it."

With a shrug, I swipe the phone open and hit the icon for speakerphone, figuring that's what he wants.

"Gabriel," a smooth voice drawls out.

"Lucifer," Gabriel says back.

Phone still in my hand, I turn my attention to my window, pretending I'm not that interested in the conversation. Though I very much am.

I recognize the name Lucifer, not only from the day I eavesdropped on Alexei and my father, but also from rumors I've heard over the years. If what I've heard is true then he's currently the most powerful and feared man in Garden City.

He has the entire city in his tight grasp.

Lucifer's smooth drawl seems to slide out of the phone as he says, "Normally, I don't interfere when one of my men sneaks off with their... blushing bride... and holes up with her until she is pregnant. But I fear, in this instance, there are important matters that need to be discussed first."

There just aren't enough *what the fucks* for today. Seriously. Blushing bride? Sneaking off? Holing up until she's pregnant?

Do his men have a habit of doing this?

I slide a glance toward Gabriel. Our gazes collide, crashing into each other. I quickly look away in surprise and hope I haven't given away my interest.

Surely, he wasn't planning on doing that...

"What important matters?" Gabriel grits out as if he's irritated.

There's a pause and then Lucifer says carefully, "We're meeting at the compound. Attendance is mandatory."

I hear Gabriel suck in a slow breath through his teeth and then release it. "I'll be there."

"Good, good," Lucifer says, sounding pleased. "I'm

looking forward to giving my congratulations to you and your beautiful bride, *in person*."

Gabriel grunts in acknowledgement and the call disconnects.

Catching movement out of the corner of my eye, I glance over to see Gabriel holding his hand out to me.

Reluctantly, I place the device in his big palm, carefully avoiding touching any of his skin.

After lifting up and shoving the phone back in his pocket, Gabriel hits the blinker and the car suddenly slows.

A couple of cars pass us before he makes a u-turn, pointing us in the opposite direction.

I look at him in alarm. Why is he suddenly turning around? He wasn't... he couldn't possibly have been planning on doing what Lucifer said...

Our situation is obviously different.

"Why are you looking at me like that?" Gabriel asks, making me realize I've been staring at him.

"Where are we going?" I ask.

"You heard, to the compound," he answers.

"In Garden City?"

"Yeah."

I bite my lip, contemplating my next question and the best way to phrase it without offending him.

He glances over and his gaze drops down to my mouth. His eyes seem to burn into me, darkening with heat.

A flush works its way up my neck.

Suddenly self-conscious, I release my lip.

He jerks his attention away.

What the hell was that?

Taking a little breath to help calm my racing heart, I ask, "Do your... associates have a habit of sneaking off with women and getting them pregnant?"

Gabriel rolls his massive shoulders in shrug. "I wouldn't know, I've been in prison."

Damn. Yeah. I guess that makes sense.

Focusing my attention outside again, I replay Lucifer and Gabriel's words in my head. So far, Gabriel has given me no reason not to trust him since he offered me his protection. You know, besides being a convicted murderer and spending ten years in prison.

Perhaps I'm being just a little paranoid.

Then he suddenly adds out of the blue, "I wouldn't put it past Simon, though. Fucker probably kept his wife tied up and locked in the house until he got her pregnant."

"Seriously?" I ask, unsure if he's joking or not.

Gabriel looks at me, not a hint of amusement on his face. "After listening to him on the phone, do you think any woman would willingly put up with his shit?"

"No," I have to admit with a sinking feeling of dread.

Perhaps Lucifer was stating the truth. That doesn't

necessarily mean though that Gabriel would do such a thing. After all, in his own words, he's been locked up in prison.

Just to be sure though, I try to joke, "You wouldn't do that, right? Obviously, you're not as annoying as him..."

Gabriel just looks at me as he deadpans, "I don't know. Depends on how much you fight me."

I laugh. "You're joking."

He has to be.

Gabriel's lips begin to curve with amusement and he arches a brow. "Am I?"

My laughter trails off and I feel the need to firmly remind him, "Remember, you agreed not to touch me without my permission."

"I did," he agrees with a nod, and then his lips stretch into a full grin. "But I didn't say anything about not getting you pregnant..."

6

GABRIEL

The moment Lucifer called to inform me of the mandatory meeting, I felt the tension in my shoulders increase tenfold. Fuck, the tension in my shoulders isn't nearly as thick as the tension in the car.

Meghan posed the question of whether I'll be touching her without her permission... and a lot of things could cause that to happen...

But what I think she means is will I be taking her against her will...

"I won't rape you, Meghan. That's not my bag," I say with a grunt as I pull to a stop at a red light.

I won't have to take her or force her. When it comes time, she'll be coming to me and begging me for it.

Watching her body, I notice she doesn't edge toward the door for escape, but the way she's riding that side of the car, I can feel she wants to get away from me as much as she wants to kiss the fuck out of me. We've got that fucking animal magnetism.

"I... I know that. I just don't understand exactly what the fuck is going on," she snaps at me.

Obviously, us turning around and heading toward Lucifer has thrown her off kilter.

Fuck, it wasn't in my plans either. I expected, at the very least, to be able to head back to the hotel room I got last night. But now the boss wants us there... At the fucking compound.

Joy of fucking joys.

"We're heading to the compound for a debriefing," I say, and my damn hand wants to reach out to feel hers.

Just touching her skin back there in the church has me itching for more contact. No one else but hers. I can smell her perfume from here and it's fucking intoxicating in this small fucking space of a vehicle.

Meghan's the first person I've touched in ten long fucking years that I didn't want to commit violence upon.

I can't stop the thoughts of how different this world is. I went in a man and came out something else. I feel like a fucking shadow of death. I can't be near people or touch them without wanting to strangle the life out of them. Something broke inside of me while I was in the supermax. Something that I can't name or even understand. Killing that fucking Russian prick last night helped though, it let me feel alive again. I wasn't the fucking one being beat up on.

I was in control.

Last night I dumped the corpse on the steps of the church, lit it on fire, and headed out to an out-of-the-way motel. That was my night. No parties or huge ass meals. I got a bottle of soda from the vending machine and a bag of chips.

John offered me a place at his house to stay. So did most of the other guys. I wasn't ready for that, though. I don't think I'd be good in a house full of kids or around happy people. I didn't do those kinds of things back then, before I went in, and I won't be doing them now.

John saw my face when he tried to touch me. He knows how much I don't want to be touched by another human being. It's something deep down and primal. I survived ten years of hell, and now I'm out here in this bright shiny fucking world. I can't seem to get a grip on the pace of the world surrounding me.

Maybe that's why I stood there when she tried to put a bullet through my chest.

There was more than enough time to snatch that gun from her tiny hands. I just didn't do it. Was I not sharp enough, was I not up to my old self? Or did I want her to put that slug through my heart so I could at least feel something besides the dead fucking husk of a body I walk around in?

Dead and full of fucking hunger.

Hunger for an outlet.

"Are you going to answer me?" Meghan asks with annoyance.

"What?" I ask as I turn my gaze to her.

"I asked what is the compound? Are you guys in a cult or something?"

"Or something," I say as I fight to keep my eyes on the road and not her.

She's beautiful, feisty as fuck, and has those lips that would look amazing wrapped around my cock. Although, in truth, I'm getting that cock-biter vibe from her all of a sudden.

Dead inside and all I can think about is pulling her over to my chest and hoping she can breathe life into my brain.

"Look, this really doesn't need to be like this..." she says as she looks out the window.

"It does," I say simply.

I don't have any other words for her. She'll learn we won't be stopping the wheel that's been set in motion.

PULLING into the compound is like going back in fucking time, except not at all. All those memories of my early days in the family are there in the back of my mind, but this place has become something so different I almost can't believe it's the same place.

The first thing I notice is the wall surrounding the house. The chain link fence has been removed, replaced by a huge stone wall with mini towers on the corners. A huge mammoth gate blocks off the private drive with a fucking guard station.

Fuck, time and money has turned this place into a fucking fortress.

Slowing down to enter the gate, I stare at the guard who motions for me to open the window. Who the fuck is this guy?

Pushing the button down, I'm half-tempted to reach out and rip his fucking throat out as he touches the trigger of his semi-assault rifle.

"Sir," he says simply, and if he was close enough I really would hurt him.

"Open the fucking gate," I growl out at him.

"Gabriel..." Meghan hisses from my side as she watches more men surround the SUV we're sitting in.

It's a tense couple of seconds before I hear a radio squawk from the guard's shoulder. "Let him in."

The guard simply turns away from me. Heading back to the guard house, he steps inside to activate the gate.

"Asshole," comes from my gritted teeth as I gun the engine of the vehicle.

Meghan quietly murmurs to me as the steering

wheel starts to groan from how hard I'm gripping it. "Calm down, Gabriel. They're just doing their job."

The blood rushing to my brain slowly abates as I pull the SUV through the gates and down the drive to the massive house. I can slowly feel my hands loosening on the wheel as her touch radiates a feeling of warmth.

"Fuck," I say with a shake of my whole body.

The red haze that started to flood my vision has abated completely when I look over at her.

Her hand slowly pulls away from me as she watches me. Is she afraid of me? I can't really tell, but she doesn't act like it. If anything, she seems to be emboldened by being able to calm me.

She should be afraid of me, not fucking smirking when I look her in the eyes.

"You okay there, big guy? We kind of need a steering wheel if we want to drive away from here," she says with that sexy fucking smirk.

"I don't like guards, and I really don't like asshole guards," I grumble before hopping out of the parked vehicle.

It's fucking springtime here in Garden City, and as fucking usual it's freezing temperatures one day and mild the next. All the same, as I go around the car to help my struggling bride out of the vehicle, I take a moment to pull my black tactical coat from the back.

It's not fucking cold outside right now, but it's not exactly warm.

Going around to her side of SUV, I start yanking out yards and fucking yards of fabric. I know my bride was stuffed into the fucking passenger side of the vehicle, I'm the one who put her there, dammit. But right now, I can't find anything but the ankle of a very pissed off woman.

"Who the fuck even wants to wear one of these bulky dresses in the first place?" she shouts as I finally grab her forearm and yank her out of the seat.

Pulling out the combat knife attached to my belt, I give her a look. "You didn't pick this fucking thing out?"

Eyeing the knife, she shakes her head slowly. "No, they had me so drugged up I had no clue I was even wearing this until right before the wedding started."

"Ah." Kneeling down in front of her, I start slicing through most of the frilly shit that I can't even remember the name of.

Hacking my way through until I see her calves, I quickly move around her, trying to trim off as much of the material as I can.

"Holy shit!" she groans when she looks down at the huge pile of white stuff. "You cut off like thirty pounds. My hips hurt so bad from all that damn weight on them."

Lifting up my jacket to her, I motion for her to take

it. "Would've been better for the both of us if we'd had a nudist wedding."

Snatching the jacket out of my hands, she tucks herself inside of it before she responds. "Not on your life "

Looking down into her eyes, I can't help but notice how small she is inside my coat. She almost looks like a lost little waif. But those fiery eyes stare back at me with a spirit that goes straight to my cock. This little one is all fucking kinds of danger bound in a little body.

"We'll see," I say as I turn toward the house.

"Fuck no, we won't." she growls at my back before jogging to catch up to me.

My silence must really irritate her though because she jabs me hard in the ribs to ask, "What are we doing here?"

"My boss wants to have a talk. I suspect it's about the marriage and what's going on with your father and your former fiancé," I say as we approach the door. "There's a lot of shit blowing around the city right now and we'd rather it be blowing in our favor."

"But I don't have anything to do with this!" she snarls. "I was being forced to fucking marry him. I didn't get to choose whether I wanted to marry him any more than I got to choose being married to you."

Reaching up to knock on the door, I'm tempted to use the knocker, but instead I use my fist as a hammer and just give it a couple of good thumps. "Yeah, well, we all have shit choices in life. You said yes, too late to back out now."

"You didn't even give me a choice!" she shouts just as the door swings open.

A beautiful young woman appears before us, her eyes taking us in quickly. "You must be Gabriel and Meghan."

Nice, she didn't even bat an eye with how either of us are dressed.

"I am," I say.

"Good, please come in. Matthew is up in his office, but I'm sure he'll be down soon," the woman says. "I'm Lily, Matthew's wife."

As soon as we step into the warm home, I can hear the distant screech of children running around the house. What the fuck kind of twilight zone did I enter? The last time I was here, I was leaving the house with handcuffs on my wrists as multiple dead bodies were being taken away.

Kids... a wife...

Fucking hell, who the hell has Lucifer turned into?

"Ah, there the two lovebirds are," Lucifer's drawl comes as he descends the stairs.

He's got a smirk a mile wide when he looks at the both of us. I haven't removed my tactical holster or vest, and looking over at my wife in my black tactical jacket and torn up wedding attire, I can't even begin to imagine what Lucifer's wife thinks of us both.

"Lovebirds?" Meghan repeats in disbelief.

"Yes dear," I say with a deep frown at the small beauty beside me.

It's going to be so much better if she goes with the flow, I think. If she doesn't, shit here could turn messy pretty damn quickly. I'm not letting her get away from me, and I sure as hell won't be letting anyone fucking try to take her away from me, not even Lucifer himself.

This sexy little woman is fucking *mine*.

"Dear?" Meghan rounds on me and stares into my eyes.

She's pissed and not hiding it.

"Remember our vows," I say.

Standing on her tiptoes in those fucking heels she's wearing must be painful, but she adds a couple inches to herself as she tries and fails to look me dead in the eye.

"I'm going to fucking kill you," she says only loud enough that I can hear her.

Grinning, I wrap my arm around her waist, pulling her in tight.

Then I whisper softly in her ear. "I'm going to fuck you so hard."

Gasping, she pulls away from me, turning a bright red. Fiery anger in her eyes mixes with something entirely different as she stares at me. Annoyance, fear, and lust all mixed in one delicious package.

A knock at the door behind us breaks the tension that's been building in the large foyer.

"That will be one of the men," Lily says with a smile as she goes to the door and opens it up.

"Ma'am," James's voice comes from behind me.

"Ah, now that we're all mostly here, we should head upstairs to talk," Lucifer says with a nod toward James and me.

Meghan may be as brave as they come, but the look of fear that crosses her features as she hears this startles me. Does she think we're going to hurt her for information? I'd never allow that.

"Meghan, you look like you could use a cup of coffee," Lily says with a smile.

"I... I think I could," Meghan stammers when she turns to look at Lily.

"Excellent," Lucifer says. "We'll be in the office."

Right now I'd rather catch a cup of coffee, but that's only because I need to keep Meghan close to me. She's mine and it feels as if she's being ripped from my hands as she walks past the staircase that I'm walking up.

One last look over her shoulder at me rips my insides out.

Fucking hell.

Rolling my shoulders, I clench my fists a couple of

times to get the blood flowing in my body. She's safe in this house, I keep telling myself. I don't like that she's without me, though.

I said I'd protect her. Not someone else.

"Where's your bag?" I ask James as we get closer to the office.

"Bag?" he asks in confusion.

"Yeah, with the thumbs in it."

"Shit!" James groans. "I just got all that fucking blood off me."

"Leave them in the car," Simon's voice calls out from the office. "My wife doesn't need to see you trailing a bunch of severed thumbs through the house."

"Agreed," Matthew says.

Shrugging my shoulders, I turn back to James and say, "Ten fucking years. Ten years and I never touched a dick but my own."

"What?" he asks.

Flinging my wrist out at his balls, I feel just the tips of my fingers connect. His eyes cross and he slowly falls to his knees. The groan he lets out is sweet music to my ears.

"Lucifer had to explain what the apps you put on my phone were," I say with a laugh.

Lucifer just shakes his head at our antics.

"Could you act your fucking ages?" Simon grumbles as he gives me a dirty ass look.

"What's got your panties in a bunch?" I ask Simon as I sit down in one of the chairs.

"You fucking taking Callahan's daughter as your fucking bride for starters," he spits out at me.

"You said bedlam and mayhem. I just married our families together," I say.

"I like it," Lucifer says from behind the desk he's sitting at.

It's the same desk that's been in this house long before I came to family. He fits well behind it. Though it reminds me of the last time I saw him sitting there. It was the first time he sat there as the head of the family, with the bodies of his father's former men splayed out around the house. A true coup.

But that coup had come at a cost.

Too many connected men died in this house that day. One of them being the mayor of Garden City.

It was the mayor's death that ended up sending me to prison.

I should have rotted away in prison and died a long miserable death. But Lucifer kept his promise. He got me out. He said he would, but ten long years was a long time to see any light at the end of the tunnel.

It turned me into the man I am now, for good or ill.

Johnathan enters the office. He walks over to a chair near mine and flops his ass down. Doesn't seem like he's changed much. He's still dressed like when I met him, jeans and biker boots with a gun at his hip.

Andrew and the rest of our inner circle make it into the office, and Lucifer looks at us all with a deep grin.

"I like having you all back together again," Lucifer says.

"Been a long time," Johnathan says as he reaches over to slap me on the shoulder.

Fucker. He knows I don't want to be touched, but with that damn look in his eyes he doesn't give a shit. Typical fucking Johnathan.

Andrew pulls a phone from his pocket and tosses it to Simon. "All the stiffs in the church. Got face pics, and tried to get as many tattoos as I could. Mix of Russians and Irish. Should be pretty evident which side they were on."

"Good," Simon says as he begins scrolling through the phone.

"So, what's the next step?" Jude asks from behind me.

"We need more intel on why they're partnering up with the Irish. Callahan wasn't even much of a player over in Bethlehem before now. Is he simply trying to take a larger slice of the pie?" Simon asks, looking up from the phone he's now got attached by some cord to a laptop.

"Bigger piece of the pie is my guess," Andrew says.

"Same here, especially since I talked to the Heralds of Hell. Their Sergeant at Arms, Cane, is pretty pissed at the Irish as well. They were getting a good supply of guns from them that's dried up recently," Johnathan says.

Looking over to him, I ask, "They still the top dog MC over there?"

"Were," he responds to me. "They got knocked down a few pegs when the leader died and his son got too big for his britches. That, and the fucking Cartel they have popping up all over the place there."

"They're going to be a problem before too long if we don't keep an eye on them," Jude says. "The Cartel is up in Ohio, and it's not exactly going well for the big cities."

"They are unfortunately for another day," Simon says as he flips the laptop around on his lap to show us a picture.

"Who'd like a deathmark on their head?" he asks with a laugh.

Looking at the picture on the screen, I see a pretty blonde woman with brown eyes staring vacantly back at us.

"I shot her at the wedding," Jude says.

"Well, one of us just pissed off a really bad woman. This is Tanya Petrov. Her twin sister is Anya Petrov. And we've just taken out one of the two deadliest women the FSB has ever produced," Simon says with a grimace.

"Meaning what, Simon?" Lucifer asks.

"Anya Petrov is going to come gunning for us, and

with her abilities, it won't be pretty." Simon clicks on another set of pictures that shows two Russian men.

"Misha Sokolov. Alexei's right-hand man when it comes to the slaver's trade since we killed off Sasha. Which is good for us and bad for them. I don't recognize the rest off the top of my head, but I'll be going through the prints and mugshots," Simon says before snapping his laptop shut.

"Next item of business, you married Meghan Callahan, Gabriel. Why is it that every time one of my men finds a woman from the wrong side of things, they marry her?" Lucifer asks with a chuckle.

"They want to be just like dear old dad," James says from the floor where he's slid himself up against the wall.

Shrugging, Lucifer looks over to Simon. "This will actually be working in our favor. We could have tortured her for what little information she probably had and then left her for dead somewhere... But this way we have more leverage. Especially in the future if we remove the Russians from the equation."

Just the mention of someone laying a finger on my woman has my vision turning red. I can feel the fucking rage flood through my veins so quickly I almost leap from the chair to throttle Lucifer for daring to entertain the thought.

"Not fucking happening," I growl through gritted teeth.

Lucifer takes a moment to look at me, and I think he's looking at me for the first time as the monster I am. "Agreed."

We stare at each other for a long time, the men around us talking and joking about the church hit. Not us, though.

"Men, I do believe dinner will be served in a bit. Give Gabriel and I a moment to catch up before then," he says while still maintaining eye contact.

Simon starts to object before Lucifer raises a hand to cut him off.

When the room clears, Lucifer says, "It's been a long time since you went in Gabriel."

"It has," I say in response.

"Do you think I've forgotten what you did for me?" he asks seriously. His eyes still have that odd fucking glow to them after all these years.

They have a way of looking directly into your soul. Looking so thoroughly through all those hidden corners of your mind.

"You got me out. I think you've done exactly what you promised," I say.

"That's not what I asked," He responds.

"No, I don't think you've forgotten what I did. You couldn't go in without this family going to ruin. Simon wouldn't have made it through. I doubt John would have been able to, either. I was the one who had what it took to get through it all," I say with a shrug.

The intensity gone now, both of us lean back in our chairs.

"Why did it seem like you were about to strangle me back there?" he asks.

"You mentioned harm coming to my woman," I say with a laugh.

"Is she yours already, Gabriel?" he asks.

Without hesitation, I answer, "Yes."

7

MEGHAN

"Cream and sugar?" Lily asks as she pours fresh coffee into a mug for me.

"Yes, please," I respond distractedly, too busy looking around and trying to wrap my head around this surreal situation.

Is this really happening? Am I really standing in this upscale kitchen, surrounded by sparkling stainless steel appliances, with this woman who's dressed like she just stepped off of a Paris runway?

It feels too strange to be real. This perfect kitchen, Lily acting as the perfect hostess. Perhaps I'm still drugged and I'm hallucinating.

Lily adds a little cream and sugar and slides the mug over to me.

I pick it up, say, "Thank you," and take a tentative sip.

The coffee is almost too hot, but my body's response to the heat is reassuring.

As I set the mug back down, though, I notice the lettering wrapping around it.

Coffee Makes Me Poop.

Yeah... there's no way this is really happening. It's official, I've lost my ever-loving mind. Any minute I'm going to wake up.

And then what?

Get married to Alexei.

Fuck.

I really hope this isn't a dream.

"Meghan?" Lily says, the thick concern in her voice pulling my attention back to her. "Are you okay? I've heard you had quite the day..."

I stare at her face for a moment, trying to determine if she's being sincere or just faking it. She's quite beautiful, stunning really, I realize. Even with her lips pulled down and her eyes narrowed with worry.

"Yeah, you can say that again." I sigh and reach for the mug again.

Lily's eyes flick down to the mug and back up to my face, the concerned look still firmly in place. "Perhaps something a little stronger is in order?"

I pause with the mug in midair then quickly put it back down and push it toward her. "I'll take the strongest booze you have on hand."

Lily nods and moves around the gleaming granite

kitchen island. Bending down, she disappears from my sight and I hear bottles clinking together.

"Is whiskey okay?" she asks.

"Yes, that's fine. Thank you," I reply and frown.

Her politeness is beginning to make me a little uncomfortable and suspicious. Why is she being so nice to me? Does she have an ulterior motive?

Her blonde head reappears and she walks back to me with a bottle of amber liquid clutched in her hand.

Untwisting the lid, she tops my mug off and gives me an apologetic smile as she stirs it. "I'm sorry, it's not Irish."

"Being Irish is overrated," I mutter before picking the mug back up and quickly gulping from it.

Lily's apologetic smile turns sad, and I'm hit with a little pang of regret for causing it. Even if she does have an ulterior motive, she's been nothing but polite, and I'm acting like a rude ass.

I quickly take another gulp of my spiked coffee to wash the pang away.

"Do you want to talk about what happened?"

My first reaction is to tell her *no*, hell no. I don't want to relive a single moment. I want to get drunk and forget the whole thing happened.

But maybe, just maybe, if she's truly sympathetic, she can help me out of this mess. Maybe, if I work her right, appeal to her woman to woman, she can help me get away.

I take another gulp of the spiked coffee and then ask, "How much do you know?"

Lily glances nervously at the door before admitting quietly, "I've only heard a little here and there. I know you were to marry that Russian, Alexei."

When she speaks Alexei's name a look of utter disgust passes over her face.

And my heart begins to swell with foolish hope.

"I didn't want to marry him," I feel the need to point out. "I was forced into it."

She nods her head, the look of disgust fading away, but her eyes are full of questions.

I decide the best course of action is to start from the beginning. I don't need to bullshit her or even exaggerate the circumstances. The truth is horrible enough to make my case.

"They drugged me. When I came to, I found myself in a back room of the church, wearing this wedding dress..."

Lily's eyes grow wide, and they only grow wider and wider as I give her every detail, not leaving anything out. I want her to have every, gritty, gory detail. I want her to know what they did to me.

As I tell my story, I notice her glancing wistfully at the bottle of whiskey, as if just hearing what happened to me makes her need a drink. But for whatever reason she never reaches for the bottle.

When I finally reach Lucifer's phone call, her face flushes with a blush.

That's interesting...

Ignoring the blush, I wrap things up quickly and end the story by spreading my hands and saying, "And now I'm here."

Lily nods her head slowly and glances at the bottle again. I reach out and nudge it toward her, but she shakes her head.

When I arch my brow, she explains, "I'm pregnant."

Of course she is, I think as Lucifer's call replays in my head. I bet that's all these men do. Lock their women up and fill their bellies with babies.

Her blush darkens as I force a tight smile, grab my mug, and tell her, "Congratulations."

I finish off the rest of my spiked coffee and almost ask for a refill, as nasty as it is.

An uncomfortable silence falls over the kitchen as we both process the story I told.

Then we both speak at once.

Lily says, "Meghan, I'm glad you're—"

As I say, "Lily, I know it's—"

We both cut ourselves off and laugh with embarrassment.

"Go on," Lily encourages me.

I hesitate, wishing I could hear what she was going to say first. It'd be nice to have an idea of what she's thinking right now. If she's even moved by my situation.

Taking a deep breath, I gather what emotional fortitude I have left, and say, "Lily, I know it's a lot to ask, but I need your help."

Lily's face immediately shuts down, becoming guarded, like a switch was just flipped.

Damn. I was afraid of that.

"What do you need?" she asks, glancing at the door again.

No doubt she's worried someone might overhear this conversation.

The little hope I had deflates behind my ribs.

I should have known better than to take this risk. She's Lucifer's wife, and if she's anything like the Irish women, above all else, she's loyal to him.

I have to ask, though. I *have* to. I already let one opportunity slip through my fingers when I gave Gabriel's phone back to him without a fight, and who knows how many more chances I'll get.

"Help me get away," I whisper. "Please."

Lily's expression softens as her eyes meet my eyes, and for a moment I almost believe all hope is not lost.

Perhaps she's different...

Then she sighs and says gently, "Meghan, you said yourself Alexei is determined to have you. And knowing what I know, what everyone knows about him, if I help you get away, do you really think he won't hunt you down? That he won't spare any resource or expense to find you and right this slight against him?"

My shoulders slump in defeat and disappointment.

"He might not," I weakly counter. "He might consider me a lost cause…"

But even I don't believe that. Even if Alexei no longer wants me as his bride, I know he and my father will hunt me down for the principle of it. They've been more than slighted, they've been downright humiliated. And in our life, in our circles, your reputation, your honor, your standing in the fucking social pecking order, is just as valuable, if not as valuable, as all the money and connections you possess.

Insults are as deadly as weapons.

"He will," Lily says firmly with assurance. "He's going to come for you, and we're the only family who has ever stood up to him and survived it. We're the only family that's punished him and made him pay for his transgressions."

With each word she speaks, I feel myself inwardly withdrawing from her more and more. She doesn't realize it, but her surety, her confidence, her damn belief, in what will play out is putting me on edge.

"So you're not going to help me?" I ask, doing my best to keep my bottom lip from quivering. Doing my best to keep the damn tears out of my eyes as the full hopeless reality of my situation sinks its claws into my brain. "You think I should just accept what happened?

I should just accept that I'm a fucking pawn that can be handed off to man after man?"

"No, that's not what I'm saying at all," Lily is quick to say in her defense. "I don't think you should be a pawn. And I don't think you need to accept others making decisions for you."

"Then what are you saying?" I ask, honestly confused.

What is her point? What the hell is she getting at?

Lily's eyes slide away for a moment before they slide back to me. "What I was trying to say," she says softly. "Is that I'm glad you're here, Meghan. I truly am."

"Why are you glad I'm here?" I press, still not getting it.

Lily reaches out, gently taking my hands in hers and looks me directly in the eyes. "Because here is the safest place you can be."

I resist the urge to jerk my hands back and scoff at her. The safest place I can be? Here? Seriously? I'm at the mercy of an organization, a *family*, that has no fondness or attachment to me. I don't even have blood on my side. Yet again, I'm a fucking pawn, a bargaining chip, for someone to use as they please.

Noticing my look of disbelief, Lily gently squeezes my hands and it's on the tip of my tongue to remind her how Alexei hurt me.

Then she says, looking deeply into my eyes once

more as if she's trying to get through to me, "Gabriel will protect you. He's your best chance at staying alive."

Her words fill me with a mixture of hot anger and cold terror.

Because she's right.

But, "Only until he no longer has a use for me."

Lily opens her mouth, no doubt ready to argue, but she's cut off by an ear-splitting screech.

Two little girls come squealing and giggling into the kitchen, playing a game of tag or chase.

Dropping my hands, Lily's lips pull down into a frown as she turns to the girls. "Evelyn and Abigail, what did I tell you girls about running and yelling in the house?"

The little blonde girl comes to such an abrupt stop that the little girl with dark curls that was chasing her stumbles into her back. They both squeak and nearly fall over, but quickly catch their balance.

The blonde checks on her friend, making sure she's okay, before looking to Lily. "You told us not to, Mommy," she says in the sweetest little voice.

Lily nods her head, switching effortlessly into full mommy mode.

She gives both the girls a stern look. "And what did I tell you the punishment would be if I caught you doing it again, Evelyn?"

Evelyn's face falls and her bottom lips begins to jut out, but then her big eyes land on me.

Her entire face suddenly lights up, doing a complete one-eighty, and she squeals, "A princess!"

I blink at her in surprise, and I only have about five seconds to prepare myself before both girls come charging at me.

I don't know why or how Evelyn came to her conclusion. It must be the dress I'm wearing, even though Gabriel has hacked most of the skirt away. Or maybe it's the gloves and all the jewelry...

"I'm not a princess," I say, taking a step back and holding my hands out as a shield in front of me.

The girls must not hear me because they both run up and wrap their arms around me. Pure happiness lights up their faces.

"I didn't know you invited a princess over for dinner, Mommy!" Evelyn says excitedly.

Her friend, whom I'm assuming is Abigail, tips her head back and beams up at me as she hugs me tightly. "I've always wanted to meet a princess. Are you here to have tea?"

I shoot Lily a 'help me' look and try my best to gently pry the girls off me. Their little arms are like bands of steel though. For being so small, they are quite strong.

"I'm not a princess," I helplessly repeat.

"Evelyn, Abigail, release Meghan at once," Lily says firmly.

She has to say it three more times, her voice

growing louder and louder over their happy squeals of "Princess Meghan," before they finally decide to obey.

Reluctantly both girls release their grip, lips jutting out and arms falling to their sides.

"That is not how we treat our guests, girls. Tell your brother Adam you are to do twenty minutes of numbers with him," Lily says to Evelyn, her voice stern and leaving no room for argument.

Evelyn's little shoulders drop and tears shine in her eyes. "Yes, Mommy."

"Next time," Lily warns. "It will be thirty."

Shoulders slumped, faces dejected, both girls shoot me a disappointed look as they begin to leave the kitchen, and I don't know what the hell comes over me.

Maybe it's because they were so excited over the prospect of me being a princess, or maybe it's just their sad, adorable little faces, but I feel bad about the whole thing.

"If you're good, I'll have tea with you later," I tell them, the words just slipping out of me.

Lily shoots me a look and I quickly realize I probably should have asked her permission first. But then her lips curve into a smile as both girls light up again and promise they'll behave.

Once the girls are gone, in a flurry of giggles and excitement, I lean against the counter, feeling tired and drained.

My day is catching up to me.

"That was nice of you," Lily says, her smile still in place.

"I'm sorry, I probably should have asked your permission first..."

She waves me off, as if it's no big deal.

"More coffee?" she asks.

I shake my head.

Nodding, her gaze drags down me, taking in my ruined wedding dress. "We should probably get you changed before someone else mistakes you for a princess."

8

MEGHAN

It's dark by the time we leave the compound. The sky is overcast, the moon smothered beneath a blanket of clouds.

I don't know exactly what time it is, but it must be late, and I'm beyond exhausted. The dinner I was forced to attend with my new 'family' felt like it dragged on forever, and I have no doubt hours and hours have passed.

In the comfort of the car, my eyes struggle to stay open as we drive to only God knows where. It doesn't help that the seat I'm sinking into is extremely soft, the leather like butter, or that Gabriel has the heater cranked up to full blast with all the vents pointed at me.

"Warming up?" he asks, his deep, rumbling voice jolting me awake.

Sitting up a little straighter, I mumble, "Yeah."

I wasn't sleeping, teacher, I swear.

Reaching up to rub the sand out of my eyes, I glance over at him, catching him looking down at my now bare legs.

"Good."

That's like the hundredth time I've caught him looking at my legs tonight.

Sensing my attention, he jerks his gaze away, focusing on the road.

The air in the car suddenly grows thick and heavy with uncomfortable tension.

I watch his fingers flex and relax against the steering wheel, flex and relax.

And for the umpteenth time, I curse myself for not accepting Lily's offer of pantyhose. After swallowing my pride and accepting a dress from her—a very nice, very flattering designer black sheath dress—I couldn't bring myself to further impose on her.

Stupid pride. I totally should have imposed on her. If I did, I wouldn't have had to endure Gabriel's little touches all night.

The man can't seem to stop touching me. Little touches that could be confused for being innocent.

But I know they're not innocent, dammit.

Throughout dinner, he found every reason and excuse to brush his skin against mine. He was constantly reaching across me for one thing or another, brushing his hand against my arm. And when he wasn't doing that, beneath the table he was rubbing his thigh against my thigh.

I couldn't escape his touch or his *heat*, and it was beyond distracting and frustrating. At a time when I should have been focused on learning everything I could about the people around me, all I could focus on, all I could pay attention to was what the man beside me was doing.

Eyes still on Gabriel's hands, I shift closer to my door to put a little more space between us.

His fingers squeeze around the steering wheel and his body visibly tenses.

I don't know what's up with him, but I don't like it one bit. The way he's acting is alarming, and more than a little bit disturbing.

Out of nowhere, the worst realization *ever* dawns on me. My tired brain putting the pieces together.

He was locked up in prison for ten years...

When was the last time he spent any significant time with a woman?

Oh god...

And now he's married to *me*.

I shift closer to my door and Gabriel glances over.

With a look of concern, eyes narrowing and forehead creasing, he asks, "Everything okay?"

I nod my head and lean against the door. "I'm just a little sleepy. Where are we going?"

He looks back to the road.

Rolling the tension out of his shoulders, he seems to relax. "To a safe house. You can sleep if you like."

Yeah, not likely, buddy.

"I don't want to sleep."

I *can't* sleep. I need to remain awake and alert so I can pay attention to where the hell he's taking me.

Peering out the window, I try to make sense of the dark landscape passing us by. It's nearly impossible though, and the fact that I'm completely unfamiliar with this city is seriously not helping.

"Do you want some music?" he asks.

I really wish he would be meaner or something. The way he's being so damn... *accommodating* is becoming annoying.

"Sure," I reply, my eyes squinting at a sign I'm trying to make out in the distance.

The radio comes on, too loud at first, and I nearly hit the roof.

"Sorry," Gabriel mutters after turning the volume down.

He begins to flip through the stations until finally settling on one playing classical music.

Really?

I took him more for a heavy metal kind of guy, but whatever.

Mentally shrugging my shoulders, I try to concentrate again on the landscape. After a few minutes though, the combination of music, the warmth in the car, and the darkness begins to affect me.

My eyelids grow heavier and heavier, and it's becoming harder to stay alert. I shift in my seat, close the vents, and try my damnedest to stay awake.

But it all seems to be an exercise in futility.

Outside, the landscape blurs into a dark smear, no matter how many times I blink my eyes.

And I swear we've passed that same sign two times now...

Are we driving in circles?

The last thing I can remember is a soft, fleeting touch against my cheek as I fall asleep.

Gabriel

While driving around, it's just as much of a challenge for me to stay on my side of the vehicle as it is for Meghan to stay awake. I know she's freaked out about being in the car with me again, not that it's her fault. She's been forced into this and it sucks for her. I can't lie and say it doesn't. Meghan's got a shitty lot in life right now. Her shitty dad and his connections fucked her over.

The Irish and the fucking Russians are going to be putting up a hell of a fight now that they're working together. Alexei's a fucking psycho bastard whose just got a strong foothold in a neighboring city.

How the fuck have they gotten so damn big? They must be trucking in some serious bankroll to keep the shit they have afloat.

We've knocked out a huge circuit of their slave trade ring. Their drug trafficking has come to a crawl. Lucifer and the boys were thwarting them at every turn until they bombed the shit out of us. I'm betting we got a shit ton of false information when we looked into who did the bombings.

The Irish were surely a part of it, not the fucking Yakuza. Irish love blowing shit up, but they're taking too big of a step forward by aligning themselves with the Russians.

They brought me out of the cage to get shit back under our foot. Get everyone off our backs. Cause enough chaos and destruction that we forever cement ourselves as the top fucking dogs. I'll kill every mother-fucker I have to, but what's going to be the cost?

Looking over to Meghan's perfect legs, I can't help myself and reach out to touch them. I have to. I have no choice in my body's reaction to her. She's like some fucking bright star and I'm a planet that's orbiting her so closely for the warmth and life she gives off.

Ten long years in a fucking cage, every single touch I felt there was a matter of life and death... But not with this girl.

I've been driving around the city in circles just so she'd fall asleep. We'd have been home thirty minutes ago if I had driven straight there, but I don't want to get into any confrontations with her right now. I'd rather just be with her than fighting and answering questions that will only fuck things up. Not to mention taking her into a house that's soon to be our home might freak her out a bit.

The rough skin of my knuckles feels so fucking abrasive compared to the silky flesh it brushes up against. A soft moan comes from her mouth as she shifts in the seat, not away from my side but closer. My breath heaves unsteadily as I switch from my knuckles to the tips of my fingers. She shifts again, but I have to pull away from her. She'd fucking kill me for taking liberties with her, and I wouldn't blame her.

Fuck. I'm not Alexei and I don't need to fucking force my way onto a woman like that worm does.

Shit, shit, shit.

Turning off the freeway, I push the SUV I've been driving back onto the road going home. I need to get out of this fucking vehicle. Being this close to her is driving me fucking insane with desire.

Desire to touch her no matter the consequences.

Meghan's not going to be easy to protect, I can feel it. She's got this spirit in her that's nearly unbreakable. It fucking turns me on so fucking badly when she fucking stands up to me. Like I couldn't dig a chick more than I do her.

I couldn't ever be with a weak-willed woman. I

want one who is as tough as fucking nails when it comes to what she wants. She's got that in her, I can see it. I just need to direct her wants and needs to line up with my own.

Slowing down to find the house that Lucifer and Simon have set up for me, I have to force myself to internalize the fucking laugh bubbling up inside me as I pull into the driveway. It's a huge fucking house in one of the more affluent neighborhoods.

This place is fucking big, and I guess some would call it attractive. If this is one of the *normal-sized* safe houses, as Lucifer put it, I want to see the fucking big ones.

Fuck me, they've got me in the fucking Ritz practically.

It's definitely a far cry from the roach motel I holed myself in last night. I figured I didn't need a house for just me. Didn't deserve anything really. But with Meghan by my side... I need more. I need things for someone besides myself.

Pushing the button for the garage door, I watch as it slowly opens up to reveal my new truck. It's a pretty nice garage, even if it's void of anything except our two vehicles. Meghan's going to need something to drive eventually, and I'm not giving her my truck, so she gets this behemoth SUV.

Meghan moans quietly in her sleep as I lift her up out of the seat. Tucking her head under my chin, I'm struck by how damn small she is in my arms. I like it. Not going to lie about it. She's small and fucking meaty in the right places. I love how her ass pops out of the black dress Lily loaned her. Her fucking curves make my mouth water.

She's a hot bundle of sexuality. Fuck. I can feel myself getting hard just holding her this close. Her hair smells like fucking heaven.

Walking through the house, I curse my long strides as I want to spend as much time with her in my arms as possible. The thought of setting her down is almost unbearable. But when I finally find a room on the second floor that feels safe and secure away from my animalistic cravings, I know it's for the best.

Removing her heels, I drop them to the floor. No need for her to sleep in those torture devices. Fuck, I bet she's even shorter than me now that they're off.

Staring down at her body, my eyes slowly trail up to those beautiful lips and my heart starts to pound in my chest. I kissed those plump lips and it fucking felt like something I didn't deserve.

Nothing as good as her should be near something like me.

Shutting off the lights, I head back the way I came. After today, I need a shower and a beer.

Meghan

Warmth surrounds me. As I come to, I realize I've somehow been cocooned in a soft, fuzzy blanket.

At first, I don't want to wake up. I'm warm, comfortable, and so very tired. It feels as if I haven't slept in weeks.

But then the memories rush over me like a bucket of ice water.

I'm not home, I'm not safe.

Oh shit, where am I?

I struggle to sit up, fighting off the blanket wrapped around me. Once I have the blanket kicked off, my eyes strain against the darkness.

It takes my eyes several seconds to adjust, and I can only make out that I'm in a room, on a big bed. The first thing I do is stick my hands out and check the bed beside me.

It's empty.

Next, I check myself. All my clothes are in place. The only thing I seem to be missing is my shoes, and maybe a little bit of my sanity.

I breathe a sigh of relief, grateful that Gabriel didn't fuck with me in my sleep. He had every opportunity. I must have been dead to world if I didn't wake up when he carried me here from the car. I didn't even wake up when he tucked that blanket around me.

Speaking of Gabriel... where is he?

The need to know has me carefully sliding out of the bed. My toe bumps into something hard and it takes me a second to figure out that it must be my shoe. Nudging the shoes out of the way, my bare feet sink into a soft carpet.

Good. The carpet will make it easier to sneak around without getting caught.

Slowly, quietly, I make my way to the door.

When I finally reach it, I find myself holding my breath as I try the handle, half-expecting it to be locked.

Thank fucking god, it's not.

The handle gives easily, and I almost can't believe it. Why didn't he lock me in? Does he want me to escape?

This is too damn easy.

Still, I ease the door open and peer through the crack I've created. Only more darkness awaits me on the other side.

I wait, holding my breath again, ears straining.

Faintly I can make out movement, but it sounds like it's coming from the floor below me.

Gathering up my courage, I open the door all the way and step out into the hallway, expecting Gabriel to jump out of the shadows at any moment.

All is quiet though as I make my way to the landing next to the stairs. No surprises. No one jumping out to scare the shit out of me.

Gripping the rail, I lean forward, watching and listening again.

A faint light comes from somewhere, illuminating some of the darkness. I can make out a living area. A couple of couches, chairs, and a big entertainment center.

No Gabriel, though.

After a couple of minutes, I decide to try my luck and quietly make my way down the stairs.

When none of the boards creak, I can't help but wonder if this is a dream. Again, this is too damn easy. It should be harder.

I creep across the first floor and finally stumble across a door with a stream of light beaming out from beneath it.

I instantly still, listening.

Someone is moving around inside. Then I hear the unmistakable sound of a shower curtain being pulled back, followed by the sound of a faucet being turned on.

I have to assume it's Gabriel, who else can it be?

And he's about to take a shower. My luck couldn't get any better tonight. I wait until I hear the shower curtain again then I quickly make my way to the front door.

My legs ache to run, to flee as fast as I can, to get the hell out of here. It's everything I can do to force myself to walk slowly, to not to give myself away.

But once I reach the front door, all bets are off. I hastily undo the lock and yank it open.

I run out into the night.

The cold hits me, and I quickly remember I'm barefoot. The morning dew chills my feet as I run through the grass of the front yard.

My breath puffs out in white clouds in front of me, but I don't care. I'm free. Finally free.

I can go anywhere I want.

I run all the way up the street until I reach an intersection and stop.

Left or right?

It should be an easy, simple choice, yet it's not. I have no clue where I am. I have no clue where I'm going.

I need to reach a phone, but who the fuck am I going to call?

Panting in the cold, I start to spin in a circle, trying to figure out what to do. I can't reach out to any of my family, not even my mother's side of the family. Nor any of the Irish. I guess the only people I can ask for help is my friends from school...

But do I really want to drag them into this mess?

Shit.

Doing that will probably get someone killed.

What the fuck am I going to do?

I guess I can try to hide on my own...

But with what money? What identification? What car?

Fuck!

I grab at my hair, tugging and pulling on it, as I try to figure out what the hell to do.

Just as I feel like I'm going to scream in angry, help-less frustration, Lily's words pop into my mind, unbidden and un-fucking-welcome.

Gabriel will protect you. He's your best chance at staying alive.

Goddammit.

I hate it, but she's right.

He might be the only person I have in the whole world...

Spinning back toward the house I just ran from, I stare at the open front door while I try to think up an alternative.

I waste precious seconds determining I have *none*.

It doesn't mean I have to accept things as they are right now, though.

Making up my mind, I run back to the house, hoping I get back before he realizes what happened.

By the time I reach the open front door, my feet feel frozen and my lungs ache. Closing the door, I have to lean against it a moment to catch my breath.

I don't have much time, though, so I straighten my shoulders and make my way to the kitchen. Steeling my resolve, I grab the biggest, sharpest knife from the block on the counter and make my way to the bathroom I passed earlier.

The light is still on and the air smells faintly of soap and water.

I try the handle, it gives easily.

Does he have something against locking the door or something?

Pushing the door open, I discover the room is not a bathroom like I expected. Rather it's a bedroom with a bathroom attached to it.

The door to the bathroom is cracked open. Steam pours out and I can hear the water still running.

Feeling like a psycho serial killer from a bad horror movie, I stalk toward the bathroom and decide to hide the knife behind my back at the last second.

Thankfully, the door doesn't creak as I push it open until I can squeeze past it. A blast of warm, steamy air hits me in the face as soon as I step into the bathroom, and after the cool night air it feels downright oppressive.

Making my way to the shower curtain, it's everything I can do not to pant and give myself away.

There's no time to waste, no time to steel myself again, so I just grab the shower curtain and rip it open.

Gabriel stands on the other side in all his wet, naked glory. He's already turned toward me as if he expected me.

The sight of all his damp, glistening skin threatens to dazzle me, and I have to shake my head to clear it.

I have a mission, dammit.

"Meghan?" Gabriel asks, sounding more confused than worried.

I take a step forward and do my best to keep my expression blank.

Stiffening, his eyes narrow at me suspiciously. "What are you doing in here?"

Lowering my lashes, I try to ignore how all his muscles clench and bulge as he tenses. He's truly a work of art. A mouth-watering combination of ink and pure, brutal man.

I take another step forward and another, until he's moving back.

Stepping into the tub with him, I say, "I think it's time we had a heart to heart."

Just as I bring the knife up, I'm grabbed and shoved into the tile wall.

Gabriel's fingers wrap around my throat as I push the tip of the knife into his left pec, above his heart.

Gaze darkening, his eyes flick down to the blade and back up to my face. "A heart to heart, huh?"

9

MEGHAN

"Yes," I exhale roughly as Gabriel's fingers squeeze around me.

The force of his hold grinds my spine into the hard tile wall and I stretch up on my tiptoes, seeking some relief.

I'm definitely starting to have second thoughts about this.

Maybe I didn't think this through, but fuck it. I have to do something. I can't just sit around, playing the helpless damsel in distress.

I fucking refuse to. This is my life and I *will* have a say in it, and if he refuses to cooperate...

Well, only one of us will be leaving this bathroom unscathed.

As I see it, we're locked in a stalemate.

When his fingers don't let up, I poke the knife

harder into his chest in warning. I don't want to hurt him, I really don't, but I will if he pushes me.

The poke of the knife seems to amuse him. Lips curling with a smirk, his fingers relax enough to let me take another breath, only to squeeze around me harder after I do.

"If you want to talk," he says, leaning forward and pushing himself on the knife. "Then talk."

Unable to stop myself, I look down as his grip around my throat loosens and watch a trickle of blood roll down his chest.

This fucker is definitely crazier than I am.

I think he has a death wish.

Shit.

Looking back up, I try to remember what the hell I wanted to say, but nothing is playing out like I thought it would in my head.

Does he have no sense of self-preservation?

"Well?" Gabriel asks expectantly.

"I can't do this," I gasp, though I don't know who I'm answering, me or him.

"Do what?"

Just when I thought I couldn't get any more disturbed by his actions, his thumb begins to stroke against my throat in a way that could be considered tender.

I'm holding a knife to his heart and the fucker is practically petting me...

"Any of this!" I hiss, trying to remember the whole purpose of this mess.

Gabriel has me so flustered though, everything is turning to shit. How the hell am I supposed to intimidate him into giving me what I want if he's not the least bit afraid of me?

"I can't do this Gabriel, I can't. I won't be your fucking captive or your tool for revenge."

Something sparks in his eyes. "Is that so?"

"Yes," I nearly growl and shake my head, trying to dislodge his thumb.

His fingers tighten around me in warning and I stop.

I take a deep breath to calm myself and hate that it burns a little. The weight of his hand around my throat is starting to feel more and more like a collar.

It's definitely a mark of possession.

This whole stupid plan wasn't supposed to go down like this. I was supposed to have the upper hand. I was supposed to be the one in control.

How did he turn this around on me? Especially when I'm the one holding a knife to him?

"I won't be your fucking *bedlam and mayhem*, Gabriel," I finally remember, and watch with satisfaction as the smirk slides right off his face.

Yeah, I was paying attention when you were explaining why you married me.

Staring him hard in the eyes, my pulses races as I

add, "I refuse to be an object you use and discard once you're done with it. I rather die than live like that."

And I fucking mean it. I wasn't going to do it for Alexei, I would have slit his throat from ear to ear as soon as I was given a chance. And I sure as hell won't do it for this asshole.

"What the fuck are you saying?" he asks, his face hardening until it's stone cold.

I fix my grip on the handle of the knife, my palm and fingers starting to sweat from holding it like this.

It's so damn humid in here from the shower, the smell of his soap, his skin, is going to my head.

"Either we do this for real...like we're a team..."

"Or?" he asks, his eyes locked on my eyes.

I push the knife into him to make my point.

"I see," he says, his jaw clenching.

Staring into his eyes, I try to figure out what the hell he's thinking. He looks angry as fuck, but also contemplative.

Seconds pass, our breaths mingling, my body flushing with heat, and my skin dampening.

As much as I don't want to acknowledge it, I can't help but be aware of how close his body is to mine. Nor can I forget that he's completely naked.

The image of him dripping wet will forever be burned into the back of my eyes.

He's truly impressive, built like a fucking god... or a devil. A devil that draws me in with his eyes.

"There's one little problem with your request though, little girl," he finally says, cutting through the oppressive silence.

Clenching my teeth at the little girl remark, I resist the urge to push the knife into him harder. "And that is?"

A slow grin spreads across his lips as I rise to the bait. "This marriage has been real to me from the beginning."

How is that a problem? I wonder in confusion.

Before I know what's happening, he's pushing the knife away way too fucking easily and pressing his body against me.

Pinning me to the wall, his mouth crashes against my mouth in a bruising kiss.

Instantly, every little nerve in my body screams to life. Crying out for something only he can give.

I'm so shocked at first, so caught off guard, I just freeze.

Then the reality of what's happening sinks its teeth in.

No. No. No. No...

This isn't what I wanted. This isn't why I came in here, or what I was trying to achieve.

I try to twist my head away, but he growls and his kiss only becomes harder. More insistent.

The more I try to fight him, the tighter his fingers squeeze around my throat, cutting off my air.

How the fuck did me wanting to ask for a secret annul-ment turn into this? I think as I try to ignore his tongue pushing past my lips.

Maybe because I never actually got around to the asking for the annulment part.

Dammit.

When I walked in here, I didn't count on him making me so damn flustered I'd fuck up the little speech I came up with in my head.

Reaching out with my free hand, I start shoving at him.

Finally releasing his grip on my throat, he grabs up the hand shoving at him and pins it to the wall above my head.

Shit. I don't know what to do. I still have the knife, but I truly don't want to hurt him like that.

I don't really want to kill the only man who's ever tried to protect me.

He begins to push his way between my thighs, using his hips to lift my ass up. And as soon as I feel something hard pressing into my sex, my body reacts as if I was just struck by lightning.

Unwanted jolts of sensation radiate from my core, zipping up my spine, and tingling through my limbs.

My fingers tighten around the knife as it almost slips from my grip.

I try to twist away, try to turn my head again now that his fingers are no longer locked around my throat.

Grabbing my face with his other hand, his fingers press into my cheeks, opening my mouth wider for his invasion.

His tongue sweeps in, claiming and conquering me without reservation.

Do something, my mind cries out as my body begins to give in, my resolve melting into his kiss just like I did back in the church.

I know from experience I can only resist his pull for so long.

I literally only have seconds left.

There's just something about him, something dark and dangerous, that *sings* to me, drawing me in like a moth to the flame.

I want to play with his fire. I want to combust in his arms, shedding the old Meghan, and be reborn as something new...

And it scares the shit out of me.

In an act of pure desperation, I bite down on his lip.

He jerks back with a grunt.

"I want an annulment," I manage to push out of my raw throat.

He stiffens with surprise then his face twists with fury.

"No," he growls low, sounding more like a beast than a man.

I open my mouth to repeat what I just said, but his

lips capture mine again, cutting me off.

He kisses me so damn hard, it's almost like he's attacking me, the force of it grinding me into the wall.

With each stroke of his tongue, with each hungry noise rolling down my throat, I find myself weakening. The fight seeping out of my bones as my brain turns to mush.

So I do the only thing I can do right now.

I bite him again to get him to stop.

"No," he growls again, lower, meaner, and angrier against my mouth.

I bite him again and again, not accepting his no after no, until I finally really sink my teeth in and taste blood.

He jolts away from me.

"I don't want to stay married! I want an annulment in exchange for my full cooperation. We don't have to stay married, Gabriel. We can work together and be free," I pant out before he has another chance to smother my words.

I watch him, heart hammering against my ribs, as he reaches up, his fingers exploring the cut my teeth made on his lip.

Stiffening, I try to prepare myself for his anger, for his retaliation. No doubt he'll want to hurt me back for hurting him.

His eyes darken, going nearly black, but it's not in anger. Oh no, it's a heated look full of lust.

Oh god, he couldn't have possibly gotten turned on by that...

Mouth curving into a disturbing grin, he grabs me by the back of the head and leans in until we're nearly nose to nose.

"Free?" He chuckles, his warm breath caressing me. "Freedom is an illusion. No one is truly free... We're all owned by someone or something."

I try to shake my head in denial, but his fingers tighten in my hair, stopping the movement.

"You're mine, Meghan. I own you now," he says firmly.

With nowhere to look but at his eyes, I find myself being pulled in, sucked into their harsh depths.

"Mine to cherish... Mine to protect... You gave yourself to me. You put yourself willingly in my hands. You took the vow in front of God."

Oh, that's rich, coming from a man who shot up a church.

I blink at him, the spell he's putting me under nearly broken.

"I was under a great deal of duress," I argue.

"You had your choice and you made it," he snaps. "No fucking take backs."

He's truly fucking crazy if he thinks he owns me now. That just because he *bullied* me into marrying him, I'm somehow his.

Growing frustrated, I decide to remind him, "I also

vowed to cut off your cock if you touched me without my permission! And you're touching me without my permission!"

Gabriel chuckles again, and the low, rumbling sound goes straight to my core, filling my belly with warmth.

How he can still be turning me on when I'm angry at him? I don't fucking understand it.

"Go ahead," he dares me and slowly leans away, all his muscles rippling as he motions at his waist. "You have the knife in your hand. Do it."

Fuck, I totally forgot about the knife for a moment. My hand is so tense and sweaty I can't believe I didn't drop it.

I shift it in my palm, getting a better grip, and seriously consider trying.

Would serve him right.

But when I glance down to see his stomach tightening with tension and his thick erection disappearing between my thighs, I'm overcome by a hot wave of pure want.

Cocks aren't pretty. In fact, they're probably one of the ugliest fucking things on the planet. But to see his, to *feel* his, hot and throbbing against my flesh, it's almost too much.

As if he's testing me, calling my bluff, I suddenly feel his cock twitch against me. The shock has me wrenching my gaze up.

"Well?" he asks, his eyes fucking gleaming at me now.

We both know I can't do it. I'm all bark and no fucking bite, and this bastard just proved it.

Dammit. Damn it all...

"You're sick," I hiss, the knife trembling in my hand.

Leaning in close, as if he can't stand the distance between us, he purrs, "In sickness and in health, darlin'."

I have the sudden urge to stab him, stab him in his fucking heart for being a smart-ass.

Instead, I clench my teeth and point out, "Funny, I don't remember saying that."

He goes still, so still, I can't help but hope I've finally gotten through to him. That he finally understands the absolute absurdity of this whole situation.

Then his eyes light up as if he just had an epiphany.

Oh, that can't be fucking good.

Pressing in closer, like a predator moving in on its prey, he curls himself around me until he's blocking out the light. He's so damn tall, so damn wide, I can't see around him.

He's literally a wall of ink-covered muscle.

His entire being, his entire presence fills my shrinking little world. Narrowing it down until I'm solely focused on him. His every breath, his every twitch.

"Is that why you're doing this?" he asks.

I just stare at him stupidly. I don't even understand the fucking question.

"You doubt my commitment to this marriage. You doubt the sincerity of my actions," he supplies, his bright, burning gaze locking on my mouth.

What the fuck?

"What?! No..." I immediately try to deny, that's not why I'm doing this.

I'm doing this because I want to be free...

But a little nagging, little fucking annoying voice in my head suggests he may be onto something.

I have been having a hard time wrapping my head around this arrangement. I don't understand the point of it. It doesn't make any damn sense.

Why bother protecting me or trying to take care of me? If he wants revenge, or bedlam and mayhem, he could have gotten that by killing me, torturing me, or locking me up.

Keeping me alive is a huge liability.

As if he can read my mind, he says almost accusingly, "You do..."

"I just don't understand why you're doing this," I finally admit in frustration, bristled by his tone. "What's in it for you?"

"Isn't it obvious?" he asks, rocking his hips forward.

His erection rubs against my soaked panties, intentionally or unintentionally finding my clit.

"No," I grit out, trying my best not to moan.

Grinning, he rocks his hips again. "I get you."

Those three words—I get you—stab right through the core of my fucking soul.

He's doing all of this because he wants me? He doesn't even know me...

Before I can even start coming to terms with his revelation, his mouth crushes against my mouth in a bruising kiss, cutting off my thoughts.

He kisses me hard and deep, so hard and deep I feel it all the way down to my toes.

My knees go weak, the will to fight back draining out of me.

"I get you, to have and to hold..." he says between pulls from my mouth.

I'm so lost in his kiss, so far gone in his taste, in his touch, I don't even realize that he's grabbing the knife out of my hand, wrestling it easily from my slick fingers, before it's too late.

It's not even a contest. One moment I have the knife and the next he has it.

Breaking the kiss, he points the knife at me and says, "From this day forward."

Panting for air, I stare at him in confusion until he fists the front of my dress, pulling it away from my skin.

As he begins to saw through the black fabric, "You're crazy," just slips past my lips.

And he is. To go through all this trouble just because he wants me... it's insane.

"Yes, we've already established that," he smirks, not even trying to deny it.

The dress splits open under the knife as Gabriel guides it down my chest. The blade comes dangerously close to my skin, but he wields it with such carefully controlled precision it never touches me.

Once he reaches my bellybutton, he tosses the knife away. It clangs loudly against the tub as he grabs the fabric in both hands and uses his brute strength to rip it the rest of the way open.

I'm not wearing a bra. Unfortunately, there wasn't one under my wedding dress, most likely due to the corset. And I'm quite a bit bigger than Lily in the chest department.

"Meghan..."

Gabriel sucks in a sharp breath through his teeth, his entire body stiffening.

There's nothing between me and his hungry, feral eyes now except for the tiny, pathetic strip of white fabric acting as my panties. I tremble against the wall, once again trapped somewhere between arousal and fear from the way he looks at me

"Goddamn," he hisses, releasing the breath he sucked in. "You should have never walked into this bathroom..."

Still gripping the tattered remains of the dress in

his fists, he yanks it down my arms, letting it fall to the bottom of the tub.

"Gabriel—" I start to protest but he cuts me off with another kiss.

Using his mouth to push me back into that foggy place of pleasure and confusion.

Once I begin to melt against the tile, he nips at my bottom lip.

"For better or for worse," he murmurs, then he begins to work his way down my neck.

A coiled weakness blooms in my veins as he kisses and suckles on the tender skin of my throat.

This is wrong in so many ways, but the way he's kissing me, as if he's worshipping me with his mouth, makes it feel too right.

"For richer and richer," he breathes against my collarbone as he drifts down, his stubble scraping across my skin.

I blink. "I don't think that's how it—"

He presses his thumb against my lips. "Shush. Be quiet while I prove my utter devotion."

I consider biting his thumb, but then he decides to skip the rest of me, and his mouth suddenly covers my left breast.

A deep, bassy sound rumbles in his throat as he pulls back a hard suckle.

On their own accord, my hands go to the back of

his head. But they don't push him away, they pull him closer.

His big, calloused hand covers my right breast and he squeezes, molding me between his fingers as I arch against the wall.

With every pull on my nipple it feels like he's tugging on a cord that's connected directly to my clit, lighting my entire body on fire.

"In safety," he groans and moves to my right breast, his tongue swiping across me before he suckles. "And in peril."

Again, I don't think those are quite the right vows, but all that comes out of my mouth is a low moan. The last thing I want to do right now is stop him.

He's making me feel so good...

Releasing my nipple with a wet sound, he begins to nibble and kiss his way down my stomach.

"In madness and sanity," he groans, his tongue briefly dipping into my belly button.

I jolt from the strange sensation and one of his big hands wraps around my hip, holding me still.

Lower he nibbles, and when it finally registers in my lust-fogged brain what he intends to do, I try to twist my hips out of his hold.

His fingers dig into my hipbones, the strength in that one hand enough to keep me from moving.

With a snarl, he rips my wet panties down my legs, peeling them away from my throbbing sex.

I shove at his shoulders, but it's not enough to stop him from pushing his head between my thighs.

"Mine to fuck and devour," he groans, his hot breath sending shivers up my spine.

Without any warning or buildup, his mouth covers my pussy, his tongue attacking my clit.

There's no gentle teasing or time to prepare myself.

No time to take a breath.

There's just immediate mind-breaking sensation.

Shoving at his shoulders again, I rise onto the very tip of my toes, trying to escape him.

But he's relentless in his pursuit.

Hands grabbing me by the back of my knees, he spreads me open wider, forcing me to completely rely on him to stay upright.

"Fuck, you taste so good," he moans between strong laps that push me to the edge of madness. "I've never tasted a sweeter pussy in all my life..."

The pressure inside me builds at a rate that threatens to destroy me from the inside out.

Grabbing him by the back of the head, I tug, desperately trying to free myself from his mouth.

"Gabriel, it's too much... you have to stop..." I plead.

I've never felt anything like this before. I've never felt anything this damn intense.

So much is expanding inside me, my body can't

contain it, and I swear my heart is going to explode inside my chest.

He growls, and instead of slowing down or stopping, his mouth works me over with a new ferocity.

Fingers digging into my flesh, he works his tongue against me so fiercely it feels like he's shoving me up the wall with it.

Higher and higher he pushes me until I can no longer fight this thing growing inside me.

"Gabriel... please..." I plead one last time.

Mercy. I need mercy.

He pauses for only a second, just long enough to command, "Come for me, Meghan."

Then he sucks on my clit *hard*.

I shatter, everything that holds me together, everything that makes me *me*, breaking apart.

"That's it, Meghan... You're such a good girl," he groans with pleasure as I cry out and come all over his hungry mouth.

So much pleasure flows through me I swear it's pouring out of me.

And his tongue is there, lapping, licking, and sucking me up.

He continues to work his mouth against me, swallowing up all my broken pieces, until every ounce of pleasure inside me has been wrung out of bones.

When I finally sag in his arms, his fingers squeeze around my thighs one last time and he breaks away.

Sliding up me, he settles my trembling thighs around his waist, then grabs me by the face.

"Look at you..." he says, his bright eyes searing into me. "So fucking beautiful... so fucking *mine*..."

He kisses me, his tongue sweeping into my mouth, forcing me to taste my own pleasure. My own defeat.

And it's sweet... so sweet...

His kiss lulls me into a false sense of security. Believing he's gotten everything that he wanted out of me, I drape my arms around his neck and kiss him back.

Then something hot and hard pushes through my folds.

I immediately stiffen against him, my mouth going slack.

Stealing one last suckle from my lips, he says, "Mine forever."

Hand still curved around my jaw, I can't look away. I can't look anywhere but at his eyes as he begins to ease his cock inside me.

And he's big... too big.

I don't think the fucker is going to fit.

My thighs tense around his waist, my body instinctively fighting his invasion.

"Fuck, you're tight," he rasps, his eyes momentarily filling with weakness.

And for a heartbeat I'm lost in that weakness, feeling it as if it were my own.

But as he continues to push himself inside me, my walls straining despite how wet I am, I fear he's going to split me in half.

"Gabriel, stop. I don't think this is going to work," I groan as my body struggles to accept him.

It's been so long since I've had sex... it's been more than a year... and I was never with anyone this big.

That bit of weakness in his steady gaze fades away, replaced by steel and determination. "I know you can take it."

I start to shake my head, but his grip quickly puts an end to it.

His voice is a husky mixture of encouragement and surety as he says, "You can handle me, Meghan."

Can I? Can I handle him? I wonder desperately as he continues to push and push himself inside me.

It's not only his size that worries me, but what he can potentially do to me if I let him inside. Will I ever be able to get him out after this? Will I be able to walk away?

Jaw clenching, his eyes flash with challenge. "Don't tell me the woman who put a gun to my chest... the woman who stormed in here and put a knife to my heart... can't take a little cock."

I suck in a shaky breath.

Oh, hell no, he didn't...

I'm not weak, and I sure as hell won't let him unwoman me.

"It's not little," I grit out in my defense.

"Damn right, it's not," he says with a cocky grin and gives another push.

At first, I want to fight him, and even stiffen in pure reflex, but then I force myself to relax.

I take a deep breath in and out, willing my body to accept him.

I can do this. Just like he said, it's only a little cock... It doesn't mean more than that.

"Yes... that's it," he groans as he sinks in another inch.

His hot length spreading me open.

Already, with so little of him inside me, I feel so full. Too full.

Pushing and pushing, he eases in another inch.

There's so much of him... I swear I can feel every vein, every little ridge of his cock as he stretches me until I feel like I might burst.

Groaning, he reaches down and grabs me by the hips, holding me firmly.

Voice strained, he orders, "Take it, baby. Take it all."

I'm not sure I can. I'm not sure I have the room inside me to give him...

I start to tense up again in fear.

Growing impatient, he snaps, "Stop fighting this, you can't stop it."

Something inside me seems to snap and I obey his demand unconsciously.

Seizing the opportunity, Gabriel thrusts forward.

Fingers digging into his shoulders, I arch against the wall as he spears me with his thick shaft.

Head dropping, he groans out, "Fuck," against my throat. "You feel so fucking good."

Before I have time to come to terms with what just happened, he drags his hips back and slams back into me again.

Completely filling me up.

There's so much of him, I don't know where he begins and I end.

My thighs tighten around his waist, my body trying to pull him back as he pulls himself out.

"You like that, baby? You like my big cock inside you..." he growls, his head lifting up.

I open my mouth to reply, whatever I was going to say strangling into a moan as he pushes forward.

"I'll take that as a yes," he grunts, his lips struggling to form that cocky smirk.

In and out, he works his cock inside me. His movements becoming faster, harder. More desperate.

It feels like only seconds pass before he's slamming himself into me. The wet sounds of flesh sliding against flesh filling my ears as he grinds me into the wall.

It's too much after everything I've gone through. His size. His stare. His sheer fucking intensity.

The way he looks like he'll fucking die if he doesn't push himself into me.

Not to mention the way he's angled so each stroke rubs against a deeply buried bundle of nerves.

After experiencing one orgasm at the mercy of his mouth, my body is eager to experience another.

Despite knowing somewhere deep inside my brain I'm giving in too easy, my muscles begin to lock up.

"Fuck... Already?" he says in a tortured growl as the walls of my pussy ripple around his cock.

I try to stop the pleasure gathering force inside me, try to hold it back.

But as he angles his hips up and slams into me like he's trying to fucking break me, my body wins the battle against my will.

White flashes in front of my eyes as a warning, then I'm clamping down on him as everything built up inside me rushes out of me in a gush.

"Shit... shit... shit..." Gabriel grunts, his rhythm jerking out of beat for a second.

Then he begins pound into me with a new brutal determination.

He's thrusts into me so hard, so fast and furious, it's not until he lets out a deafening roar that I realize he's pumping me full of warmth.

So much warmth.

My ears ring as another of explosion of pleasure

rips through me, and it's not until I begin to float back down from the heavens that I realize what he roared.

Until death do us part.

With one last warm pulse of his cock, Gabriel stills.

Panting, I stare at him in disbelief. Did that really just happen? It couldn't have...

As if he can sense all the shit going on in my head, his voice breaks through the sound of my panting, coming out as a raw growl. "I mean it. Until death do us part, Meghan. The only way you're going to get rid of me is by killing me."

His cock suddenly twitches inside me and then he slowly rolls his hips.

I gasp, my oversensitive nerves screaming in protest.

He grins and begins to roll his hips deeper.

I swear he hasn't gone soft at all. No, he's just as hard as when he started.

"And if you want to go that route, I suggest skipping the guns and knives..."

"Oh yeah?" I groan back, somehow pushing the words out as I struggle against the fire he's trying stoke to life inside me. "How do you suggest I kill you then?"

Eyes lighting up, his grin stretches wider. "I suggest trying to fuck me to death..."

10

GABRIEL

Pre-dawn light filters though the curtains directly on my closed eyes. I've been lying here awake for the past half hour, trying to determine exactly where my place is right now in the world. I've gotten married, tortured and killed men, and been released from prison in less than forty-eight hours.

It's been one hell of a week so far.

Opening my eyes and looking at Meghan, my body feels that now familiar ache of desire and longing. We fucked in the shower, then again in the bed before we both collapsed well after the clock showed midnight. I'm not tired though, I'm awake and *alive*. I can feel the tiny cells in my body coming to life for the first time in a decade.

I was dead in prison, I can't deny that to myself. I was dead and mentally ready for the end. I've questioned how much longer I would have been able to hold out before I attacked the guards so badly they would have had no choice but to end my life sentence. I wouldn't have killed myself directly, nah, that shits for the birds. No, I would have gone down doing what I do best.

Causing destruction.

Now all that shit's out the fucking window.

Meghan's curled up next to me in a tiny little ball. She went to sleep with an arm draped across my chest, but when I woke this morning she was turned the opposite way, her ass pressed hard against my hip. I've been in those clingy fucking relationships where the girl has to be attached at the hip in bed.

Fuck that noise.

We need to be fucking comfortable. I don't have a fucking worry in the world about us not being *attached*. I married her and flat-out claimed her on our wedding night. Ain't nothing else going to break that apart.

Fuck, even her trying to kill me didn't stop my ass from claiming her.

My hand slides over the gouge she made in my chest, right above the fucking heart. She definitely broke the skin last night. And I loved the fuck out of that shit. I want a woman who's got that fucking killer instinct. I'm not into those fucking shrinking violets, or whatever the fuck they're called.

A small groan comes from Meghan as she slowly rolls to her back. "When did I get into a fucking car wreck?"

Rolling to my side, I look at her delicate facial features scrunched up into a grimace.

"Fuck, you don't look so good, you alright?" I ask.

"Welcome to the world of morning-after, asshole," she whines as she rubs the palms of her hands against her eyes. "You should never marry someone if you don't know what they look like in the morning."

"I didn't mean in the looks department," I say with a chuckle.

My fingers trail lightly over her chin as I lean over to kiss her temple.

Whimpering, she says, "Even that fucking hurts."

"Fuck," I growl out. "Did he knock you around before the wedding?"

I don't see any bruises on her face, but that doesn't mean she wasn't shaken or thrown around like a rag doll.

"Not exactly," she whispers, a small sound catching in her throat. "But the fucker drugged me, so I don't really know."

Fucking dick-less, pile of shit. At least I make my women marry me drug-free. Not sure that's something I need to bring up now, though.

"Fuck. Any idea what they put in you?" I ask.

"No clue, they just made sure I was very compliant." A line of moisture seeps down her cheek as she turns her head away from me. "I'm missing a lot of time."

Fuck. I knew the outline of it all, I suppose. With the way she fights for what she wants, there's no way she would have married that sack of slime willingly. Which, I guess, is a good sign for me, even if she has tried to kill me twice.

Fuck, the thought of her trying to kill me causes a stirring between my legs, my cock wanting to thicken. I want to find out if she's still as tight as I remember from last night. The way her legs felt wrapped around my hips still leaves me without words to describe how damn good it felt.

Her body is so much smaller than mine, but it fits so well. It's like she was born just to be melded against my own body. She isn't fragile by any means. She's got the hips and breasts that are meant for a good hard pounding.

Soft and tender lovemaking are going to happen... eventually. But until we get our fucking beasts under control, I'm going to love pounding the shit out of her.

"Sorry, is there anything I can get for you?" I ask quietly.

"No... yes? Maybe some Tylenol?"

She turns her head to me look me in the eyes.

"I'm going to have to leave the house for that," I say. "This place is empty as can be. No food or anything. All we have are towels, sheets, blankets, plates, silverware, and cups. Not even the stuff to clean any of that shit with, though."

"Fuck."

"Yeah. I'd say that you need to come with me.... But we don't have any clothes for you, either. I've got what was in my bag but that's about it."

She lays there for a long time, looking into my eyes.

"Can I see your phone?" Meghan asks out of nowhere.

"Huh?" I ask in confusion.

"I'm hungry and I need panties. You fucking destroyed them last night," she grumbles.

"I don't think the pizza places are open yet, Meghan," I say as I roll toward the nightstand to grab my phone. "And how exactly are you going to get panties? I'm not letting some pizza boy buy them for you."

"Oh god, you're such a fossil. Things aren't like how they used to be."

She snickers.

Handing the phone to her, I watch her roll to her back. Her large breasts flatten somewhat, but they still look heavy and full.

My tongue moistens my lips as I start edging toward her.

Glancing over at me, she stops typing on my phone.

Pushing at my head, she says, "Not a chance. My body is one giant fucking bruise."

Showing me her wrist, she says, "Alexei wasn't very nice to me. Every time he touched me, he made sure it hurt."

Shuddering, she goes back to typing.

I growl out his name, "Alexei... that fucker is going to die. I'll break his fucking neck."

"I wouldn't mind watching that," she says.

"What are you doing?" I ask, watching her face.

I could easily check the screen, but I'd much rather watch her lips.

"I need your credit card. Do you even have one of those?" she asks as she pushes against my ever-encroaching mouth.

I know she said she was hurting everywhere. Maybe a kiss on some of those spots would help...

"It's in my wallet," I say.

"Grab it real quick," she says, still typing and scrolling through things.

"My wallet is in my pants," I grumble.

"Well, get it out and give it to me."

Her eyes lift to look at me again.

She's way too fucking beautiful in the mornings. It's a weapon I'm sure she knows she has.

"My pants are downstairs in the bathroom," I say, and my eyes drift lower to her breasts.

Her voice cuts through the lustful fog that's beginning to cloud my brain. "Not a chance, Gabriel. I'm even sore down there. It feels like you put a fucking baseball bat in me."

A white sheet slowly covers her breasts, and I swear I can feel my cock screaming in rage at the injustice of the world. Covering up breasts like hers should be a capital crime.

Looking up at her face, I frown. "Why do you need my credit card?"

"Because I need clothes and food. I'm willing to bet you need some stuff too. I can't imagine the Incredible Hulk can go without his spinach for too long. All those big muscles might turn to fat," she says, and there's snippy humor in her eyes as she pointedly looks at my chest and arms.

"You mean Popeye, right?" I ask and start trying to tug down the sheet.

Holding it tightly, she glares at me. "Wallet, food, clothes, and then maybe sex."

"Fuck," I grumble as I start sitting up. "How the hell are you going to get all that stuff through my phone?"

"There are multiple services that will deliver food

from restaurants for a small fee. There are also these things called online stores that will deliver books, clothes, and anything else you can practically think of the same day if you pay enough. Other than that, I'm going to try and call Lucifer's wife, Lily," she says before she returns her attention to the phone.

Those last words stop me dead in my tracks. "Why the fuck would you want to do that?"

Shrugging those beautiful shoulders of hers, she says, "Because she told me to call her if I needed help setting up the house."

"I wasn't aware you had been discussing our home yet."

"You were in that office for over an hour and a half. We had to talk about something."

She makes a shooing motion with her hand.

"Are you fucking shooing me?" I ask.

Treating me like some fucking kid, what the fuck?

"No. I'm telling you to hurry up and help feed your fucking wife. Remember those vows you reamed into me last night while you were plowing me?" she asks without the faintest hint of a laugh or smirk.

"Fucking hell's gates," I grumble as I turn back to the door of the bedroom.

"I thought it was funny... reamed and plowed..." She laughs at my back.

She's going to find it real funny when I'm cramming my thick ass cock so far into her she starts to fucking choke.

TIMES SURE HAVE FUCKING CHANGED since I went in. Just the fact alone that Meghan can have food, clothing, and I'm pretty sure anything else on the planet delivered to us is amazing. For most of the morning, I was answering the door. First came the food she ordered from some local mom and pop place. She must have ordered half the damn menu with how much food showed up.

Sitting there, watching as she demolished everything in front of her as quickly as I did, was an interesting turn of events. She's not the type of woman to order water and salad. No, she eats what she wants and doesn't apologize for it.

"Quit fucking staring at me," she says when she finally looks up from the phone and plate in front of her.

"No," I say before I take another long look at her.

She's fucking beautiful, why shouldn't I?

"Ugh," she grumbles at me before looking back down to the phone.

"What are you doing now?" I ask as I go back to eating the last of my breakfast, still watching the way she sits there, her eyes flaying across whatever it is she's doing.

"Ordering more clothes. I had no idea how much influence Lily has with this city's retailers. All I have to do is mention her name and the clothes practically fly themselves to this house."

"What's wrong with what you have on?" I ask, and from the look she gives me, I obviously haven't been paying attention to something.

She's got on a pair of black fleece-lined leggings and a tight heavy metal band shirt. And while I've got no clue about when these things came in style, I'm damn thankful she loves wearing them. She should, at least, since she ordered ten pairs of them. Fuck me, I've never seen a woman order so much clothing.

It's mind-numbing to think about until I ask the one question I should have asked in the first place. "How much is all this costing?"

"Madness and sanity... You said those words. So, therapy it is. Retail therapy," she says, looking back down at the phone. "Also, I need a phone too. Can you ask for one on this plan or do I need to order that too?"

"That's not exactly what I meant," I growl out as I stretch out my arms. "I'll check on the phone. Operational security is going to put a lot of restrictions on what you can get."

"I've had this phone the whole time and you haven't once checked on what I'm doing."

"No need. Nine-one-one has been disconnected, and I'm pretty sure all the stuff you're doing is being monitored by that prick, Simon," I say with a lazy shrug of my shoulders. "Besides, we've established you're in this for the long haul, just like me. I'm going to trust you. That's not something I do much of. You could try to run like you did last night, before you came into the shower... But you came back."

Looking up from the phone, I can see she's contemplating my words. Her eyes narrow as she realizes everything I said.

"How did you know?" she asks.

I smirk. "Did you see all the grass on the bathroom floor? Your feet had clippings on them."

"Shit," she mutters.

"Pretty much. You came back, that shows you're smart enough to know what's best for you, and us. Also, you could have tried killing me in earnest."

"I thought me trying to shoot and stab you would give you more pause," she frowns at me.

"Nah, that shit was just foreplay," I say.

Food has made me sleepy. Now all I need to do is get Meghan out of those clothes. A day spent in the sack sounds perfect right now.

The loud shrill of my phone hits my nerves like a fucking atomic bomb. Fucking hell.

"A guy named James is calling... Is he the one who did the thumbs?" she asks with a wince.

"Yeah," I say, motioning for her to give me the phone.

"That was..." she starts before shaking her head at me. "Do you know how to answer it?"

I shrug my shoulders. "I push the talk button?"

Laughing, she presses the button and says, "Hello, Gabriel's answering service. How can I direct your call?"

I don't hear the response, but by the way her face flushes, it probably wasn't a nice request to speak to me.

"Do you kiss your mother with that mouth?" she asks before handing me the phone.

"With tongue," I hear James say as I press the phone to my ear.

"What do you want, James?" I ask as I push away from the table to stand up.

"I was figuring you'd want to go out to the cemetery today. Should be a good time to get shit done... Well, shit done before all the madness you start," he says.

He's got a point, I guess. Shit's going to get hectic soon enough. The calm before the storm is right now. Might as well take advantage of it.

"Alright, where do you want to meet up?" I ask.

"I'll see you over at the cemetery next to Father Coss's church in about an hour," he says.

"Sounds good, bring another load out for me. I

need a hip holster and a forty-five," I say before hitting the red button on the screen.

Arching my back, I stretch out the stiffness that formed in my shoulders from sleeping on such a soft mattress.

Looking to Meghan, I feel another form of stiffness starting up as well. Not enough time for it, though. We're out in the suburbs of Garden City, and it's not going to be a quick trip to the cemetery when it's on the opposite side of the city.

"What's up?" Meghan asks.

"Gotta go see some old friends. You dressed warm enough to be outside for a bit?"

"I think so," she says as she pushes away from the table.

"Good..." Staring at the food and stuff all over the table, I grimace. "We need to hire a maid. I hate fucking doing dishes."

She picks up her empty plate. "I can check with Lily, if you want."

Heading toward the garage after a quick sweep up of the kitchen table, we stand inside, looking at the black Tahoe and the black F-250.

"We'll take mine. The mom-mobile is yours," I say with a grunt.

"Mine?" she asks as we head toward the truck.

"You wanted in, you're in now. That's your SUV,

keys are on the kitchen counter. We're taking mine today, though," I say as I pull myself inside the truck.

My ass feels good behind the wheel of this baby. John did me proud when he got me this big bitch.

"Why the hell are you calling it a mom-mobile?" Meghan asks when she gets settled in the truck.

"What the fuck does that Tahoe look like? It's the new soccer mom car. You're going to love it when you're running our brats to practice," I say with a grin.

"It's really early in the day for me to shoot your balls off, Gabriel," Meghan snarls at me.

11

GABRIEL

The cemetery next to St. Michael's looks the same as it always has—old and full of dead and fucking useless carcasses.

That's all we are in the end. Dead weight.

Fuck, I think most of us guys in the inner circle would have been lucky to even have someone mourn us over the grave, or I used to think that. Now everyone's getting married and has fucking soccer mom cars. Fuck, I even did it myself. None of us are thinking of the repercussions from doing this shit. It's going to affect our families one day... it's just how shit is in our way of life.

Just like all those stupid fucking movies, the bad guy always gets it in the end.

I'd like to think the fucking weather matches my mood as I get out of the truck, but it doesn't feel like fucking cooperating, I guess. Fucking sunshine and blue skies for as far as the eye can see.

The ride over was pretty damn quiet. I guess kids aren't in the near future with Meghan. Can't say I blame her, fucking things are a death knell. She'd look good knocked up, though, with a big belly and those luscious tits...

"I thought you said we were visiting some old friends," she says as we walk toward James's BMW.

"We are, in a way. Gotta pay my respects. Lots of guys are gone from my family since I left."

"Oh," she says, and I think I can detect a hint of understanding or something.

I don't know what it is. But when she grabs my hand and squeezes it tightly, I know she's here with me. With me and not because of me.

"Gabriel, how's the air on the outside?" James asks as he steps out of his car.

He's dressed in his usual black fancy jeans and tight-fitting shirt.

"Good, pretty boy. How's life with a tiny dick?" I ask him.

"Eh, less chance of catching something when I don't even get inside." He smirks at me.

Turning back to go to his trunk, he continues, "I wasn't sure how much of a load out you'd need, so I brought a mix of everything."

"Sounds good. You able to fit her with a vest?"

He pops his head out from behind the trunk lid, reminding me of one of those movies where some kid is looking around a corner.

"The runt?" he asks with a quirk of his eyebrow. "Yeah, I got one that will fit her, I think. Though, with her bust, she's gonna be squeezed in until I can get one fitted properly for her."

Looking down at the confused but blushing bride of mine, I nod. "Yeah, she's short as fuck and busty as hell. Kinda like a Texas woman from a country song, just needs the hair."

"I'm going to castrate you and make you an ox in your sleep," she growls at me.

"Jesus, you're just like fucking John, man. Dude's always cutting someone's junk off," James says with a chuckle as he motions us over to his trunk.

Walking to the back, my heart gets that little stutter as I look at all the beautiful weaponry he has stashed inside. It's like the boy wants to arm half a platoon and invade a small country.

"Jumping fucking Jesus, you going to war?" I ask.

With a snicker, James, shrugs his shoulders. "Nah, I just follow the good ol' Boy Scout motto."

"What's mine from all this?" I ask.

"Anything and everything. I was at the compound, so I grabbed all the shit I thought you might want. I'll resupply later," he says and steps back so that I can get in and start loading up.

Looking at my little fucking sexy woman, I spot our first problem. "You order any jeans when you were shopping?"

"A couple. Why?" she asks as she peers down into the trunk.

Pulling up my shirt, I motion to the holster I have on my hip. Nodding over to James, I watch as he does the same thing.

"Arm holsters are impractical for how we dress, unless you're that fuck Simon," I say.

I motion to her leggings. "Those aren't going to hold a belt holster, and carrying a gun around in a purse is asking to get yourself fucking killed."

"Oh." Her mouth makes that a-ha movement, and I could so see myself sliding my thick cock in between her lips.

Clearing my throat, I say, "Were probably not going to need most of this today, but since you tried putting a bullet through my chest a couple of days ago, I figure you can at least shoot a gun, right?"

She nods that beautiful head of hers and gives me a grin. "I get a gun?"

"Yeah, and bullets too," I say.

She grimaces. "A girl tries to shoot someone one time without bullets and you never let her live it down."

"We'll see," I say, and pull out an empty black bag.

Spotting the large sticks of C-4, I grab a few stacks, as well as three bags of metal ball bearings.

Looking over at James, I ask, "This C-4 civilian or military grade?"

"Military grade," he says, looking up from his phone.

"Good," I say.

Grabbing the rest of the gear we'll need from the trunk, I smile as Meghan's eyes grow wider and wider with each weapon I pull out. Most of the guns I won't need anytime soon, but it never hurts to have a couple of M4 assault rifles. Grabbing four more pistols, I shove them into the bag I've filled up.

Hefting the large black bag of goodies onto my shoulder, I hand a modified M4 assault rifle to Meghan. "That one is yours. And we'll get it set to your comfort in a couple of days. I'm sure we've got a range we can train at."

Walking over to the truck, I say to James, "I'm surprised I didn't see any surface-to-air missiles in there."

"Simon and Lucifer have a stock of those at the compound. They won't let me play with them, though. Something about children and blowing the house up," he says with an annoyed shrug.

Meghan

Pistols, assault rifles, and explosives, oh my. Gabriel pulls so much from the back of James's car, my head starts to spin.

There's seriously enough weaponry packed between him and James to start a war.

At first it all seems a bit like overkill. After all, how many weapons does one man need? Especially a man as big and powerful as Gabriel?

But when I remember Alexei and the threat he poses to me, it almost doesn't feel like enough.

"Try this on," James says and tosses a black vest to me.

The vest hits me square in the chest and I just manage to grab it without falling over or dropping it to the ground.

"Gee, thanks," I grumble.

"You're welcome," James says, giving me a smirk before turning his attention back to his trunk.

Hefting the vest up, I'm surprised by the weight. The thing is *heavy*. I swear it must weigh at least ten pounds.

I struggle a bit to undo the Velcro straps. My hands trying and failing to pull them off not only because my hands are sore and my arm still hurts like a bitch, but because it feels like someone must have superglued them on. After loading the last of the weapons up in the truck, Gabriel notices and walks up to me.

"Here, let me help you with that," he says as he takes it from my grasp.

Yesterday was hands down the worst day of my life, I think as I watch him easily rip off all the Velcro straps.

Once the straps are open, he settles the vest over my shoulders and begins to strap me in, binding me in tight.

Yet today seems to be shaping up to be one of the best.

I've gone from having nothing. No money, no car, no allies, and no way to protect myself.

To having it all...

In a blink of an eye, I have everything I need to survive.

And it's not lost upon me why I suddenly have so much.

Not only has he given me protection, Gabriel has also given me my freedom and dignity back. And for what?

Because he thinks I'm his?

Warmth washes over me as I remember the words he spoke last night in the heat of the moment.

So fucking mine...

"How's that feel?" Gabriel asks, dropping his hands and taking a step back.

"A little tight," I mutter, hoping he doesn't notice the color warming my cheeks.

I don't know if it's the vest or the weight of his possession that's squeezing around my breasts right now, but whichever it is, it's uncomfortable as fuck.

"I was afraid of that," James says, popping up from his trunk.

Both men turn their scrutiny on me and it's everything I can do not to squirm.

Gabriel's gaze sweeps over me slowly, much more slowly than James. Roaming not only over the vest but also dropping down the length of my legs. I watch that look I've become familiar with over the last few hours spread over his face.

Even bound up in this too-tight vest, he looks like he wants to fucking *eat* me. Eat me, throw me down on the ground, and take me right now, right here.

And I'm half-tempted to let him.

Shit. I'm really starting to sink into the deep end now. After last night, I'm not even sure I remember where the surface is, or if I'll ever be able to find it again.

Do I still want to get away from him? I don't have a fucking clue. I wish I could say with one hundred percent certainty that last night didn't change a thing, but it's changed *everything*.

We connected on a level I didn't think possible.

With his body, with those damn eyes, he showed me more than words ever could.

And I believe him. I believe every truth he pounded into me.

But instead of reassuring me, or even comforting me, his truth has only filled me with more confusion and uncertainty.

This thing between us... it's too big for my head to wrap around, but I can't deny that it's there. I can feel it even now, pulsing just beneath the surface of my skin. Drawing me to him. Making me care about him...

And just the thought of trusting it, of putting my faith in it, scares the shit out me.

He's still a stranger. He could kill little kids for all I know.

And my immediate instinct is to run like hell.

But I know I can't let fear rule me. I've let fear rule me for so long... and where did that get me? It got me here.

So I'm trying my best to just go along with all of this and see where it takes us. But he makes it hard not to run when he looks at me like that.

"I'll need to take her measurements," James frowns.

Turning back to his trunk, James reaches in and quickly pulls something small and black out. He takes two steps toward me before Gabriel stops him dead in his tracks.

Voice low and harsh with the beginning of a growl, Gabriel says, "If you touch her, I'll cut your fucking hands off."

Immediately, all my skin seems to tighten, that tone in his voice causing my core to clench with arousal.

Holy shit, just a moment ago he and James were all buddy-buddy, and now Gabriel looks like he's ready to dismember him.

"Woah, man," James says throwing his hands up in the air and taking a step back. "Getting a little possessive already, aren't we?"

Gabriel just shoots him a look that's full of violence.

James mutters, "Damn. I thought you were cool. Now you're turning into the rest of those crazy fuckers."

He tosses the little black plastic thing to Gabriel with a look of disgust.

Ignoring the look, Gabriel snatches the thing out of the air and returns his attention to me. He hands the plastic thing to me before he begins to rip all the straps on my vest off.

As soon as the last strap comes undone, my ribs expand and I feel like I can take a full breath again.

Damn, if he's really going to be this protective of me, shielding me even from his friends, then I guess he really does deserve a chance.

"We'll keep this one as an emergency backup," Gabriel says, dropping the vest to the ground.

I nod my head, good with that logic. A too-tight vest is better than no vest at all.

I hand him the plastic thing back, expecting him to start taking my measurements, but his eyes drop to my chest and stay there.

At first, I think it's just because he's sizing me up, but when his eyes burn hotter and hotter, I find myself glancing down.

Dammit, my nipples are hard and poking right through my shirt despite my bra.

James clears his throat loudly and Gabriel shakes his head as if he's coming out of a daze.

"I need her underbust and overbust measurements in inches to get a good fit," James says with a laugh, looking between us.

"Turn the fuck around," Gabriel snaps back, his voice dropping to a full a growl.

I can't resist the urge to throw James's smirk back at him. Maybe being Gabriel's possession isn't so bad after all. Given all the grief James has given me today, he deserves a little grief in return.

"Fucking hell," James grumbles as he turns around.

Once he's satisfied James isn't looking at me, Gabriel returns his attention to me. Grabbing the end of the black plastic thing, he yanks out a strip of measuring tape.

Moving closer, he starts to bring the tape up to my chest only to hesitate.

It takes me a second for me to realize he probably has no clue how to measure a bust.

"It's just like measuring for a bra," I offer and lift my arms up.

Gabriel nods his head but he's still looking confused and cute as fuck.

Of course he doesn't know how to measure for a bra, unless there's a side of him I don't know about...

I feel myself smiling as I explain, "You wrap it around me, under my breasts first."

As if he's afraid of hurting me, Gabriel wraps the measuring tape around me, just over my ribs.

"A little higher," I encourage him and swallow back a chuckle.

Given what he did to me last night, you'd think he'd have no reservations about measuring me.

But he's so unsure, so hesitant, I have to tell him, "Higher," a couple of times before he finally has the length of thin tape where it needs to be.

Eyes quickly noting the number on the measuring tape, he calls out, "Thirty," to James.

"In inches?" James calls back.

Gabriel checks the number again. "Yes."

"Got it. Now measure over her boobs."

Gabriel growls deep in his throat, so deep it reminds me of thunder rumbling. "Stop thinking about her boobs."

James laughs. "I wasn't, man, until now..."

Gabriel starts to pull away, probably to throttle James, but I reach down and grab his hand to stop him.

"Come on, we're almost done. Let's get this over with."

Gabriel looks down at my hand on his hand and the strangest emotion passes over his face. I yank my hand back, something about that emotion making me feel uneasy.

His eyes lift, meeting mine again, and burn right through me.

Damn. I forgot he has a weird reaction to my touch. Sometimes it almost looks like it hurts him when I touch him.

"Sorry," I mumble and drop my hand before I remember I need to keep my arms up.

"Don't be sorry," he rasps and then clears his throat.

He keeps staring at me until my arms start to become sore.

My one arm is really starting to bother me, so I have to remind him, "You need to measure my over bust now."

His eyes cut away, but not before I see the flash of heat inside them.

And now my damn body is burning all over.

Just what I need when he's going to be touching my breasts.

"Yeah, hurry it up. I've got chicks to do and people to kill." James snickers.

Gabriel shakes his head and finally seems to relax a

little. "What chicks? Who was it... Johnathan? He told me you were hung up on one of Beth's friends."

Gabriel must have hit a nerve because James immediately tries to deny it. "I'm not hung up on Sophia."

"Oh, *Sophia*. So that's her name." Gabriel grins.

James mutters something about a donkey, a horse, and Gabriel's mother under his breath.

Gabriel chuckles, not the least bit offended.

Then all his focus is on me.

Lids lowering, Gabriel steps into me. Moving in even closer than he did to measure under my bust. I'm don't know if it's intentional, but his presence, his sheer size and heat, is enough to make butterflies take flight in my stomach.

I find myself sucking in a breath and holding it as he wraps the measuring tape around me without my guidance, right over my breasts.

"Thirty-seven," he calls out.

James lets out a low whistle.

Gabriel's arms start to drop, but the tape is a little loose so I tell him to, "Tighten it."

He immediately freezes then cocks his head as if he's not sure he heard me right.

"It's too loose, Gabriel. Tighten it," I'm forced to repeat, my face burning like it's on fire.

Time seems to slow down as he moves in even

closer to me. It's completely unnecessary, but I don't have it in me to tell him to give me more space.

No, this close, his shadow engulfs me, and there's something strangely comforting about the darkness.

I become painfully aware of my nipples as he tightens the tape around me, the pressure of the tape digging into them and finally smashing them down.

I become aware of every nerve of my body trying to break free to reach him.

"Thirty-six," Gabriel chokes out, and that sounds about right.

But he doesn't loosen the tape and I don't ask him to. If anything, my lips are poised to tell him to tighten it again.

To bind me up further. To keep me. To protect me. To never fucking let me go.

It's as if I've suddenly become bewitched.

And thankfully James is here to break the spell. "Fuck, I'm going to get pregnant just watching you two."

I pull away first, breaking Gabriel's hold on the measuring tape. As the tape drops away, I bring my arms down, crossing them protectively over my chest.

Disappointment and irritation creep over Gabriel's face before he clenches his fists and shoves it back down.

His lips part, and I swear he's going to say something cutting to James, but then he presses his lips together.

Looking very much like a man who's suddenly had an epiphany, his gaze scours over me, giving me another once over.

Then he asks, "Do these vests come in kid sizes?"

Assuming he's talking about me, I narrow my eyes at him. "I'm not a kid."

Yeah, I'm short, but how could he even think that after looking at me the way he was looking at me?

"I wasn't talking about you," he assures me, his eyes glinting with amusement and the corners of his lips curling. "I'm asking for our future children."

Oh boy, here we go again.

"I don't know," James answers thoughtfully. "I'm sure they do. I'll look into it."

"There will be no *our future children*," I say firmly to Gabriel, hoping he finally gets it.

Gabriel bends down and at least has the decency to drop his voice to almost a whisper as he says, "Are you sure? Because I don't remember using any protection last night..."

Lord have mercy, is he purposely trying to make me die of embarrassment?

Puffing his chest out, Gabriel straightens, looking entirely too sure of himself.

And it's on the tip of my tongue to tell him he may not have used protection, but I did. I've had an IUD for a couple of years now, and I can't even remember the last time I had a period. In fact, last night, after sex, was the first time I've had some cramping and a little spotting in a long time.

But I figure that was just because Gabriel was so rough and my body wasn't used to it.

"No kids," I repeat, trying to drill it in without revealing my little secret.

"We'll see," Gabriel says smugly and tosses the tape back to James.

Yeah... no we won't. Unless he has some way of removing my IUD without me knowing it... And I seriously, *seriously* doubt he'd resort to that unless he's a sick fuck.

Sighing, I shake my head and roll my eyes.

James slams his trunk shut. "Ready to pay Thomas a visit?"

Gabriel's face instantly grows grim and I feel a little pang of regret that I gave him shit about the kid thing.

I totally forgot we were here to visit his fallen brothers today.

Nodding his head, he sighs like a man who's been carrying too much weight, and says, "Lead the way."

12

GABRIEL

Walking toward the graves, I glance over at Meghan. "You don't have to be here for this. You can wait in the truck if you want."

Shaking her dark hair from her eyes, she looks up at me. "No, I don't have to be. I want to be."

Not entirely sure what to make of that statement, I look down to Paul's headstone. It's simple and unadorned. His life condensed down to two dates. Right beside his, I see Thomas's. Brothers in life, and now in eternity, if there is one.

Will I be next to them? I used to think when I finally died in prison, my body would be burnt in some crematorium.

Then my ashes would be thrown in a dumpster.

Heaven or hell... I don't really believe all that bullshit. I won't be repenting for the shit I've done. I'm not sorry for any of it. But what happens after I die has started to itch in the back of my head. What happens to Meghan? I'd do that whole corny I'd come back from hell to keep her safe thing, but what's that really mean?

James stands to my left. He points to an area past a strand of trees and a small hill. "Peter's on the other side of the hill with his grandmother. It wasn't in his will, but she left a spot for him beside her if he wanted it."

"How'd Paul and Thomas get these spots?" I ask, motioning around us.

It's nice, I guess, in this part of the cemetery. Trees with shade and somewhat close to a small lake. Although there seems to be a lot of unused land around these two plots.

"Lucifer bought out this section," he says with a small shrug and looks around us. "Any plot that doesn't have a stone is ours. He's keeping us together, I guess. Family and all that shit."

Even in death, we'll be his hellhounds and soldiers.

"That's comforting..." Meghan says with a hint of sarcasm.

"Where did Bart end up?" I ask James.

"Andrew dealt with him and he didn't offer any answers," James says as we both turn toward the sound of a vehicle driving up the road.

Hand slowly sliding to the gun on my hip, I move just enough to put myself in-between Meghan and the blacked-out Cadillac that slows as it gets closer to us.

"Expecting friends?" I ask James quickly.

"No, but I know who it is." James grumbles quietly to me.

Meghan goes to step up beside me, but I shuffle in her path. "Hold on there, little bit. Need to see first what we're dealing with."

"Seriously?" she whispers at my back.

"Y'all relax, this one isn't dangerous in the shoot-us sense." James chuckles as he looks to us both.

"Who is it?" I ask.

James doesn't answer though, he just starts walking toward our vehicles where the black Cadillac has come to a stop at. As the back door opens, a loud sigh comes out of me like a huge gust of fuckery.

Stepping out of the car, an old man slowly straightens up with the aid of a wooden cane. His gnarled hands are time-worn and he has a thick bearded face.

Ten years ago, before I went into prison, I remember seeing the old man looking at me much like he does now. Sad and regretful. His thick black beard has grown whiter and grayer, though. The wrinkles around his eyes have transitioned from laugh lines to old man lines. He's hunched more now, where he used to stand tall and proud. Time seems to have worn on him. His black coat, black pants, and black shirt all neatly pressed, and the white of his priestly collar looks out of place on him.

"Is that a priest?" Meghan asks with confusion.

"Yeah, Father Coss," James says.

"He looks like a bear that got really old," she says, "or... something... He's really a priest?"

"Yeah, just like all the other ones. Corrupt as the day is long and full of fire," I say.

He doesn't leave the concrete of the drive, just stands there waiting for us to make our way over to him. He does that fucking majestic wait shit, as if us peasants shall march up to him like he's the fucking Pope.

When we get close enough for my tastes, I stop Meghan, and say to the man, "Coss."

"Gabriel. James." He nods to us all, then he smiles at Meghan. "Miss?"

"Meghan, sir." Meghan says quietly and for some fucking reason she's being almost shy about it.

"Ah, Meghan..." Father Coss looks at us all. "It's good to see you. I'm glad you came to pay your respects to Paul and Thomas, Gabriel. Have you had a chance to stop by Peter's?"

"Some other time," I say.

James moves to my side as he nods his head toward Father Coss. "I'll be heading out. I've got places to be and sins to atone for."

Father Coss gives James a frown. "When's the last time you thought about coming to confessional, James?"

"Same time the priest asked to see my no-no spot."

"James Alexander Po—" Father Coss exclaims before being cut off.

"You finish that sentence, Father, and I'll nail your bits to the alter like I did the last priest," James says with a laugh as he walks past the priest and heads to his car.

"What do you want, Coss?" I ask as I watch James make the lucky getaway.

"I came to speak with you now that you're out of that damnable prison. Simon kindly told me where to find you, since I highly doubted I'd be able to get you into the church just yet," he says almost fucking magnanimously, as if I seek his fucking forgiveness.

"I'll make sure to shoot Simon in the leg," I say as I reach down to grab Meghan's hand.

"Gabriel, what happened ten years ago... We need to talk about that day... Perhaps we could have Miss Meghan give us a moment to talk," he suggests, and I can see he desperately wants to do this alone.

He wants to do this in private, where his fucking past sins don't have to be brought out into the light of day.

"Nah, she stays by my side, Coss. I met her in a

church, if that helps any, but as James said... Sins to commit and nothing to atone for."

Pulling Meghan with me, I start to pass Coss before he reaches out and grabs at my arm.

"I was there that day too, dammit!" he growls.

"Yeah, you got sent to the fucking priesthood. I got ten years in a supermax. You committed the sins just as much as I did. Don't fucking think for a moment I owe you a thing," I snarl before ripping my arm away from him. "Just because you wear the costume doesn't mean you're forgivable."

Yanking Meghan along beside me, I pull us quickly to the truck. Helping her get in, I shut her door before heading back to the priest who stares at me with something akin to fear in his eyes.

Standing before me, the old man is a shell of his former glory, but he sure thinks he's bigger than me now.

"You pulled the trigger on how many of your brothers that day?" I ask before going on. "I've killed a lot of men in the name of Lucifer, and I don't for one fucking moment forget that. You should remember all your past fucking sins sometime, Father."

"I've come to terms with what I've done, Gabriel," he says as he pushes a finger into my chest. "And I've tried to bring each one of you back into the light. It's been too damn long for you men to go on this way."

"Yeah, well, we've got a way to go," I say, smacking

his hand away from me. "And if I remember correctly, *Dad*, you took the cloth as soon as it was offered. The bodies hadn't even cooled before you went straight into the priesthood."

"I did this as a way to show penance for my misdeeds—" he tries to tell me before I burst out laughing in his face.

"You took the cloth because it was that or death. You didn't give two shits about your past misdeeds," I say.

"You damnable cuss. I'm not too old to put you in your place," he growls as he straightens to his full height.

"Just like you did to Simon and me after Miriam died? I've still got the scars from the coat hangers. Simon's got them all over his back from laying on top of me, trying to shield me from your righteous anger. Our drunk mother even took a couple of those blows in the early days... Before she drank herself to death and put a bullet in her brains to end *her* suffering," I say with a growl.

Scars are all over our backs because of this shithead's rage. Because he couldn't fucking deal with being a parent anymore. Because he wanted us to grow up as hard me.

"I..." he stutters.

"Get fucked, Father Coss," I say to him, using the name he chose to start his life over with.

PUSHING the call button on my phone, I wait for Simon to pick up.

"What is it, Gabriel?"

"Fuck you. Next time you set me up for seeing, Coss, I'll break your fucking spine."

"Tsk, Tsk. Keeping talking to me like that and I'll —" Simon tries to respond.

"Fuck off. Is that Russian restaurant over in Bethlehem still a front for their laundering services?" I ask.

"To an extent. It's fallen to mostly old men regaling each other with stories from their former glory days," he says.

"They do any business there?" I ask.

"Yes, it still launders about a million every three months," he says, and I can hear the tapping of a keyboard.

"Good. Do me a favor and turn off all the traffic and surrounding cameras around the restaurant. I'll probably need a change of license plates this afternoon," I say.

His voice is slow and careful as he says, "I can do both. What do you have planned?"

"If they've got inside security feeds, get yourself into them and you'll see," I say and then disconnect the phone.

WHEN I'VE HAD a moment to bring my simmering anger down a notch, I get into the truck and take a look at Meghan. She's far too beautiful, so much so it makes my tongue feel thick with unsure feelings for her.

"What was that about?" Meghan asks as I pull out of the cemetery.

"My asshole brother set us up for that little fucking visit," I growl out as we pull onto the main road.

James hightailed it pretty damn fast out of there. No chance in catching up with his ass.

"Why and who was he? I mean I know he was a priest... but why is he coming to talk to you guys?" Meghan asks.

When I don't immediately answer her, she pokes my arm with her slender fingers. "What was that about? I thought you said we're in this together?"

"Coss was a power behind the throne when it came to the family business. He stood just to the right side of Lucifer's father," I say as I get us onto the highway heading towards Bethlehem.

"You mean Lucifer's father had a priest working for him?"

"No. He was one of Lucifer's father's men, one of the best hitmen around. Lucifer gave him the choice of the church or the graveyard," I say and try to ease the fucking tension in my shoulders.

It's been a long fucking time since I saw that fucker, and he still makes me want to commit violent fucking murder. I want to wrap my calloused hands around his old, weathered fucking throat.

That motherfucker stayed out of the grave and prison, while I spent ten long fucking years inside a cement fucking block. I'm not fucking mad at Lucifer, Simon, or any of the other guys. They had their lives stretching before them like a beautiful sunrise. I was in my sunset. I'd killed too many men to clear the way for the family.

To clear the way for Lucifer to take over as the unmitigated leader.

Father Coss, that fucker was left alive for appearance's sake. At least that's how he got Lucifer to spare him. He did some of the dirty work with me and in return he got to live. It also kept the status quo with the surrounding families. He was kept around to guide Lucifer...

Like that would have ever truly fucking happened. Lucifer took full control the day he smothered his fucking father, and I put a bullet in anyone who objected. I killed eleven men that day for Lucifer. Father Coss killed two. Might as well have killed me, or so I thought. Wouldn't have been much to kill off a son of his.

The wheel groans again as I start trying to bend it

into something beyond the circular shape it's supposed to be.

"Gabriel. Stop," Meghan says quietly, her small fingers tracing the popping veins of my arms. "Stop for me."

Slowly I pry my fingers off the steering wheel. I don't know if I could truly bend the fucker in half like I want to, but I'm willing to bet it wouldn't be good for the car if I did.

"You're going to have a heart attack before you're forty..." she says quietly. "Which reminds me, exactly how old are you?"

"Thirty-one," I grunt as I shift in my seat.

Meghan has a way of bringing me out of my rage, even if I still want to fucking kill Coss. That high-horsed motherfucker thinks of us as fallen soldiers, and we probably are. But him trying to fucking redeem us is a fucking joke. He's got more than enough blood on his hands.

"Shit, I robbed the retirement home!" Meghan groans loudly. "You're going to keel over any year now from old age. Do we need to get one of those stair-escalator things? You know, the ones the old people sit in to ride up a flight of stairs..."

"I'd fucking break one of those things just by sitting on it," I growl out as I latch my hand onto her inner thigh. "Besides, I didn't see your young ass caring about me being so old last night."

"Oh..." she murmurs as I start to stroke her thigh. "What... What about family? Brothers or sisters?"

My hand stops roaming so I can grab the steering wheel again with it.

"Simon... That asshole you've met already is my brother. Had a sister, but she died very young to an infection that wasn't caught in time," I say.

"Gabriel... I'm sorry."

"It's alright," I say.

But it's not really. I think back to then and I don't remember as much as I used to. It fucking hurts some- where in my stomach that I can't remember the last time I allowed myself to think of Miriam.

Simon was about ten when she died, old enough I guess to know that his little sister was gone forever, but not old enough to know why. I think that's where he got his obsession with being clean from. All he was told was that it was an infection that killed her. Some bug. He started washing his hands at the funeral and couldn't stop. My parents weren't any help, the death of Miriam broke something deep in them.

I had to take control of Simon after that. A six-year- old who just lost his twin sister taking care of a ten- year-old who was getting fucked in the head...

"You don't look like it's alright," Meghan says softly.

"I don't much think of her. No use in remembering someone like that. She was the good one, the white to my black," I say, and I can feel the anger rising up in my throat.

It's like a fucking sickness trying to crawl its way up and be unleashed.

"You sound like you were really close to her?" she asks.

"She was my fraternal twin. Thank whatever god for that. I can't imagine she would have been very happy looking like me as a chick," I say with a chuckle. "She was the bigger one in the womb, from what my mom said. I was the runt."

"Fuck me, I can't imagine trying to push out two babies," she says.

"Only child then?" I ask.

"Yeah, just me. My parents tried for more, but I'm the only one."

"So, if you don't mind me asking, where's your mom?" I ask, and I can see instantly it's not going to be a good answer.

"She... died... in a... a car bomb," she says, and looks away from me like it's some dirty little secret.

"When was that?" I ask.

This time it's me taking her hand. Shit like that sucks to relive.

"Five years ago. My dad says it was the Italians from Garden City trying to take over more space," she whispers.

Why the fuck would they even try that, is my first thought.

Killing off a wife isn't a good idea, not when it comes to wars. You don't kill the spouses or kids, not if you don't have to.

"Fuck, that sucks, Meghan. I'm sorry."

"It was pretty hard after that. I don't have any siblings... So my dad became a bit of a nightmare. Very overprotective. I barely talked him into letting me go out to California for school."

"I went out there once, had to do a job there. I stayed for a couple of weeks, waiting around. Lots of sun and beaches out there," I say.

Lots of sun, beaches, and blood, is more like it though. I had to track one of Lucifer's father's debtors. It sucked. Too many damn people around, too many damn distractions.

Then again, I got to see the shitty underbelly of Hollywood. That was fucking eye-opening. There were more sleezy scumbags than I could believe. Fuck, everywhere I looked I saw drugs, prostitutes, and thieves.

I thought Garden City was bad, but Hollywood was worse. It seemed like the higher someone was in the social circles, the dirtier they played. Too many of those men and women out there thought they owned the world. It wouldn't be a picnic trying to keep that fucking city under control.

"I can just imagine you laying on a beach, drinking piña coladas," Meghan says with a chuckle.

"Nah, that shit tastes foul. I tried my hand at surfing though, for about a week. It was interesting trying to find a board big enough for me," I say with a laugh at the memory.

"You, surfing?" She snorts.

"Yeah, I wasn't too bad at it. I spent a week after my job just sitting in the ocean from dawn to dusk. First time in my life I found my hands clean from dirt and blood. Saltwater washed a lot of shit off me," I say.

Those fucking waves out there... it was peaceful. I'd just sit on the board and watch the swells coming in. Take in the horizon. Two months later, I was in prison. It was fucking hell being shoved into a six-by-eight-foot cell after seeing the ocean.

Being in prison... it was like living on pure adrenaline for years. But... fucking Meghan... She walks over all those deep-seated instincts and touches me with no fear. I touch her now just to make sure she's real, that she isn't some figment of my fucked-up imagination.

"Wow," she says as she looks over to me in something akin to surprise.

"What?"

"I never pegged you as the surfer boy type."

Chuckling, I say, "I'm not."

"Don't worry, I won't tell anyone. I know you've got a rep to protect."

"So, what were you going to college for?" I ask.

"I was pursuing a degree in Business Administration. It was the only path my father would permit me to take."

"What did you want to take?" I ask as we begin to pull off the interstate, taking the Bethlehem exit.

"I don't really know. With my mom's death shaking my whole world up, I wanted to do something that wasn't related to the family. But my father had plans for me, regardless of what I wanted. Alexei being the prime example," she says with some heat in her voice.

I think she's been bottling her shit up for some time now. It was just the icing on the cake when her father tried to force her into a marriage she didn't want. I have no clue how the fuck what I did was any different. Then again, she's tried to kill me since then... Maybe she gets off on the violence just as much as I do.

She sure fucked like it last night.

"Well, we'll be doing something with him as soon as I find the little dick bastard," I grin as I look at her.

She smiles, but it's not exactly a warm one.

"I just want to see how he fucking responds to being drugged up while someone pushes his ass around."

"I doubt I'll be doing much pushing. I've got a feeling my fists will be doing most of the work."

We travel through the city in silence. This city is a lot like Garden city, except smaller and a little poorer.

Lots of vice, though. I think at one time there were plans on taking over this city like Lucifer did with Garden, but I'm guessing the Russians are fucking that up.

"So, being Callahan's daughter... Besides the whole Russian pricks coming into the city, what else has been happening?" I ask.

Shrugging her shoulders, she says, "I don't know much. I know that a Mexican cartel has been pissing my father off because the uneasy truce with the Heralds of Hell seems to be breaking down..."

"They're still around?" I ask. "The Heralds of Hell? I remember they were having issues before I went to prison."

"Yeah, they've been operating on the fringes for some time now, but they offered help to my father when the Italians bombed us. He took them up on it, but with the Mexican cartel trying to take over all the drug trade in the city, it's put a strain on him. The Heralds want more guns and manpower to fight with, and the Irish have been struggling to keep what property they can to themselves. Then you have the Russians pushing their way into the mix. It's a powder keg, one match and this whole city will be at war."

Well, fuck me running. She's knows more than I thought she did.

Looking around the street I'm on, I spot a parking spot close to the Russian restaurant The Little Bear.

"Gonna need you to take over driving in a minute," I say as I reverse the truck into the parking spot.

Directly ahead of us the sleepy little restaurant sits. It's a small building, thankfully nothing on either side of it.

"What? Why?" Meghan asks.

"I need to go say hello to some friends, and I need you at the wheel," I say as I pull the black bag from the backseat up to my lap.

"I thought we did everything together," she says with a frown.

"We do, so that means you need to get us out of here as soon as I get in the truck," I say and pull out four sticks of C-4.

Grabbing the bag of ball-bearings, I hand Meghan two sticks of the explosive.

Setting the bearings bag between us, I grab a handful and start pushing them into the explosive, trying to give it a good covering.

"Can you do those two sticks?" I ask as I start on my second bar of the grayish plastic explosive.

"What exactly are we doing?" she asks as she takes a handful of bearings and starts pressing them into the explosive.

"Collateral damage. I want to make sure this place doesn't get rebuilt."

"Oh."

Looking over the four long bars of C-4, I grin as I

stuff them into a small black bag. After thinking for a moment, I end up pushing the rest of the metal ball bearings into the bag with it. Pushing detonators into each stick, I set them to blow from the little receiver I have in my pocket.

"Be right back, keep the engine running," I say.

Jumping out of the truck, I look back and see Meghan climbing into the driver's seat with a pensive look on her face. She's more than likely questioning what exactly she signed up for. She's about to see. I haven't exactly killed anyone in front of her eyes yet, or had her kill anyone, but it's only a matter of time before it happens.

Putting a pleasant smile on my face as I cross the street, I head directly for the front door of the dimly lit restaurant. It's looks just like I remembered, old and out of date. Still clinging to the past. Fuck, that sounds a bit like me if I'm being honest with myself. Old and out of date. Clinging to a past full of hurt and anger.

Pushing the door inward, I stand there for a moment, allowing my eyes to acclimate to the dim lighting inside. The décor is straight out of a 60's upscale restaurant. Except now it's comes off as skeezy. The old-world tiling has lost its luster, and the paint on the walls has a thick coating of cigarette smoke. Even the chairs and tables look out of step with the world outside.

Walking toward the small waiting area, I poke my

head around the corner to peek inside the dining area. As I thought, it's half-full of old men, relics of the Soviet era. More than likely a few old KGB sitting there.

I watch as they all eat food slowly from their plates or take long drinks from glasses containing a clear alcohol. Vodka. They sure do love that shit.

Looking down to my bag, I grin. This should work out just like I want. I don't give a shit if these old men are really connected to Alexei. I just want to fuck with his money operations, and I want him to know I don't care about collateral damage. I'm just here to have a fucking good time while I hunt his dumbass.

I've got enough C-4 in the bag to level the whole building, and probably more than that. Haven't used it in a long time, so my memory is a bit fuzzy on what kind of damage I'm getting ready to cause.

Kneeling down to the floor, I push the bag across the old world tile then grin as it quietly reaches about the midway mark of the dining room.

Standing up from where I'm crouching, I head back to the front door. Time to move.

And fuck.

Some little old lady is getting ready to come in the door.

Stepping quickly to the door, I flip the closed sign before I open it just enough to let myself out of the door.

Looking down at the woman, I give her a frown.

"Sorry, ma'am. I was just informed they're closed for the day. Something about a gas leak from one of their grills," I say, trying to be as unoffending as possible.

As small as Meghan is, this little old lady looks even tinier.

"That's no good," she says with a frown, looking past the door.

"No, ma'am, but better safe than sorry, I think."

Turning to get her to move away from the door, I suggest, "How about I help you back to your car?"

"You're a good boy. My grandson used to be, now he's too busy for me," she says with a sigh.

Reaching up, she takes my arm, and I slowly walk her toward the street light. "I'm sure he still thinks about you, though."

"Bah, he thinks of me for my money. But I'm too smart to give it away," she ends with a grin.

As we slowly cross the street, I look up to see Meghan gawking. Her eyes are as round as saucers as I wink at her.

"Thank you, young man," the little lady says as we reach her car.

"My pleasure. As I said, better safe than sorry."

Walking back to my truck, I wait until I hear the little old lady's car take off down the street before I push the detonate button on the little device in my pocket.

The resounding concussion effect nearly knocks me off my feet as I jog over to the truck.

Hopping into the passenger side, I give Meghan a grin. "She was a really sweet woman. Said I remind her of an old movie star," I say as I motion for her to start driving. "Time to go, babe. No need to stick around here any longer.

"Holy fucking shit," Meghan mutters as she puts us the truck in drive and whips us out of the parking spot.

When a second booming sound goes off, I snicker. I wonder if that was a gas main.

13

MEGHAN

A huge cloud of smoke darkens the sky behind me. The street is littered with chunks of stone and other debris. People run out of the surrounding buildings with looks of shock and worry on their faces.

My foot presses hard on the gas and the engine of the truck rumbles as I race away from the scene of the explosion.

Once I'm a few blocks away, I manage to sneak a quick glance over at Gabriel.

He's leaned back in his seat, wearing the biggest shit-eating grin on his face.

I almost do a double take, but there's so much traffic in front of me I'm afraid I'll rear-end somebody.

How can he be so fucking relaxed? So fucking happy after what he just did?

My foot pushes harder on the gas, the need to get away from what's behind me causing my heart to beat frantically.

When he talked about collateral damage, I stupidly assumed he was blowing something up with no one in it. But I know there were people in that restaurant. I watched him walk an old lady out for Christ's sake!

Bile rises up in my throat and I have to swallow it back down a couple of times before I manage to ask, "So, how many people did I just help you kill?"

Fuck. I've never killed anyone before.

Out of the corner of my eyes I see Gabriel shrug his shoulders nonchalantly, like the body count is no big deal. "I'm not really sure."

"Can you at least guestimate?" I ask a little too shrilly, the need to know bordering on hysteria.

How much blood do I have on my hands?

I sense him stiffening beside me before he offers slowly, almost carefully, "I don't know. Probably less than a dozen."

Probably less than a dozen... So I just helped him kill at the most eleven people...

My hands tighten around the steering wheel, finding the grooves he's already made in it.

"Meghan," he says, his voice heavy with worry. "Pull over, I'll take over."

I shake my head and my foot pushes harder on the

gas. I can't let him take over. No, I can't let him have control.

Who knows what he'll do next?

First it was the church... and now this... and who knows how many before I even met him...

He's a psychotic murderer, and I fucked him.

Oh god.

I'm married to him.

I blow through three more lights, seriously considering pulling over, popping the door open and shoving his big ass out.

Guns don't work, nor do knives. He's like some horror movie monster that can't be killed.

I doubt he'd survive though if I ran him over with the truck.

But then again, maybe he would...

"Take the next left," he says, but I'm so stuck in my head I miss the turn.

He repeats my name a few times, trying to get my attention as I think of all the ways I could off him.

I know he didn't use all the C4. If I can get my hands on what's in the back, I could shove it down his pants...

"Meghan," he finally growls menacingly.

My eyes snap to him.

"Take the next left."

I'm half-tempted to take the next right out of sheer obstinance, but maybe once I get him to wherever he wants to go, he'll get out of the truck and I can drive off into the horizon.

A girl can only hope.

"Now take the next right," he says after we drive down the road a mile or so.

With a sigh, I hit the blinker and slow the truck down as I pull us into a parking lot.

He jerks his chin toward a dark building sitting at the edge of the lot. "Park in front of there."

I do exactly as he says. I pull into one of the empty spots in front of the building and then put the truck in park.

Releasing a deep breath, I stare ahead at the building. The place looks like some kind of grungy dive bar. The sign reads: The River Waters.

I avoid glancing over at Gabriel as I wait for him to make the first move. I'm hoping he'll get out without realizing I still have the truck running.

As if he knows exactly what I'm thinking, he reaches over and twists the keys out of the ignition.

Damn.

"Get out of the truck, Meghan," he says, so close his warm breath brushes against my ear.

I shiver and immediately hate myself for still being affected by him. He's a murdering monster, yet my body doesn't seem to know or care.

The stupid thing still wants him.

Seeking to escape his presence, I yank on the door handle and quickly slide out of my seat.

Once my feet hit the ground, I'm filled with the overwhelming need to run. To escape this fucking madness.

Before I even realize what I'm doing, my knees are pumping and my lungs are aching as I take off across the parking lot.

Gabriel bellows my name.

I don't stop though, I can't stop.

I run so fast, so hard, I gas myself within a couple of minutes. I manage to make it to the very edge of the lot before I feel the ground thundering beneath my feet.

A second later what feels like an iron bar wraps around my chest.

I scream and flail as Gabriel yanks me off my feet and begins to drag me backward.

My heels drag across the asphalt as I wail out, "Let me go!"

Another iron bar wraps around me and his big palm slaps over my mouth.

I try to bite him, try to kick him, but it's fucking hopeless.

Once again, I'm forced to face the crushing reality that I'm not strong enough to fight him off. This isn't an action movie, and I'm not a genetically enhanced superwoman. Pure physics is working against me, and it sucks so fucking bad.

Gabriel drags me all the way back to the truck then pushes me up against the door.

Flipping me around, he drops one arm from around my chest.

"Where the fuck are you going?" he huffs out as he cages me in.

With his hand still slapped over my mouth, all I can do is snort and glare up at him.

His jaw tenses with frustration. "What the fuck is the problem now?"

"You," I pant out as soon as he slides his hand off my mouth. "You're the fucking problem, Gabriel. Just let me go!"

I take a cheap shot at his shin, catching him off guard. He grunts and slaps his hand back over my mouth.

Shaking his head, he looks at me like I'm some kind of alien creature he doesn't understand. "How the fuck am I the problem? What the fuck did I do?"

How can he not know?

Without giving me a chance to respond, he keeps his hand firmly against my lips and asks as if he's finally figuring it out, "Is it because I blew up that restaurant?"

I glare up at him some more.

"Are you fucking kidding me? You're pissed because I blew up a bunch of fucking Russians?"

Ding, ding, ding. We have a fucking winner.

"What the hell, Meghan?" he growls as he slides his hand off my mouth.

Still panting, I take a second to lick my dry lips, then immediately regret it when I taste a hint of his skin.

"It's not that you blew up a bunch of fucking Russians," I explain, though Lord knows I don't owe him an explanation. "It's that you just killed a bunch of people and made me an accomplice!"

He frowns as he stares at me. "So you're worried about getting busted and doin' time? Well, don't you worry your—"

"No... yes. No!" I cut him off. "I don't want to get busted and don't want to do time, but that's not why I want you to let me go."

His eyes flash, growing colder, icier, and he presses his body into me, crushing me against the truck. "I'm not fucking letting you go. Do I need to remind you again what you mean to me?"

I swear this is just an exercise in futility. He just doesn't get *it*. How can he when he's a psycho? But I push on.

"You... you... you tricked me into helping you kill people!" I finally blurt out while hot tears start to sting my eyes.

Goddammit, I hate that I feel like this. Hate that I'm on the verge of crying over this. I'm not fucking weak, and never thought something like this would bother me, but it does.

It's one thing to imagine killing someone, especially someone who deserves it. Someone who's hurt me.

It's another thing being deceived into helping someone kill a group of strangers.

Gabriel reels back from me as if I just slapped him in the face. "You held a gun to my chest and pulled the trigger...'

"Yes!" I snap at him, not denying it.

He'd be dead if there was a bullet left in the chamber.

"You held a knife to my heart and threatened to cut off my balls..."

"I did," I agree, blinking my eyes to fight back the tears.

Gabriel shakes his head slowly, his confused gaze never leaving my face. "You're sending me mixed signals here, babe. Have you never killed anyone before?"

"No!" I snap out and then suck in a deep breath.

I've never killed anyone before. There's never been a reason to. As a woman in my family, I was sheltered, protected while the men did all the dirty work. The risk, the danger, never touched me until my mom was killed in that car explosion.

Gabriel's eyes soften, filling with sympathy, and I

instantly can't stand it. I don't need him feeling sorry for me over this.

Stiffening my spine, I explain, "All those things I did, I did them in self-defense. It wasn't cold-blooded murder."

There's a difference, a huge fucking difference. One is done for self-preservation.

And one stains the soul.

"There was nothing cold-blooded about it..." Gabriel says defensively, the softness fading from his eyes as he pushes back into me.

I shake my head and look away.

Grabbing me by the hair, he tugs, forcing me to look up at him. "This is war."

I almost laugh. So that's his excuse? That's his reasoning? The route he's going to take to make me feel less guilty about this?

"War is full of atrocities," I counter. "It's full of sick, powerful men who use it as an excuse to get off... to fulfill their depraved fantasies."

Gabriel's blonde brows begin to inch toward his hairline and his lips twitch with amusement. "I don't need war to get off when I have you."

I open my mouth to tell him he doesn't have me, but he tugs on my hair, stopping me.

"This is kill or be killed," he practically croons.

I snap my mouth shut and stare up at him.

"And I'll kill every motherfucker on this planet to

protect you. The streets will run red until I know you're safe."

I know he probably meant that statement to be reassuring, but honestly it's rather terrifying. I search his face, search his eyes, for any sign that he's joking, but he looks completely serious.

My skin prickles with goosebumps and a chill travels down my spine.

"How does blowing up that restaurant and killing innocent people protect me?" I ask, hoping to push him more towards reason.

He doesn't even blink before he states gruffly, "Not a bastard in there was innocent."

"Yeah, but how do you know? How you can be sure?"

Both brows pulling down, he practically growls as he pushes his hips into me. "Because I know, Meghan."

That answer just isn't good enough for me. I need proof. I need something, anything, to relieve my conscience.

"Did you look them up beforehand? Was that entire thing planned?" I continue to push.

Gabriel makes a frustrated noise. He's pressed so close, I can feel almost every muscle in his body tightening with tension.

Grabbing me by the face, he stares hard into my eyes as he says, "You're just going to have to trust me on this."

Trust him? How can I trust him when he didn't even let me in on what he was doing in the first place?

I open my mouth to tell him just that when he cuts me off. "If you don't, we're dead men walking."

That brings me up a little short.

I blink up at him. "What do you mean?"

His lashes lower and his eyes pierce through me like two sharp shards of ice. "It's them or us, Meghan."

Them or us... a familiar excuse I've heard my father give for his decisions. His whole reason for going after the Italians and starting the feud in the first place. A feud that took my mother's life.

All of a sudden Callum's face flashes through my mind, followed by all the dead men in the church. My father... my father was shot. I don't even know how injured he was. He could be dead for all I know.

I start trembling as the reality of what happened yesterday washes over me. So much has happened to me since the wedding that I haven't really had time to think about it. To process it.

Scowling, Gabriel drops his hands from my cheeks and reaches down, gathering me up in his arms and pulling me close. I stiffen at first, not wanting his comfort, but I'm so cold all of a sudden, and he's so *warm*.

I'm drowning... sinking... and the only thing I can grab onto is the fucking shark in the bloody waters.

His hands travel over me, tender, soothing.

Too fucking tender and soothing for a man so willing to commit murder.

"I don't want anyone else to die," I admit softly.

Especially in a fiery inferno...

I shudder, unable to repress the memory of what happened to my mother... what probably happened to those people in the restaurant.

Gabriel releases a huff of air that whispers across the top of my head and gives me a tight squeeze before he pulls back.

Eyes finding my eyes again, he looks almost regretful as he asks, "Not even Alexei?"

I suck in a breath and just stare at him, the truth of that question slamming into me.

Fuck.

I do want Alexei to die, and it probably makes me the biggest fucking hypocrite in the world.

I try to look away, try to hide the truth inside me, the bit of shame I'm feeling, but his gaze traps mine, holding me captive.

"People are going to die, Meghan. A lot of people are going to die before this is over with, but I'm doing my damnedest to make sure it's not us."

I stare at him, my own personal battle raging inside of me. Part of me still wants to rebel at all of this. To refuse to accept it because it's morally *wrong*.

If this were a book or movie, we'd find some way to take out the bad guys without anyone else getting hurt.

But this isn't a book or movie... this is my fucking life we're dealing with here.

"Fuck..." Gabriel suddenly groans and leans down, pressing his forehead against mine. "You're so fucking sweet and innocent."

Instantly I try to scoff. Me? Sweet and innocent? I've been accused of a lot of things in my life, but never those two words, especially together.

His voice drops to a growl. "Don't try to argue with me on this. You are."

I roll my eyes and his grip tightens on me.

"You are," he insists. "You're fucking pure compared to me. And if there was any way I could spare you from all this shit, if there was a safe cage I could lock you in to protect you, I would."

Bristling at the thought of him locking me in a cage, I narrow my eyes at him. "Just try it..."

Gabriel chuckles, and before I can completely comprehend what's happening, his head dips down and his mouth covers mine.

He forces a kiss from my lips. Pulling and sucking with determination until I finally stop fighting and start to give in. "And that's exactly why I need you. I need you by my side, Meghan."

He kisses me again as I struggle not to completely melt in his arms. His teeth find my bottom lip, tugging and pulling at me, but the nip is rather gentle.

"I need you with me on this," he groans.

Another kiss is pressed to my lips, so hard my head starts to tip back. I grab at him, holding on so I don't fall over.

His mouth continues to ravish mine until I'm breathless and I'm dizzy. Until I'm struggling to remember why I'm upset with him.

Pressing me up against the truck, he fits himself between my thighs and drives his tongue into me like he's fucking me with it. Reminding me of what his cock did to me last night.

Reminding me of his devotion and commitment to this unholy union.

When he finally tears his mouth away from mine, it's like it takes every bit of strength in his body to do so.

"I need you to put your faith in me, Meghan. Put your faith in me and stand by my side while I do what I've been put on this planet to do."

My chest rising and falling as I pant for air, my voice sounds breathy as I ask, "What were you put on this planet to do?"

No shame, no anger, no remorse crosses his face as he answers without hesitation, "Kill."

14

MEGHAN

I should be running away, screaming. I know I should be running away and screaming, yet my feet won't move.

I stare at Gabriel as he looks at me expectantly. He probably wants me to say something. Give him some kind of reassurance or promise that I'll stick with him.

Words fail me though.

I've never been more confused or conflicted.

After that kiss, my body throbs with the need to press closer to him, while my head just wants to float far, far away from this mess.

Thankfully, I'm saved by the sudden and jarring ringing of his phone.

He tries to ignore it, his gaze burning into me, his eyes demanding.

And I know if he kisses me again, I'll give in. I'll make promises my soul can't keep.

I'll doom myself to damnation.

The phone rings and rings until falling silent, only to start back up again.

I squirm under Gabriel's stare as it grows more and more intense before I point out, "You should probably answer that."

He lets the phone ring again until it falls silent. It's not until it starts back up again that he makes a move to answer it. Cursing under his breath, he digs the phone out of his pocket.

"Yeah?" he snaps in irritation as he places the phone against his ear.

I can't hear the person on the other end of the line, but whatever they say causes Gabriel's face to tighten with anger.

"No shit," he mutters and pushes away from me. "I'm not a fucking idiot."

His head starts to whip around, his eyes searching as if he's looking for someone watching us.

He grunts a few times in what I'm assuming is an answer to the other person, then he hangs up the phone. Shoving the phone back into his pocket, he reaches up and rakes his fingers through his short hair.

"Creepy fucker," he grumbles, then his eyes land on me again.

Sharper than daggers.

Before I can ask *who*, he's dropping his hand and telling me to, "Get in the truck."

Hesitating, I ask, "What's going on?"

"Too much heat,' he answers and steps into me. Grabbing me by the hand, he uses it to tug me around the other side of the truck. "We need to head back to the house and lay low for a while."

I dig in my heels as he swings the passenger door open and resist his nudge to get inside. "Are we going to get busted?"

He looks at me for a moment and then his mouth curves into a slow smirk. "Nah. Simon is just being paranoid."

He gives me another nudge and I decide I've wasted enough time. I'm not entirely sure I believe him about the us getting busted part, but standing around and asking questions isn't going to prevent it.

Once I climb into my seat, he makes sure I do up my seatbelt before shutting the door. Then he stomps around the front of the truck and slides into the driver's seat.

The drive back to the house is quiet and tense.

Gabriel keeps shooting little glances at me and I feel his need for a commitment from me hanging like a sword over my head.

I wish I could alleviate his worry. I wish I could alleviate this ball of tension growing inside me.

But I can't.

I'm so torn up and confused, I don't even know where to begin. I'm stuck in this awful mental place, trapped somewhere between an existential dilemma and a crisis of conscience.

After our little heart to heart last night, I thought the worst was over. I thought we were on the same fucking page.

The two of us against the world.

I made the decision to trust him to protect me. To trust him not to hurt me.

But he ruined that illusion, blew the fucker up when he blew up the restaurant.

As bad as it is, part of me wishes I never witnessed it. Wishes that he did it without me around. Because now I'm back to square fucking one.

Things I could overlook, that I could forgive, like mowing down those gathered for my wedding in the church, are weighing heavily on me now.

Was I simply letting them go because all those men wronged me? Because I didn't actually see him kill anybody? Or did I do it because it was simply in my best interest?

Fuck... I don't even know....

I don't even know what I believe in anymore.

Turning my gaze to the window, I look out but I'm not really seeing anything. It's bright and sunny, but everything is gray. As gray as a fucking graveyard.

Before today, the last time I visited a graveyard was to pay respects to my mother.

Fuck... my mother.

That hole her loss left inside me throbs and aches. More than anything I wish she was alive. I'd give anything to talk to her, to touch her, to smell her, even if it was only for a few seconds.

She would know what to do. What decision I should make so I can live with myself after this.

Despite being married to my father, she was gifted with seeing the world in black and white. Seeing right from wrong.

My father and her used to joke about her being my father's angel on his shoulder.

She kept my father in line, kept him human... up until the feud with the Italians.

The car begins to slow down, and it takes me a moment to realize we're pulling into the garage.

Great. We're here and I still haven't figured anything out yet.

Gabriel inches the truck forward before throwing it in park and shutting off the engine. He hits a button and the garage door rolls down behind us.

I don't even have to look over to know his attention is riveted on me. I can feel it bearing down on me, the pressure of it nearly crushing me into my seat.

Afraid I might crack, I undo my seatbelt and grab

the door handle. I push my door open and hop out before Gabriel can stop me.

A second after my feet hit the ground, I hear his door pop open.

"Meghan..." he says, his voice deep with a hint of warning.

Rushing up to the door that leads inside the house, I say over my shoulder, "I'm not trying to run. I just need some space, Gabriel... some time to think..."

I take the two steps leading up to the door in one step and grab the handle.

My fingers twist, and nothing happens.

Of course the damn thing is locked and I don't have a key.

It's the fucking story of my life.

Groaning, I lean my forehead against the door, fighting the urge to bang my head against it.

It seems no matter how hard I try to be in control of my own destiny, the universe itself will step in to stop me.

I'm fucking cursed to be at the mercy of men.

Gabriel's door slams shut behind me and I jump in surprise, rattled by the loud noise. Heart pounding in my throat, slowly I spin around to face him.

All it takes is one look to know he's not going to give me the space I'm asking for.

Stalking forward, he moves with the sinister grace of a natural born predator that knows he's at the top of the food chain. Unlike most of the big men I've come across during my short life, there's no clumsiness or overcompensation in his movements.

No, he's a man that's completely comfortable in his skin. He probably even relishes the advantage it gives him.

"Gabriel, please..." I can't help but plead one last time. "I just need a little time."

Eyes nearly white-hot with heat, they land on my face and I shrink back.

"There's no time, Meghan," he says with a finality that causes my heart to instantly drop to my stomach. "I've already wasted ten years of my life. I won't waste another second because your fear is holding you back."

He steps up to me and for once we're nearly eye to eye.

"I'm not afraid," I bluff, forcing myself to meet his gaze.

"Don't lie to me, beautiful," he growls and reaches out, grabbing me roughly and pulling me close. His knuckles brush tenderly down my cheek. "It's not a good look on you."

He wants the truth? Fuck it. I won't lie.

Fighting my body's need to give into a shiver, I tell him exactly what I told him last night, but seriously mean it this time. "I don't think I can do this."

In fact, I'm pretty sure I can't.

I watch his emotions blow across his eyes like storm clouds rolling in. Anger flashes like lightning across clouds of determination.

Instinctively sensing the impending danger, I try to squirm my way out of his grip.

"Fine," he grits out between his teeth, his hold on me tightening. "I'll do it for the both of us."

Before I can ask what the fuck he means by that, he's picking me up off my feet and throwing me over his shoulder.

"What the hell, Gabriel?" I huff out as my stomach meets his shoulder.

"Stay still, I don't want to drop you," he growls and gives my butt a hard smack.

I stiffen in surprise, the pain radiating through my cheeks.

Did he really just spank me?

The unmistakable soft beeps of a code being punched in hits my ears and a second later I feel a breeze of warm air as the door to the house swings open.

He moves forward and my self-preservation kicks in.

"Put me down, asshole," I snarl and kick at him.

Grunting, he ignores my attempts to hurt him.

Hands finding purchase on his back, I try to push up, to slide out of his hold, but he suddenly lifts me up as if he's adjusting my weight. Tossing me into the air like I'm a sack of potatoes.

My stomach leaves his shoulder before I come back down in an even worse position.

I'm so far down his back now, I'm afraid I'm going to fall on my damn head.

"Put me down!" I screech, both furious and terrified.

"No," he says, his arm tightening across the back of my legs.

As he stomps through the house, I have to grab at his damn pants to keep from bouncing all over the place.

Tears of anger well up in my eyes.

Just when I thought he couldn't push me further past my breaking point, he has to go and do something like this.

My feet kick uselessly at him as I helplessly watch the floor scroll by. It's probably stupid of me to keep fighting him, given my precarious position, but I just can't help it.

"I hate you," I mutter when he comes to a stop.

"No, you don't," he sighs and pushes a door open.

The hardwood floor transitions into carpet.

"I do!" I insist.

The door slams shut behind us. He takes two steps forward, and before I can prepare myself, he's tossing me onto a bed.

I let out a shrill screech as I land on the mattress on my back.

I bounce once, twice, before my body can get its bearings. Scrambling into action, I try to sit up only to have him push me back down by the shoulders.

"You don't hate me, Meghan," he says, looming over me.

He keeps me pinned downed until I stop struggling. Until I accept that fighting his strength is futile.

Then he brushes some of the hair out of my eyes. "You just wish you did."

The truth of those words cut right through me in a way that leaves me shaking. I do wish I could hate him. I wish I could despise him for the situation he's put me in with all my heart.

Lord knows I've tried, but for some reason I can't.

He's just like every other monster in my life... and yet he's not.

And I can't fucking figure out what makes him different.

Taking in his face—his piercing eyes, his strong jaw, that bit of blonde scruff—I decide it's not his looks. He's fucking edible, yes. I'd love to sink my teeth into every inch of his body and bite down, but Alexei is arguably almost just as handsome.

His fingers tighten around my shoulders and his gaze continues to bore down on me.

It's certainly not his personality. He's just as overbearing and bossy as every other man I've ever dealt with.

He's no saint, that's for sure. Willing to kill... and even taking pleasure in it.

I want to say it's because he's tried to help me in his own, selfish way, but I'm not even sure it's that.

No, it's something else... It's this damn spark between us. This intangible thing I can't control, manipulate, destroy, or wish away, no matter how hard I try.

Even now it throbs inside me, pulsing through my limbs.

"Okay, I don't hate you," I grit out. "But I certainly don't like you. So please, get the fuck off me."

He seems to relax once I admit I don't hate him. The look in his eyes even softens to something close to tenderness.

But he doesn't move. He remains poised above me.

And the longer he looks at me, the more aware I become of the position I'm in. I'm pinned beneath him, completely at his mercy. We both know that he can do anything he wants to me.

We both know I can't stop him.

For some strange, awful reason, my body finds this terribly exciting. My breath begins to quicken and a tingling sensation creeps over my skin.

I try to ignore it, but the longer he just stares down at me, the worse it gets.

Fuck, why does he have to be so damn handsome?

"Gabriel, please get off me," I plead softly, switching tactics and hoping playing nice will get me my way.

"Well, since you asked so nicely..." he drawls out and suddenly pushes up.

He rises above me and grabs the bottom of his shirt before tugging it up and over his head.

Tossing the shirt away, his attention snaps back to me as I gasp.

"What the fuck are you doing?" I ask, frozen in place.

The sudden sight of his bare chest and all the naked skin is such a shock that I forget that I can move now.

"Finishing what we started in the parking lot," he says as he reaches down to undo his pants.

"We didn't start anything in the parking lot," I sputter.

I know I should look away as his fingers yank down his zipper, but I can't bring myself to do it. Instead, I watch, almost entranced, as he shoves his pants down to the floor and steps out of them.

Straightening, his expression darkens as he says, "You tried to run..."

"Yeah? So?" I push out of my throat.

The damn thing is closing up as my eyes take all of

his glorious body in. He's so damn big, all over, and so damn intimidating.

My thighs twitch with the muscle memory of him between them, and I squeeze my knees together in an attempt to stop it.

Lashes lowering, his already dark expression twists into something that's downright feral. "Never run from me, Meghan."

Suddenly he lunges for me.

Before I'm even aware of what I'm doing, I'm scrambling backward. My brain screaming for me to flee.

I don't get far enough away, though. Grabbing me by the leg, he yanks me down the bed.

"Not only does it make me angry," he grunts as he comes down on top of me.

I smack and slap at him as he releases my leg and slides up my body. I get one good slap in on his cheek and we both freeze.

I slapped him so hard my palm stings, and I seriously consider smacking him again, but fear holds me back.

One heartbeat passes, then another.

A slow, maniacal grin stretches across his lips. "It makes me hard."

Grabbing up my hands like it's no effort at all, he pins them above my head.

I writhe and twist, trying to escape his grip.

Bringing his weight down on top of me, he rolls his hips, his hard cock grinding into my sex. "It makes me need to stake my claim on you."

Despite my panic, that rolling grind of his cock sends a spike of pure pleasure through me, and all it does is make me angry.

Did I say I didn't hate him? Well, I think I change my mind...

"You already own me, asshole. We're married," I snarl at him. "What more do you want?"

Head dipping down, he licks and nips at my ear before he purrs, "I need to be inside you, Meghan."

A wave of pure weakness flows over me and for a moment I'm dangerously close to melting beneath him. But then that fear, that pure, icy cold terror of all the things he could do to me rears its ugly head.

Switching both of my wrists into one of his hands, he begins to lick, nip, and suckle his way down my neck.

"I need to be buried so tight and deep, I know you can never get away from me again."

My toes curl inside my boots even as my brain strains to think of a way to get him to stop before it's too late.

If I let him in again... if I open myself up... he'll completely destroy me.

His hand drags down my side and then his fingers grab at the waistband of my pants.

"I'm sorry," I blurt out in a panic. "I promise I won't run again."

Slowly his head lifts up and his eyes clash with my eyes. It takes only one breath before I see doubt and mistrust staring right back at me.

I swear it looks like he can tell I'm lying.

"Oh yeah?"

I try to push down the thought that I'm running at the first chance I get, and say more firmly, "Yes. I won't run, I promise."

"That's good," he smiles, but the smile doesn't move past his lips.

That should tip me off that he doesn't totally believe me, but a bit of hope lights up inside me, regardless.

I find myself smiling back at him, even relaxing a little bit as his grip around my wrists loosens.

But then his hands are suddenly dropping down to my waist and he's grabbing me by the hips.

He flips me over before my dumb brain can even process what the fuck is happening.

And then his hips are against me, his erection digging into my ass.

"Because the next time you run, I just might have to shove my cock up this juicy ass to feel better again."

Gasping with a mixture of outrage and shock, I try to push up, try to crawl away from him, but he wastes no time in grabbing up my wrists again. Wastes no time shifting them into one of his hands so the other can yank down my pants.

"Don't you dare. Don't you fucking dare," I cry out.

All his weight comes down on me, crushing me into the mattress.

I whimper as his mouth finds my ear. "Don't I dare, what? Don't I dare shove it in your ass?"

His hips grind into me, the hard length of his shaft sliding through the now bare flesh of my cheeks.

And I hate to admit it, but there's something secretly thrilling about feeling him there, where no man has ever touched me before.

Despite my anger and fear, my core clenches and I feel myself getting wet.

"Or don't I dare remind you that you're *mine* and you don't get to fucking run away from me?"

"Both!" I nearly wail, desperate to get out from underneath him anyway I can.

I'm already dangerously close to completely shattering. His weight alone stirring up the primal need to bend to him.

My body remembers last night, no matter how much brain wishes it could forget it.

Rocking his hips again, the crown of his cock slides down, pushing against my entrance.

"I have to, Meghan," he growls into my ear, causing all the little hairs on my body to stand on end. "I have to... because I can't fucking lose you."

Hearing those words and the edge of desperation to them, the doubts that have been plaguing me suddenly feel so far away. Floating out of my reach. I want to grab them, I want to hold onto to them, but it's becoming harder and harder to care about anything but how he feels against me.

That despite all our differences, we just seem to fucking *fit*.

Working that hand that pulled down my pants around my hip, his fingers push between me and the bed, exploring me. Sliding through my slick folds and spreading me wider for him.

"I can't lose the best fucking thing to ever happen to me," he groans, his fingers dragging up and finding my clit.

He begins to work them against me, and it's everything I can do to keep from moaning and grinding myself into him. To keep myself from giving into this sickness he's infecting me with.

Now that I know what he's capable of, what kind of man he truly is, I shouldn't be getting off on his touch.

But I am.

Even knowing that the very fingers that are giving me pleasure have caused pain and death isn't enough to stop me from enjoying it.

If anything, it only amplifies it.

His fingers swirl around and around in my wetness, and I can no longer stop myself. My hips begin to move in rhythm with him until I'm practically humping the bed.

"I can't lose the little slice of heaven I've found after ten fucking years of hell," he breathes into my ear.

The rough tips of his fingers suddenly pinch down on my clit and my hips buck as a jolt of pure pleasure shoots up my spine.

Madness. Pure madness has taken ahold of me. It's the only explanation that makes any sense. To enjoy him pushing me... using his strength to overpower me... is so fucking wrong on so many levels, but I can't help it.

It's almost like I need this. I need to be shoved past my lines drawn in the sand.

I need someone strong enough to fucking throw me over them just like this for my own benefit.

Without giving me a chance to catch my breath or recover, he thrusts his hips forward, pushing himself into me.

Though I'm wet, I'm still too tight to take him, and this position certainly isn't helping.

"Goddammit," he grits out, rolling his hips and swirling his fingers against my clit as he tries to squeeze his thickness inside me. "Stop fighting me, baby."

"I'm not... fighting..." I pant out in my own tortured frustration.

I'm so far beyond fighting him, I'm nearly delirious for him.

My body is desperate to feel his cock pushing inside me, breaking down the last of my defenses.

"You are," he insists then releases his grip on my wrists.

Grabbing me roughly around the waist, he rolls us both onto our sides.

My chest expands, and without so much of his weight on top of me, I can finally take a full breath.

"You're still fighting me, Meghan. Still trying to keep me out..."

With everything going on between my thighs, somehow I'm still able to sense him shoving my leggings further down my legs.

"And I'll be damned if I let anything come between us."

As soon as the elastic of my waistband makes it past my knees, he's forcing my legs wider. Just wide enough that he can thrust up, his cock spreading me open.

I stiffen against him, my spine going ramrod straight as my walls struggle to stretch around him.

There's so much of him, my belly fills with this strange flipping sensation. I try to swallow it back down, but it crawls over me until I'm uncontrollably trembling.

And just when I think he's gone as deep inside me

as he can go, he pushes in even further, making me feel as if I just might burst.

Finally, he reaches the spot where he can go no further without truly damaging me and stops, going completely still.

His strained breath in my ear, I realize I'm stretched so tightly around him I can feel my pulse throbbing around his thickness.

"This..." he pants, slowly withdrawing from me only to thrust his length back in. "This is what makes this life worth living..."

Slowly he works his cock in and out of me, gliding easily along my wetness.

And the most intense, most incredible sensations begin to build inside me. Ramping up with each deep stroke.

"I won't let you push me out," he grunts, picking up speed. "I won't let you run from us."

Little mewling sounds begin to slip from my lips, joining with the wet sounds of our joining.

There seems to be this one vulnerable spot inside me that he keeps hitting, so hypersensitive it steals my breath.

Faster and faster, he pumps inside me. His hips slapping against my ass. And all the sensations growing inside of me suddenly become so strong and overwhelming I can't handle it.

I try to pull away only to have his arms suddenly come around me.

"No," he nearly roars as his arms pull me back, clutching me against his chest. "Don't you dare fucking run."

"It's too much, Gabriel!" I wail as he keeps me trapped against him as he rolls onto his back.

"It's not enough," he counters, his arms wrapping over my breasts. "It will never be enough."

Heels digging into the bed, his arms tighten around me as he begins to slam himself inside me like he'll die if he doesn't.

Trapped against him in the embrace of his arms, I become frantic to escape. All the things assaulting my body feel so good, I swear he's killing me.

Clawing at his arms, I shake my head back and forth as I sob, "Gabriel, please! I can't, I can't."

"You can," he insists. "You fucking can, Meghan. Stop fucking fighting it, stop holding back."

But I can't stop fighting it or holding it back. The pleasure he's inflicting on me is so good, so fucking strong, it almost *hurts*. And the orgasm looming in front of me is so steep, I don't think I can survive the fall.

Then he kisses my cheek and says, "Trust me, baby. I've got you."

I shouldn't, but my entire body is throbbing in agony, my pussy quivering with the need for relief.

Releasing a hair-raising growl, he begins to piston himself inside me furiously, determined to push me over the edge, despite my refusal.

"Come for me. Come for me, goddammit," he demands, and there's just so much inside me I snap.

I go soaring over the edge, and the fall is so glorious, so fucking terrifying, I scream.

I scream because I'm afraid. I scream because it feels so good. But most of all I scream because there's so much built up inside of me it's the only way to release it.

"Yes," Gabriel says in triumph as his hips slap hard against my ass. "That's it, baby. I got you."

I fall and fall, screaming the whole way down. But instead of crashing and breaking, he's there to catch me.

I reach the bottom squeezed in his arms.

With a groan, he slams his cock deep one last time, and is warmth floods me as he murmurs sweet words of devotion.

And for once in my fucking life I feel safe.

I feel protected.

15

GABRIEL

The shrill ring of my cellphone yanks me out from under the hot showerhead. I'm not entirely sure how long I've been standing under the heat. I've probably used up most of the hot water in the tank, but it's been worth it.

I've been able to silence all the thoughts that rage and tear through my mind. I need to stay in the moment right now, to be the hand of destruction that Lucifer pulled me from hell to be.

The ringing ends as I step out of the shower and pull a towel around my waist. I can hear Meghan's sleepy voice as she walks to the door. She's talking to someone quietly before she opens the door and thrusts the phone toward me.

She's definitely not a morning person, I think as I

watch her grumpily walk back to the bed and practically thrown herself down on top of it.

"What?" I ask as I push the phone up to my ear.

My eyes stare down at Meghan's panty-covered ass. It looks so juicy and delicious, I'm half tempted to bite it. Bite it and leave a bruise.

Mark this chick as mine.

"Russians took out a bank we own. I need you down on the scene. We need to figure out what the fuck happened," Simon snaps in my ear.

"When?" I ask as I contemplate whether or not Meghan will kick me if I slap that ass.

I want to do so many fun things to it. I wasn't joking when I said I'd fuck it if she ever tries to run again. Fuck, I want to fuck it regardless of her trying to run.

"At five-seventeen this morning. Killed an onsite guard we had in the building," he mutters over the sound of keys tapping on a keyboard.

"Is that the only casualty?" I ask.

"Yes. Are you fucking leaving yet?" he snaps at me.

"Soon, I need to get some gear. Who's my onsite contact?" I ask as I turn away from Meghan.

She grumbles loudly, her head buried under a pillow.

"Detective Sommers will be leading the investigation. Unfortunately, someone called in the bombing before we could call in our version of what happened," he says.

"Fuck, so the news outlets will be trying to climb over each other to get the story?" I grumble.

"Yes, so leave your wife at home. We don't need her face plastered all over the news. I've called what contacts I have in the media and I'm trying to get this downplayed as much as possible. But it's the fucking media."

"Fuck, I'm not exactly fond of the idea of leaving her here alone," I say as I walk over to the dresser.

I grab a pair of jeans and a t-shirt out of it.

Meghan moves and I'm pretty sure she's listening in.

"I don't give a shit, get the fuck over there. I'll text you the location now," Simon snaps before he disconnects the phone.

"Fucking douchebag," I growl as I slap the phone down on the dresser.

"What's going on?" Meghan asks, fully awake now.

"Someone bombed a bank we own," I growl as I yank the t-shirt over my head.

I'm not fucking happy with Simon right now, not when he tells me to leave Meghan home alone. But I can't fucking argue the logic. While she needs to be attached to my hip, this isn't the time for her face to be shown. Too many unknown variables.

Sitting up straight, her eyebrows lift almost up to her hairline. "Did you say someone bombed a bank?"

"Yeah," I say while pulling my pants up.

"You forgot your underwear," she points out quietly.

Looking down, I push my junk into the jeans and carefully zip up. "Nah, I don't like wearing 'em."

Shaking her head, she forces her attention away from my cock. "Someone blew up a bank... because you bombed their restaurant?"

"Looks like it. The risk of retaliation was always going to be high no matter what we did. That restaurant was a money laundering front for them," I say as I sit down to pull on socks and my boots.

"Oh god," she mumbles.

Reaching over, I grab her ankle and pull her to my side.

"Stop!" she pushes at me.

"No," I say quietly.

"But... but all this violence..." she croaks as she looks up at me.

"Would have been happening with or without you. Your father insulated you from the world he operated in. Lots of things were happening you never got to see."

"But..." she whispers, shaking her head.

"Right or wrong, it happened, Meghan. Whether you knew it or not, shit was going down," I say and wrap an arm around her shoulder.

"I just don't..." she starts but stops. "How much of what's happening now is my fault?"

"Don't even try to follow that path, Meghan. Just

don't. Fucked up shit's always going on and it's not going to stop anytime soon. This shit's been going on long before you came along. Long before I was around," I say, and try to stop the anger inside me that wants to reach out and murder anyone who makes her hurt like she does.

"Is this all there ever will be? Pain and death?" she asks. "Blood and innocents dying?"

"No," I say with a growl. "I aim to make sure these fuckers are all six feet under."

"But that just means more killing."

"It does, but I was brought out for a purpose. I'm the dog let off the leash. It's Lucifer's way of showing the world that playtime is over."

Hugging her tight to my side for a moment, I almost start shaking with the inner turmoil of leaving her here without me.

"I gotta go check out what's happened, and I need you to stay here and keep out of trouble for a few hours," I say.

Looking up at me with a frown, she asks, "Why are you leaving me alone? I didn't think that was something you were comfortable doing..."

"I have to trust you sometime, Meghan. Trust that you know doing what I tell you is in your best interest. They want you back. Alexei is pissed that I took what he thinks is his property."

"I'm not just some piece of property, dammit!" she

snarls at me before standing up from the bed. "I still have my head on my shoulders. It's up to me to make decisions, not you, and definitely not that asshole."

"Decisions that could cost you and others by making the wrong choices," I say.

Pacing back and forth in front of me, she stops cold.

"What do you mean?" she hisses at me, her anger palpable.

With a small grin, I say, "Do you really think you'd be so lucky as to be the only one hurt if this goes to full-scale war? That you're the only one affected by this?"

"Again, what do you mean?" she snarls out.

"Beth," I say with a shrug.

"What does this have to do with her?" she asks, and that righteous anger is fading away at the mention of Johnathan's wife.

"You met her. From what I remember, you liked her and their son Charlie, right?" I ask.

"Are you threatening them!?" she asks, balling up her fists.

Her posture stiffens as she stalks toward me.

"Fuck, no. I don't kill kids, Meghan. But Alexei sure does. Ever wonder how Johnathan and Beth met? Does she look like she's old enough to have a boy Charlie's age?" I ask. "Think about how old he looked, then look at those two. They've been married for less than a year.

Beth's only just now hitting her twenties. Charlie doesn't look like either of them, does he?"

"What the hell are you saying?" she asks.

"I caught a bit of their history. Alexei, the same guy who wanted to marry you, was running a slave ring," I say.

Eyes wide, she says, "What?"

"Yeah, that same slave ring was floating through Garden City, and more than likely Bethlehem. Lucifer didn't take kindly to that shit going on. Beth got snatched right outside of Johnathan's bar."

"Oh my god," she says as she stands there, looking at me in shock.

"The inner circle staged a quick operation to take down that slave ring and got Beth back, along with some of her friends. Charlie, it seems, was a tag along on that. The Russians were going to sell the boy off to someone who would've done some truly dark shit."

"He's just a small boy..." she says.

"A small boy who's seen more bad shit in his life than most."

"And Beth?" she asks.

"One of her friends got in the way and paid the price. The others... I don't know. I think her friend Sophia is okay. Beth got her pound of flesh, but they didn't catch Alexei."

"Alexei..." she whispers.

"Yep, the one and the same. You're not the only

innocent out there that's been hurt by that fuck. He's out there right now, planning or doing more shit. Like I said, you need to listen to what the hell I say."

"I'm your guardian fucking angel," comes out of my mouth as I stand up before her.

"How long will you be gone?" she asks.

"A few hours. We've got food in the house now... Don't answer the door," I say, and take her delicate hand in mine.

Pulling her forward, I wrap my arms around her shoulders. I don't think I'll ever get over how fucking small she is compared to me. Or the way it feels like she was made for my body. Made to fit me perfectly.

"Okay," she murmurs into my chest.

"I'm leaving the handgun and the AR-15 with you. I'll pick up your body armor after I check out the bank. Then we're going to head out to the gun range. You need to show me what you can do."

"Promise me we'll get Alexei," she whispers, looking up into my eyes.

"I promise we will."

A BURNT-OUT HUSK of a building looks pretty fucked up in the dawn's early light. If Alexei wanted to send a message, he sure as fuck did it right.

Message received.

Putting the phone to my ear, I stare at the smoldering building while the fire department slowly combs through it.

"I have Lucifer on the line with us," Simon says.

"How's the property?" Lucifer asks.

"You can't see this shit from all the security cameras we have around here?" I ask as I look up to one and shoot the middle finger.

"We do, but what's your impression? You're the explosive expert," Lucifer says with a growl.

"They used some seriously heavy materials to hit this level of devastation," I say.

Even the vault and safety deposit are in bad shape. Everything was blown to fucking bits. This was a tough job to do. You could have used a rocket launcher and not have gotten these results.

"I've put out to the media that this was a disgruntled person we foreclosed on," I say as I start walking around the building.

I'm surprised that Alexei had this kind of team working here in the states. This is some heavy fucking shit he's blowing up.

"It's a good enough excuse as any," Lucifer says.

"They knew where to plant the bombs. Knew where to get the biggest bang for their buck," I say as I bend over a couple of bent and charred metal beams. "Someone gave them the blueprints. I'd get on the line and find out who. They came here to put a dent in us, this wasn't for show."

Rubbing off the dark burn marks on the metal, I sniff at the acrid smell. "This wasn't C-4. I'd get the fire department to take samples so that we can start trying to identify exactly what was used."

"Will do. Have you spotted any faces in the crowd?" Simon asks.

"None. At least, none that look out of place. I doubt whoever did this is still in the city," I say.

"Do you think this was one of Alexei's men?" Lucifer asks.

"Is he recruiting former FSB or SVR?" I ask.

Standing up from the metal, I start heading back to the truck.

"Yes, from the intel we've amassed, he's been recruiting heavily from their ranks," Simon says.

"If that's the case, I don't think he used an outside contractor for this. This was too well put together, and in such a short period of time.... I can't believe they managed to pull it off this quickly."

I hear a new voice in the background. "Agreed."

"That Andrew?" I ask.

"It is. Meet us back at the compound," Lucifer says.

"On my way. Get me a new vehicle, Simon. This one's not going to be good for much longer. I can guarantee the Russians got eyes on me right now. They're probably in a building somewhere. I wouldn't be surprised if they don't have a message for us sometime soon. They want to talk."

WALKING DOWN one of the many hallways in Lucifer's home, I see Simon standing outside of the office, talking on his cellphone.

"It's time to come in from the cold, Eric," I hear him say as I get closer.

Walking past him, I stop and look into the office, spotting Andrew sitting in a chair across from Lucifer. Johnathan looks up from where he's perched on the side of a chair and nods at me.

"Think about what I've said," Simon says into his phone before he disconnects.

"I've put out a call to a man I know and want to bring into the circle," Simon says as he walks past me.

Following him, I'm tempted to trip his ass, but right now I'd rather just get this shit over with so I can get back to Meghan.

"What kind of guy?" I ask as I take a seat.

"Hitman. Very good at his job, and very trusted. He's worked for us in the past, out east. Reliable, and isn't afraid to get his hands dirty. He's had a spot of trouble with some of the heavy hitters, got shot up in Cincinnati. But with the time and healing he's had, he's ready to land somewhere permanent," Simon says as he gets comfortable in a chair with his laptop in his lap.

"Get him here as soon as you can. If you vouch for him personally, I'll meet with him," Lucifer says, then motions to me. "So what do you have for us, any more thoughts?"

"Nothing beyond these guys are going to start hitting more and more targets. I've seriously pissed them off if they've gotten their shit together quick enough to hit us like this," I say as I look down at my hands.

Something doesn't sit right, though.

Looking back up, I add, "I wouldn't be surprised if this wasn't in the plans all along. They had to work too quickly to get shit like this planned out. I know I've been inside of a cage for ten years, but I can't imagine they were able to get all the shit they needed in the scant hours they had."

"How long would it take to get the materials for something like this, Simon?" Andrew asks.

"For us? In our own backyard, six to eight hours," Simon answers without hesitation.

"We've got eyes and ears everywhere. Shit like this would take some time to set up, especially if they needed the building blueprints, materials, and the right guys to pull it off," Johnathan says.

"They had it in the works then. Perhaps even before the wedding. What if this is just a continuation of the bombings they started with Lucky Tails?" Lucifer asks.

There's a long silence as we all think about that.

"Then it's time for me to ramp shit up," I say with shrug. "Where's James and Jude?"

"James is with the police chief, smoothing things over. It seems that Sommers isn't as useful as he used to be," Simon says. "Jude is watching over a few guards for a couple of investment properties we can't afford to lose right now."

"Strip joints?" I ask with a chuckle.

"Our other banks," Lucifer says with a smirk of his own.

"Fuck, we're going that legitimate now?" I ask with a raised eyebrow.

"For our progeny. We're still the disreputable crowd, as always," Lucifer says.

Well, fuck me running. Being legit is a scary fucking thought.

"You're not expecting me to wear suits like those two fucks?" I ask, pointing at Simon and Andrew.

A large grin spreads across the evil fuck's face as he says, "Of course, in due time."

"I'd rather fucking choke," I snort.

"Back to the business at hand. The new tech that Sommers has talked about is now on every police vehicle in Garden City. It's called an LPR, or License Plate Reader. We've known about the software and hardware since its inception, but until recently it's been tightly controlled," Simon says.

"Isn't that thing the little mod they have affixed to the cop cars now? Reads the plates of every car they pass?" Andrew says.

"Exactly," Simon says. "Going over the video feeds around the church, I was able to pull two license plates numbers. Although I'm unable to ascertain which exactly is Alexei's, I've put in a tracking request for those two plates."

"As soon as they start moving, we should be able to find them?" I ask.

"Yes, with time I should be able to follow them through Garden City and Bethlehem. If a police car picks them up, I'll be able to link them through traffic cameras and such," Simon says with a grin as he flips the laptop around for us to see. "Two black Audis. One was riding with enough weight to show it had at least four passengers, perhaps five. The second had two or three men in it."

"You don't think they'll swap plates?" Johnathan asks.

Simon shrugs his shoulders. "More than likely, no. They don't have our developed contacts and information. If they do, it will make our job of tracking these men down much harder."

I nod my head. "Figures. Any trees you need me to shake?"

Lucifer shakes his head. "Not yet. With the hit on the restaurant and the bank, we need to keep our actions more covert. Let's see what kind of message they try sending us. It should be soon."

"Sounds good, but I've got a feeling the Irish aren't going to be happy with us no matter the outcome of this little war. We're working with the Italians. From what Meghan has told me, her mom getting hit with a car bomb has put a huge rift between the two factions," I say.

"I don't buy it being the Italians. They had no reason to when it happened, and it's not their style anymore," Andrew says.

"Really?" I ask as I turn to look at him.

"Yeah, the Italians weren't even trying to take over territory in Bethlehem. They were busy fucking around with the Russians when that shit went down over here in Garden. Why the hell would they go for a war on two entirely different fronts?" Andrew says and points to Lucifer.

"He's got a very good point," Lucifer says as he looks over to Simon. "Put a call over to our Italian contacts. Let's see what they have to say. I think us befriending the Irish would go a long way in offsetting what the Russians have been doing."

"If the Italians didn't do the hit, who did?" I ask the room.

Snickering, Johnathan says, "They don't call the drink the Irish Car Bomb for no reason."

Laughing, Lucifer says, "Now that would be interesting."

"It would," Simon says, "This could be falling back to the troubles the Italians and Irish were having over in Ohio. Two of the best hitmen in the world dropped off the map after the big dust up over there. What if the Irish were trying to take over more space and needed to pin serious damage on the Italians?"

That's some convoluted thinking, if you ask me. But if the Irish killed the wife of an Irish boss... fuck me. That'd be a mess to deal with. They'd have to have a damn good reason for doing it.

"Any chance it was the Russians?" I ask.

"Blame the Italians, cozy up to the poor little Irish and get their allegiance?" Andrew asks.

"I've got a thousand bucks right now that says it wasn't the Italians who did it," Johnathan says with a laugh.

Snorting with a chuckle, I say, "Not taking that fool's bet."

As soon as we start standing up to go about our tasks for the day, Lucifer's phone starts ringing on his desk.

Looking down at the phone, he frowns at it. "It's an unknown number, Simon."

"I'll start a trace," Simon says quickly.

Lucifer picks up the phone and waits a moment before saying, "Hello."

Simon makes a thumbs up gesture from his laptop and motions for us to stay.

Lucifer grins as he says, "Let me put you on speakerphone."

Pushing a button, he sets the phone down in the cradle and a Russian voice comes over the line. "Of course."

"Now that we're all here, how I can help you... Alexei?" Lucifer says in a smooth drawl.

"It's been an exciting week so far, for the both of us. Too much excitement. Perhaps we need to come to an understanding," Alexei says.

"What kind of understanding?" Lucifer asks.

"You have property of mine. You stole it, and I want it back," Alexei says with a small growl to his voice.

"Ah, you speak of Mr. Callahan's daughter," Lucifer says with a grin.

"Yes," he says. "Give her back to me, and all will be forgiven."

My eyes widen with anger as I stomp toward the phone. A growl of anger begins to work through my throat.

Then a strong hand grips my bicep, stopping my forward moving progress.

Lucifer looks into my eyes then, his grin only widening as he says, "No."

I'm not sure who he's speaking to, and I don't really care. Meghan's mine. Anyone who tries to take her will die. I won't be creative in my killing, either. I'll simply put a bullet through their heart and stop them dead.

"No?!" Alexei spits out through the line, and I can imagine his face turning beet red from his anger.

"Correct," Lucifer says in that smug way of his.

"I'll fucking murder you all. I'll take your women and rape them to death. I'll have my men fuck your children. All of your lives are forfeit!" Alexei screams at us through the phone.

"Hmm, let me think about this, Alexei. I'd hate to be rash," Lucifer says quietly.

"You better. You have no idea what kind of hell I will bring on your heads!"

All around me, the inner circle bristles with fury. It's one thing to threaten one of us. But to threaten our families....

Alexei has gone too far.

"Here's my offer, Alexei," Lucifer says after a moment of quiet. "You will give us all the properties in Garden City that you still hold."

"Done," Alexei says a bit too quickly.

"You will give us all the properties in Bethlehem, as well," Lucifer says.

"Sure—" Alexei tries to say.

"I'm not finished," Lucifer snarls. "You will then remove all of your men from my country. You will return to Russia with your hands empty and your testicles left on my desk. You will each put a bullet through your brains, and then, when you reach hell, you will submit my name as your fucking Master."

"I will fucking end you all," Alexei screams. "I will blow—"

Lucifer pushes the disconnect button and looks to all of us. "I want them all dead. I do not care how much blood is spilt. They all die."

Nodding our heads at Lucifer, we look to Simon.

"The tracer failed. He's hiding behind too many firewall layers. He used a satellite phone that's former Russian military hardware. I could hack their systems, but it's unlikely I'll be able to locate him. The phone is used to latch onto as many satellites as possible to give it a broad reach. Triangulating will be next to impossible," Simon says with a sigh.

"I fucking hate Russians," I say with a deep growl.

16

MEGHAN

I begged Gabriel for space, and now that I finally have it, I don't know what to do with myself. The house is quiet and empty. Too fucking quiet and empty.

Every little noise has me on edge.

Every shadow is a person who wants to hurt me.

All alone with my thoughts, I feel like I'm going a little crazy.

I pace the rooms, the halls, passing time until Gabriel returns to me, and find myself missing his presence.

I try to convince myself it's only because I feel safer with him, but it's more than that...

Much more than that.

Dammit, I think the fucker is growing on me.

Shaking my head at myself, I stop in the bedroom

and stare down at the bed. His scent still lingers in the air, a raw, unapologetic masculine scent, and there's an imprint in the shape of his huge body in the ruffled sheets.

Reaching down, I trace the outline of his back, remembering that blissful moment of feeling safe.

What we did last night, the things he said, the way he desperately thrust himself inside me and held me in his arms afterward... I think it's completely broken me.

Broken me in a way that can never be fixed.

There was truth in the way our bodies joined, an unmistakable truth I can't ignore or deny.

Despite the circumstances that brought us together, despite everything against us, he honestly wants me and needs me.

And worst of all, I think I need him in return.

It's insane, so damn insane.

And wrong on so many levels.

He goes against everything I've ever believed.

But after everything I've been through, I can't stop myself from wanting him to be someone I can lean on. Someone I can count on.

The one person in the world who will never abandon me. The one person who will always stand beside me.

After he said it, I'm honestly starting to believe that he just might be my guardian angel.

God's fucked up answer to all my prayers.

Stalking back into the living room, I pull the curtain back on the front window just enough to peek my eyes out. The neighborhood is alive with activity. Kids playing, riding their bikes, or chasing each other and being noisy. Neighbors working in their gardens, chatting, and doing other things.

I search for anything suspicious, anything that could be out of place.

It's not lost on me that despite all that's going on outside, that if Alexei has been watching us, if he knows I'm here, then this would be the best time to grab me.

Fuck... Alexei.

Just thinking his name sends chills through me. Reaching down to my hip holster, my fingers squeeze around the handle of the pistol Gabriel left me.

I didn't think I could hate the man more than I already do, but after Gabriel told me about Beth, her friends, and Charlie, I was filled with this mix of sheer anger and horror.

I knew that pathetic slimeball was selling kids. I fucking knew it. Yet meeting one of his victims face to face makes it more real.

More awful.

The pain, the suffering he's caused, can't go unpunished. And if Gabriel ends up being the one to punish him, I hope I'm there.

I hope he lets me put a bullet between his soulless eyes.

Dropping the curtain, I force my fingers to release the butt of the gun and pace my way back down the hall.

I must wear a thousand more steps into the floor before I hear the sound of the garage door sliding up.

Rushing back over to the front window, I flick the curtain to the side and peek outside.

I don't recognize the car.

Shit.

A million things run through my head in my panic. Alexei found me. Something happened to Gabriel. Some other asshole wants me dead.

His own men are stabbing him in his back.

The garage door begins to slide back down, and I try to force my racing heart to calm.

It doesn't matter who's out there, I decide. All that matters is that I protect myself.

Fingers trembling, I take a deep breath and ease the pistol out of my holster as I silently walk over to the door and position myself.

I don't hear the car door open, but I hear it slam shut.

Gabriel loaded the gun for me, I know he did, but I double-check the loaded chamber indicator before I lift it in front of me, just to be sure.

Heavy footsteps thump up the two stairs and the

soft beeping of the entrance code being punched in comes through the door.

My finger eases over the trigger as the door swings open. I'm a split-second from squeezing it when Gabriel steps through the doorway.

He takes one look at me and freezes.

I'm so worked up, so freaked out from being left alone, in that split-second of time Alexei is in front of me and I want to shoot him.

I want to blow his fucking head off.

And I almost do it.

"Holy shit!" I cry out as I drop my arms and point the gun at the floor.

I'm so fucking scared, so fucking terrified of Alexei, I almost killed Gabriel. Like seriously fucking killed him.

I was a hair away from squeezing the trigger.

I start to shake uncontrollably, and if I didn't think the gun would accidentally go off, I'd throw the damn thing away from me.

Staring at Gabriel, I'm utterly helpless and unable to move.

I came so close to killing him, to losing him, I've petrified myself to the bone.

And there's such a look of rage on his face, such a dark, twisted expression of anger, I don't know what to do.

"I'm sorry," I say after I gulp in a mouthful of air,

and it doesn't feel like enough. How could sorry ever be enough? "I didn't recognize the car."

He walks up to me, his expression darkening even further, and still I can't fucking move. My damn feet are glued to the floor.

I know he won't do it, but I half-expect him to lash out at me. To retaliate. To hurt me for what I almost did.

It's what my father would do.

He stops in front of me and I inwardly flinch as he reaches out.

Hand dropping down, he grabs the barrel of the gun and helps me tuck it safely back into my holster.

"It's fine," he grits out and releases the gun.

As if he can read all the shit that's going on inside me, he stares into my eyes, his harsh face threatening to give into softness.

And for a moment, he looks like he's going to touch me. Lifting his hand up, he nears my cheek, but then, as if he's suddenly remembered something, he squeezes that hand into a fist and whips away from me.

The loss of that touch hits me like a punch in the chest.

It's not fine. None of this is fine. Not by a long shot.

If the fucking Russians and Irish don't kill us, my dumbass probably will.

Gabriel begins to stomp around the house, checking all the doors and windows.

"Did anyone bother you while I was gone?" he asks, peering out the front window after checking the lock.

"No," I push out of my throat.

He grunts and snaps the curtains shut.

Once he's satisfied with the exterior entrances, he moves deeper into the house.

Eventually, my thoughts and heart begin to calm down enough for me to wonder what the hell he's doing.

Putting one foot in front of the other, I walk down the hall, keeping a safe distance as I follow behind him.

There's so much anger in the way he moves, I can practically see it radiating off him. Pushing into each room, he checks it before closing the door behind him.

Ever since that first night, I've never seen him close an interior door before, I realize. In fact, he has this awful habit of leaving them all open.

"Gabriel..." I say to get his attention but trail off as he keeps stomping around in his big black boots, ignoring me.

Oh god, did I just ruin this thing blossoming between us with my panic? Have we ended like we began? I wouldn't be surprised if he's decided to wipe his hands of me now. After all, how many times can I expect him to put up with me pointing a dangerous weapon at him?

The need to apologize, to make him understand

why I did what I did, causes the words to tumble out of me as I follow behind him.

"I didn't recognize the car. I've never seen it before. I thought you were still driving the truck and expected the worst."

Without glancing back at me, he says, "I know. You did good, I'm proud of you."

That brings me up short.

What the hell is going on here?

If he's so proud of me, why does he seem so pissed off?

He begins to stomp up the stairs, taking them two at a time, and I race to catch up with him.

"I almost killed you. I thought you were Alexei," I huff out as I grip the banister.

Suddenly he stops before reaching the top and I hear him take a deep breath. I watch the muscles in his neck, his shoulders, and his back bunch up through his tight black shirt as his entire body tightens with tension.

He's so rigid, I'm surprised I don't hear his bones crack from the stress of being so stiff.

"Gabriel, what's wrong?" I ask, reaching out to touch his back.

I feel his muscles tighten even more before they relax.

Both hands squeezing into fists, he cracks his neck to the side, then he slowly turns around to face me.

The black look etched into his rugged features is so terrifying I find myself taking a hasty step back.

Glaring down at me, his lip curls up as he says, "If you fucking killed me because you thought I was that cockroach, I'd still be proud of you, baby girl."

His words don't match his expression at all, and I don't know how to reconcile what I'm seeing with what I'm hearing.

Is he truly not angry with me, or is he only saying it for some unknown reason?

He takes a step down, and I find myself instinctively taking another step back.

"Then why are you looking at me like that?" I finally ask.

"Looking at you like what?"

"Like you want to kill me and bathe in my blood."

Stilling at my question, he closes his eyes for a moment and then lets out what I think is supposed to be a sigh but it comes out more like growl.

"It's not for you," he says, and spins back around.

He moves back up the stairs with a renewed purpose, and I hesitate, wondering if it's wise to chase after him.

He's upset about something, and perhaps it's best to give him some space...

But the need to know what's made him so angry has me pumping my legs to follow him up the steps.

"Who is it for?" I ask, but he doesn't answer.

He ignores me, pulling the door open to the bathroom. He pops his head inside before slamming the door shut.

"Gabriel," I frown, trying to step in his way.

"I have to check the house, Meghan. I have to make sure it's secure," he grits out, then the big fucking ogre literally picks me up by the waist and moves me out of his path.

My jaw drops and I stare after him as he walks away.

Snapping my jaw shut, I grind my teeth together as he checks on the bedrooms, still treating me as if I don't exist.

Well, fuck him if he's going to be that way. Picking me up and moving me like I'm a damn child...

Shaking my head, I turn around and walk back down the stairs.

When I reach the bottom, I can still hear him prowling around upstairs, so I head to the kitchen to get a drink.

I'm pulling open the cabinet above the counter and stretching up on my tiptoes to grab a glass when I sense his presence filling the small space.

Still annoyed by the way he treated me, I decide to give him a taste of his own medicine and ignore him as I pull the glass down.

Suddenly his shadow rolls over me, swallowing me

up. He shuts the cabinet for me and then his fingers lightly brush down my arm.

Jerking away from him, I move over to the sink and hold the glass under the faucet.

"Is the house secure?" I snap as I turn the faucet on.

"Yes," he replies, that one word dropping from his lips as if it's somehow both significant and insignificant.

Whipping around when he moves closer to me, I lift the glass between us. "Well, I suppose that's good then."

I take a drink and begin to lower the glass back down when he decides to yank the rug out from beneath my feet. "Alexei contacted us. He's demanded you back."

The glass slips from my fingers and shatters against the floor.

At once every fear I've been carrying around inside seems to grow, looming larger.

Water splashes against my ankles but I don't care. It doesn't matter.

"What?" I gasp, hoping I heard him wrong.

Gabriel looks down at the floor, at all the glass, then he grabs me by the hips.

Picking me up, he sets me on the counter with a thump.

"What did you say?" I repeat, my voice a harsh whisper as I tip my head back to look up at him.

The glass on the floor crunches beneath Gabriel's boots as he steps into me. "Alexei has demanded you back."

Those words drive into me like nails in my coffin.

I'm dead... dead...

So fucking dead.

I thought... Well, I guess I secretly hoped that Alexei wouldn't want me now. That he'd consider me not worth the effort and move on.

But if he wants me back...

Gabriel's thighs bump into my legs as if he's seeking permission to press closer, but I leave them closed to him.

I can't let him in until I know if he's going to betray me. If he's going to give me up.

I don't think he will, but I've been betrayed by so many people I thought were looking out for me, I have to be cautious.

Before I can ask the question that's sticking in my throat, he bends over me, grabbing the counter with both hands. "He's threatened to take our women and rape them to death. He's threatened to have his men fuck our children."

"Oh god," I moan and try not to sway.

One hand comes up to my neck as if I'm some fucking damsel in a movie.

But the fear, the terror, it's real. It's *alive* inside me, each threat feeding its power.

Gabriel's eyes lock on mine, the intense hold of them the only thing keeping me from fainting. "He's threatened to murder us all if we don't hand you over."

Of course he did. I'd expect no less from a monster like him.

He'll probably even do worse... if given the chance.

Fuck.

Fuck. Fuck. Fuck.

This is the worst fucking thing that could happen. There is no doubt in my mind that Alexei will try to make good on his threats. He's probably working on them right now.

Gabriel's entire family is in great and immediate danger, and it's all because of me. All because Gabriel took me and didn't kill me.

"Are—" I start and stop.

I have to fill my lungs with air several times before I can get the question out.

Gabriel watches me, his face growing more and more furious as if he knows exactly what I'm going to ask.

"Are you going to hand me over?"

Gabriel says, "*No*," so violently it's jarring.

My skeleton jolts beneath my skin.

And I'd probably accept that answer, I'd probably leave that statement as it is, even take comfort in his protection, but I'm highly aware that I'm not the only one in danger here.

This goes beyond me, just like he pointed out earlier, and I don't know if I could live with myself if anyone else got hurt.

"But—" I start to argue, shredding all sense of self-preservation.

There's a loud crack and I have no clue where it's coming until I glance down. Somehow, with his grip alone, he's managed to crack the countertop.

Or maybe that crack has always been there...

There's no way he could physically do that.

My eyes travel back up his body, taking in his taut muscles and popping veins.

Face strained as if it's taking everything inside him to keep from erupting, he snaps, "I'm not handing you over, Meghan. You're mine, and this shit doesn't change that."

Those words should be reassuring, but the way he says *mine* sounds more like a threat than an endearment.

"But—" I try again, only to have him stop me.

Pushing his way between my legs, he grabs me by the face. His grip is too frantic, too harsh at first but immediately gentles when I wince.

"I won't say it again. You're mine and I'm not fucking giving you up."

I should accept that. I should even be happy with it, but I can't. "I don't want anyone to get hurt."

Especially on the account of me.

I've met the wives, Lily, Amy, Beth, and Meredith. And their children. And their husbands. There are too many people to protect. Too many possible causalities.

.

Fingers tightening behind my head, Gabriel pulls my face up. "The only people that are going to get hurt are the fucking Russian cocksuckers who think they can threaten us and get away with it."

I open my mouth to argue with him, to point out that the odds are against us. That the odds are that at least one person is going to get hurt.

But once again the fucker cuts me off, a strange light flickering to life in his eyes. "I'm going to kill them, Meghan. I'm going to fucking kill them all."

His thumbs stroke tenderly against my cheeks as if he's saying something emotional, something sweet. "I'm not only going to exterminate them, I'm going to abort them and everyone connected with them from this world. Abort their walking carcasses and use their blood to baptize their taint from this city."

He lets that sink in, lets it sink into the very marrow of my bones before he finishes with, "And I need you at my side. I need to know you'll stand with me."

My gut reaction is to tell him *no*. To rail at him for asking that of me.

How can he? How dare he?

Not only does he plan on killing Alexei and all the Russians, but he's also going to kill everyone connected to them. That includes my father and all the Irish.

Everyone I've grown up with, whether they've personally done me wrong or not, is in jeopardy.

"It's them or us," he reminds me as I hesitate.

So we're back to this again. We've come full circle, and this time I know he won't let me off without answering him.

The way he's looking at me, his eyes boring into me, I can sense his desperate need for a commitment from me.

And, oh god, I want to give it to him. With all my heart I do. He's given me so much, he's given me *everything*. But the thought of helping him kill my former family makes me sick.

I'm not a murderer, and I don't know if I have it in me.

But what's the alternative?

Abandon Gabriel? Spit in the face of everything he's done and sacrificed for me?

His thumbs continue to stroke against my cheeks, urging me to choose him.

Choose him over all the fuckers who've tried to hurt me.

Choose between him and my fear.

"Meghan," he says, his head dipping down, his nose rubbing against mine.

He continues to say my name over and over

again, nuzzling at my face, and there's so much pleading in the way he says it, he might as well be begging me.

I hate to him hear beg, but I know in the very depths of my soul that this choice will forever change me. I'll never be the same again.

I might not be able to look at my face in the mirror after this.

I might fucking hate myself after this.

Tears fill my eyes as I make my choice.

Dragging in a shuddering breath, I'm afraid something inside of me is breaking, a fundamental part I need to survive, to exist as I have.

But as I say the words, "I'll stand by you," out loud with tears spilling down my cheeks, I suddenly feel free.

Free of the chains that have been holding me back.

Gabriel pulls slowly away from me, and I catch a flicker of hope in his eyes, but it quickly fades away.

Something inside me desperately needs to see that flicker again.

So I find myself saying, "I'm with you, Gabriel. I choose you. I choose *us*."

I didn't know joy could be found inside darkness, but that's the only way I can explain the emotions that play over his face.

Bone-deep, endless joy.

He looks like I've just handed him the sky.

Then a hair-raising, animalistic sounds rumbles out of his throat just before his mouth slams into mine.

Any other time, I might not be prepared for the force of the kiss he lays on me.

But I'm ready this time.

Grabbing at him, I meet him push for push. Determined to not let this thing between us break me.

Determined to stand by my choice.

Our lips, tongues, and teeth clash and tangle together in a frantic need that makes time fade away.

There is only him, me, and the overwhelming desire to take him deep inside my body.

To make my promise complete.

As if he's afraid I might change my mind, his hands grab at my shirt, ripping and tearing until the fabric falls away in shreds. I try to do the same to his shirt, but I don't quite have the strength.

When I whimper into his mouth, he reaches down and bats my hands away.

Grabbing where I grabbed, he yanks his hands apart, ripping his black t-shirt open for me.

Greedy for the feel of his skin, I slap my palms against his bare chest. I explore, rubbing my hands over the hard planes of his sculpted pecs.

But it's not enough. I have this visceral need to dig into his flesh. To leave my mark.

Clawing at him, I scrape my nails down to his waist.

With a smothered growl, he thrusts his hips hard into me, grinding his trapped erection into my sex.

Hoping for another thrust, I drag my nails back up, raking them across his stiff nipples.

His entire body jolts and a purr of pleasure rolls down my throat. Then he's grabbing up my hands and yanking them behind my back, forcing me to thrust out my chest.

He rips his lips away from mine, and before I can gasp out a protest, he's nipping his way down my neck.

I want to beg him to kiss me again, but he bites at the hollow of my throat and a flash of delicious weakness courses through me, forcing me into silence.

Lower, his mouth travels.

Biting at my collarbones and nipping a path down to my breasts.

Sucking in a breath and holding it, I half-expect him to bite at my nipples, given what I did to his.

But his hot mouth completely covers me and he groans with pleasure as he pulls back a gentle suckle.

Warmth floods through my veins, burning like molten lava, and I begin to melt beneath his mouth.

Back and forth, between both breasts, he hungrily and frantically suckles on me, until I'm squirming against the counter and my breasts feel heavy.

Just as I begin to relax, tipping my head back and letting him have his way with me, his teeth clamp down on my nipple.

Pinching down on the tender flesh.

I jerk, my head snapping up.

With a grin, he soothes the pain away with his tongue, swirling it against me.

I watch him with wary eyes as he moves to the other breast, prepared for the pinch. But all he does is suckle until I start to relax again.

As soon as my head tips back and a low moan flows out of my throat, his teeth are clamping down.

"Gabriel," I gasp, finally breaking the silence between us as the sting settles in.

"You taste so fucking good," he groans, "I just want to eat you up."

His tongue lashes at me as if he's in a hurry to soothe the pain away.

"I want to leave my mark all over your body."

Then he's kissing, nipping, sucking, and biting his way down my stomach. My muscles tighten against the onslaught of his mouth and I don't even realize he's released my hands until he's unbuckling my holster and shoving down my pants.

My pants, panties, and shoes hit the floor and his head dips lower. Teeth scraping across my mons.

"Don't you dare," I warn and feel his smirk.

Shoving my thighs apart, I tense up in fear and excitement as his warm breath drops lower, hitting my wetness.

If he bites me there, so help me—

That thought inside my head is cut off as he suddenly straightens, towering over me again.

Before I have a chance to react to the sudden change, he's grabbing me by the back of the head and pulling me in for another brutal kiss.

I become so lost in the taste of his mouth, I throw my arms around his neck and cling to him.

Reaching between us, he undoes his own holster and pants one-handed.

Then his fingers are wrapping around my hip and jerking my ass to the edge of the counter. There's no warning, no time to brace myself, as he begins to push his thick, velvety length into me.

My tongue and lips begin to falter as my walls stretch around him.

So big... will he ever stop feeling so big?

"That's it," he encourages me between pulls of his mouth. "Don't fight me, Meghan. Let me in."

I spread my thighs wider to accept him and even wrap my legs around his waist, pulling him closer.

He groans with primal satisfaction as he slides all the way in.

Once he's completely inside me, he stops and tugs on the back of my scalp.

"Who do you belong to?" he asks, his voice deep and guttural.

His grip on my hair forcing my neck to arch almost

painfully, I stare up into the blazing depths of his blue eyes and say without hesitation, "You."

He makes a sound deep in the depths of his throat and pulls his hips back.

I start to whimper at the loss of him, then he suddenly slams back in.

"Say it again," he demands. "Who do you belong to?"

"You. I belong to you. I'm yours, Gabriel," I moan as he grinds his hips against mine.

"That's right... that's fucking right," he grunts as he begins to pump in and out.

But even with me seated on the counter, he's so tall he has to angle himself downward.

Growling with frustration, he suddenly picks me up, his fingers digging into flesh of my ass.

Then he slams me up against the front of the refrigerator.

"You're mine... fucking mine..." he grunts as he slams his hips into me so hard I begin to bounce. "And I'm never fucking letting you go."

I've given myself over to him so completely that it's only seconds before the beginning of my release is upon me.

Gathering force in the center of my core like a coming storm.

Each little sound that falls from my mouth seems to encourage him to fuck me harder and faster.

So hard, I feel his balls slapping against my ass and the door of refrigerator bending against my spine.

I writhe, my sweat slick skin sliding against his.

And then the force inside me is unleashed.

White lightning flashes in front of my eyes, and I swear I hear the roar of thunder in my ears.

But then I realize that's Gabriel roaring.

My pussy squeezes around him, desperately pulling him deeper as he declares, "Even if you tried to run from me, even if you chose not to stand beside me..."

Grabbing me by the chin, he forces me to stare into his eyes as I'm trapped, lost and powerless, inside my throes.

"I wouldn't let you go."

His words chill me even as his cock pumps me full of warmth.

And I start regret my decision.

But then, as he reaches the last seconds of his release, that angry mask of his slips off face.

And so much dark, twisted love stares back at me, I'm lost.

Utterly fucking lost.

"I fucking love you, Meghan," he declares.

And god help me...

I think I love him in return.

17

GABRIEL

It seems like I'm the one always getting out of bed first. Meghan lays behind me, sprawled out on the bed in just a pair of tiny panties. I swear she sleeps on her stomach like that on purpose. It's like she's begging me to slap that tight juicy ass of hers.

Times like these in the still moments before the death that's to come, I feel almost holy. I feel almost righteous. Maybe sinfully righteous.

Murder and mayhem isn't exactly the heavenly way. But I've never questioned my destiny. Never questioned the decisions that lead to the end of my rope. I don't plan on starting it now. Meghan agreeing to be by my side has filled that final piece I've been needing. Not that I knew I needed it.

When I got out of prison, I was dead inside. Rage was there in my body, but it wasn't like it is now. Now

I've got a purpose to keep moving, to do something proactive with my life.

I have someone I have to protect now. Someone I love and need to keep safe.

Words aren't always trustworthy. Meghan said she was mine, but I needed to see it in her eyes. To see that she truly meant it and felt the full bearing of those words. Her eyes told the truth, they showed the commitment we found with each other. Words after that were pointless. We're in this together now, good or bad, together.

The last three days since we've formed our bond have been at times quick, and at other times too slow. We've alternated between acting like we're on our honeymoon, to sitting on the couch speculating about what the fuck's been happening in the outside world.

The tension at times has been palpable. Both of us want to be out there getting this fucking war over with. We want the same thing, even if I'm more a little more bloodthirsty compared to her.

I truly believe she thinks this can be ended if we just all back down. I know for certain that won't appease either side. The Russians have been taking over too much land and vice around the cities. They're thirsty for territory and they hate us for kicking their asses at every turn.

Daily reports from Simon are vague at best. Nothing's happening out there. The Russians and Irish are bunkering in and keeping us guessing at their plans. It's a wait and see for the time being.

A *bzzt* sound rattles my nightstand as I stare out the back window of the bedroom. It looks out into a large wooded area, and I make sure I don't have any nasty surprises coming toward me before I turn back to the nightstand. The sunlight that guides me back to the phone tells me we've slept half the morning away.

"Who's that?" Meghan asks, her face buried in a pillow.

"No clue," I say before picking up the phone.

Letting out a growl, I press the connect button. "Can't fucking go twenty-four hours without you fucking bothering me, Simon."

"Listen here, you fucking cretin..." he snaps out at me before letting out a slow breath.

"Aw, that's all you got to say?" I ask with a grin.

"Get to highway forty heading east out of town towards Bethlehem. We've got a hit on the LPR for both cars," Simon says.

Instantly switching from fucking-off mode, my brain rattles a question out, "What's the coverage of the vehicle?"

"One unmarked police vehicle with the chief of police in his personal vehicle are in a loose tailing formation. They'll be joined soon by Detective Somers in another unmarked. Once we have enough men in the area, we'll pull them over."

"Any chance we have Alexei in the vehicle?" I ask as I motion for Meghan to get up.

"Yes, confirmed from a quick traffic light camera shot before they got on the highway. Also, there is a good chance Meghan's father is in the vehicle, but we can't be sure."

Grabbing my jeans and t-shirt off the floor, I say, "We'll be out the door in two minutes."

Dropping the phone to the bed, I quickly begin to pull my clothes on. "Get ready, baby. They got a location on Alexei."

"Oh god, it's starting up again, isn't it?" Meghan asks as she stands up from the bed.

"No," I say quietly to her. "It's getting ready to end. I'm through fucking around with these guys."

I watch as Meghan quickly yanks on a t-shirt and a pair of jeans. Since I talked her into using a hip holster for her gun when we go out in public she's taken to wearing some of the tightest jeans I've seen on a woman.

Tight clothing is good on Meghan, very good.

Both of us race through the house, grabbing our gear from the kitchen as we go. I strap on my vest before I hop into the black Lexus with tinted windows, and we squeal out of the garage.

CONNECTING to Simon through the car's phone system, I ask, "What's the distance between Alexei and me?"

"Five miles, no traffic in-between," Simon responds.

"Who's all in this parade?" I ask.

"We've got Johnathan and Andrew a mile ahead of you. James is enroute, but at the present he's fifteen miles out from the current target," Simon says.

"What about Jude?" I ask.

"He's on a different task. We've still got Alexei's father to deal with," he says.

"So, he's guarding the guy's incapacitated body?" I ask.

"Yes, even though we're positive that the location is secure, we're not taking any chances."

"That's so fucked," Meghan mumbles as she looks over at me.

Shrugging my shoulders, I say, "It's a good bargaining chip for us. We've not used it yet, and from what Simon says about the gas line explosion they caused, Alexei more than likely thinks that he was killed."

"Agreed." Lucifer comes on the line. "Although we'll be letting that little secret out soon enough. I think if we're careful and use it at the right moment, we'll cause quite the shitstorm back in Russia."

"Bringing the rest of the crew on comms, one moment," Simon says.

While we're waiting, I reach over to Meghan's leg and squeeze her thigh. Taking my eyes off the road for a brief look, I see that her body is tight and tense. Her hands keep squeezing themselves. She's as wound up as can be.

"Calm, Meghan. Take deep breaths," I say as I squeeze her thigh again.

This time, though, my hand slides up close to the parting of her legs.

Looking down at my hand and then up to my eyes, she gives me a small laugh.

Then she whispers, "You're thinking about that even now?"

"Yep." I smirk at her before turning my eyes back to the road.

It's a partial lie though. Sex is always going to be on my mind when I have her anywhere near me, but right now I'm thinking more about what I'm going to do when I get my hands around Alexei's throat.

"On another note, I've spoken with the Italians. They've adamantly denied any and all actions against the Irish when the bombing happened. They've also requested a sit down with us to discuss the matter," Simon says through the speakers,

Meghan freezes up beside me.

Turning my attention to her again, I see anger flash through her eyes.

Well shit. I was planning on talking to her about

this, but hadn't had the time or information to go further than my suspicions of what might have happened.

"What... what..." Meghan growls out.

"They weren't in a position to do what they were accused of," Simon says quickly, before he curses loudly. "Shit! The damn undercover officer is pulling the lead car over. Get moving now!"

"We're about thirty seconds from them," Andrew says through the speakers.

"All parties switch to ear comms," Simon says, and the car suddenly falls silent.

Pushing the earbud deeper into my ear, I look over to Meghan as she does the same. Her expression is a mixture of shock and anger.

Fucking hell.

I'm going to fucking wrap my hands around Simon's fucking neck and slam him into a fucking brick wall the next time I see his stupid fucking ass. I'll have to shove my fucking boot so far up his ass, he can fucking feel it coming out of his big fucking ears.

"Meghan," I say quietly, trying to get her attention.

Ignoring me, she starts fussing around with her gun holster.

Her hands are shaking horribly.

"Focus!" I shout at her as I watch her try to get her vest even tighter around her chest.

Her eyes snap over to me and for an instant I swear

she would slide a knife right through my neck. She's got a fire burning deeply in her eyes.

"Focus," I say gently this time. "Focus on what's going to happen now. Don't think of anything past the next ten minutes."

"Tell me what Simon's talking about," Meghan says, and from the tenseness in her voice, I know she won't be dropping this.

"We were talking about the bombing and how it didn't make sense to us... Especially since at the time of the bombing the Italians were weak on all fronts. They were dealing with a ton of shit out in Ohio as it was. None of us think it was them, so we're looking into it," I explain.

"But my father said it was them. Said it was a message from them," she states to me.

I shrug my shoulders. "I don't know, Meghan. I don't think he's right. Something else was going on."

"What?" she asks, incredulous.

"Look, we'll talk about this as soon as we can," I say, then point up ahead to the highway.

The highway's not too busy right now so we have the perfect view to see a swarm of cars pulled over on the side of the road. A police officer is facing the wrong way though, and he's walking toward Andrew and Johnathan's car with his hand on his pistol.

What the fuck?

"Simon, we have an issue," Andrew says over the radio.

"Yeah, fucking cop is trying to tell us to go away," Johnathan says.

"Shit. I'm getting a bad live feed from your vehicle's cam," Simon says.

Slowly pulling off to the side, behind our guy's vehicles, I make sure to pull far enough over that I'm in the grass and able to get a better view of what's happening.

"He's radioing something in," Andrew spits out.

"Motherfucking simple-minded fucks," I spit out.

The chief of police exits his vehicle and starts walking over to us.

Fuck!

Hitting reverse, I slam on the gas while saying, "They're going to bolt if we don't get ahead of them."

"Get around them and hold them there!" Simon hisses loudly in my earbud.

Meghan whimpers loudly as I tear back out of the grass and then shift into drive. Pushing the peddle down hard, I whip us around the cars in the back.

What a fucking mess this shit is. Everything's going to going to hell in a handbasket.

Slamming on the brakes in front of the cars, I twist the wheel so that my car is almost fully sideways as we come to a stop to block them. Looking at the cars, I yank my door open and grab Meghan by the shoulder strap of her vest, pulling her along with me.

"What the fuck?" she yelps as she finally gets her body under control and exits the car through my door.

"Soon they're going to know exactly who the fuck you are and I want a car between us if the bullets start flying," I say as I yank the back door open and pull out my AR-15.

Switching the safety off the semi-auto machine gun, I resist the urge to aim it at Alexei's car and start pulling the trigger.

"Oh god, what the hell are we going—" Meghan says, worried, then suddenly falls silent as she motions to something behind me.

Turning to look around, I groan inwardly. Two fast approaching state police cars are heading our way with their lights flashing.

Then their sirens suddenly turn on.

"Fuck!" I yell loudly. "Simon, we've got two state police cars coming in hot."

"Goddammit!" Simon snarls into the comms.

"Can you get rid of the extras, Simon?" Johnathan asks.

Turning back to the car Andrew and Johnathan are trying to exit, I see that this whole fucking thing is turning into a shit show.

Especially when I spot Meghan's dad climbing out of Alexei's car and standing behind a door.

Fuck me.

The two state police cars screech their tires behind me, and it's in the moment that I turn to see them that I also see a flash of gunfire.

Ducking down behind the car, I aim my AR-15 down at the ground as the police behind us jump out of their cars and aim their pistols at us.

"Chief's down. Someone in one of the Russian cars shot him," Johnathan yells in the ear comms.

"Goddammit!" Lucifer bellows into the ear comms as well.

A couple of shots ring out behind me and then I see Meghan taking a step around the back of our car before she starts rushing toward her father.

18

MEGHAN

I know what I'm doing is stupid. I know it will probably get me hurt or killed. But once I lay eyes on my father, there's only one path forward for me. I need to reach him. I need to know who the fuck killed my mother if it wasn't the Italians.

And if was him...

I need to fucking kill him.

Gabriel told me to focus, and that's exactly what I'm doing. Focusing on my target.

Orders to *freeze* are shouted behind me, but I ignore them. Gabriel roars my name, but I ignore him too.

Gunfire erupts from somewhere close by, but I don't care.

Dashing across the fifteen feet that separates Gabriel's Lexus from the black Audi my father ducked out of, all the craziness that's going down is just background noise.

I don't see the flashing red and blue lights. I don't smell the blood and lead on the air.

I only have one purpose, one goal. To reach my father and get the truth out of him before someone else kills him.

"Meghan!" Gabriel roars again, and I almost hesitate.

Almost.

But then my father slowly turns my way.

"Meghan," he gasps as I run up on him, his face draining of color.

He looks at me like he's just seen a ghost.

Multiple blasts of gunfire suddenly ring out and my father shakes his head, seemingly snapping out of it.

"What the hell are you doing?" he hisses as he jumps forward, grabs me by the arm and yanks me down behind the car. "Are you trying to get yourself killed?"

Shots ping off the front of the Audi and my father curses under his breath.

I let him drag me down. I let him think he's protecting me. But when I hear a car door opening behind me, I grab my gun from my holster.

My father turns away, his wide, anxious gaze

darting around, seeking out the sources of danger surrounding us, and I bring my gun up.

I aim it at the back of his head.

When he finally turns back to look at me, he's got the barrel of my pistol in his face.

"What—" he starts to say and then looks in my eyes.

Whatever he sees there causes him to freeze.

Taking a deep breath, I slip my finger over the trigger and resist the urge to pull it now.

For so long he lied to me... lied to my fucking face. Lied to me while he held me in his arms as I sobbed over my mother's closed casket. The betrayal cuts and burns like nothing I've ever felt before, eating me from the inside out like boiling acid.

The words want to stick in my throat, unsure if they want to be a whisper or a shout, but I force them out, my voice cracking. "Who the fuck killed mom?"

He turns his face away and tries to hide the flash of panic in his eyes, but I catch it. I fucking latch onto it. "Why are you asking me this? You know who killed your mother, it was the Italians."

Looking back to me, he meets my eyes again and tries to hold my gaze, expecting me to buy his bullshit.

But I'm not buying it.

As I just stare at him, he must realize it.

Switching tactics, he acts as if I'm a child and he's exasperated. "We don't have time for this, lass..."

"Don't call me *lass*," I snap out and take another deep breath, trying to keep myself calm.

Trying to keep my hand from shaking.

There's just so much going on inside me, though. A maelstrom of anger, confusion, and hurt is swirling inside me and I'm on the verge of completely losing it.

Steadying my hand, I lift the barrel up, aiming it between his blue eyes. "I know it wasn't the Italians. Stop fucking lying to me!"

This time my father can't hide the panic he's feeling as he looks to the barrel of the gun and back to me.

It's plain on his face.

He knows the truth, has known it all along, and doesn't want me to know it.

"Meghan, love, now is not the time to be discussing this. We can talk about this later," he says calmly, completely avoiding the question.

I shake my head. With all the shit going on around us, there might not be a later. And I've believed his lie for so long, I need the truth now.

"Was it you? Did you kill her?"

Just speaking the words out loud causes tears to prick at the corners of my eyes.

I think deep down a part of me has always suspected he did it. Did it because she wasn't onboard with starting a war.

"No," he breathes out in shock and then shakes his head in denial. "No. I didn't kill her."

"Why should I believe you?"

Why should I believe anything his lying mouth says?

One heartbeat passes, then another as we stare at each other. So many emotions pass over my father's face, I can't keep track of them.

Then he seems to crumble in on himself with a look of pure devastation. "Because I loved her, lass. Loved her with all my heart. She was my sun and my moon."

Something inside me rips open to hear him say that. I can't even count how many times I heard him calling her his sun and moon over the years with pure adoration.

And god, the way she would smile at him just before she kissed him...

His own eyes full of unshed tears, his voice cracks. "I still love her. I love her as much as I love you."

I've never seen my father cry before, not even at my mother's funeral. I always wondered if it was because he didn't feel enough to do so, or if it was a front for the rest of the family.

But that's what he's doing right now. Crying and standing in front of me with the posture of a broken man.

And I believe him.

I believe him so much I start crying with him.

He didn't kill her, I'm sure of it now, and I should be relieved, but all I feel is the same devastation mirrored on his expression.

Oh god, how did we come to this? What the fuck happened?

"If..." I start and have to stop to swallow back a sob. "If you didn't kill her, who did?"

I watch my father's mouth open. I watch as a shadow passes over his face and it doesn't even register why that might be happening. I'm so focused on him, on the answer he's about to give me, I don't realize the danger before it's too late.

The hair on the back of my neck suddenly stands on end as my father closes his mouth, pressing his lips together with a look of resignation.

I straighten as I sense someone behind me and then a body is pushing into my back.

I try to whip around, but I'm too damn slow. A strong, hard arm comes around my middle, locking me in place while a hand covers my hand over the gun.

As the hand covering mine presses against my trigger finger, I freeze, afraid I might accidentally fire my weapon.

Alexei's voice slides into my ear, chilling me to the very marrow of bones. "Hello, Meghan. So glad you've decided to return me."

Everything inside me shuts down in shock. I can't breathe, I can't think.

I can't fucking fight back.

Alexei's nose rubs against my ear before he asks, "Did you miss me?"

My body begins to tremble and I squeeze my knees together, afraid I might embarrass myself like that damn priest.

Alexei chuckles, his breath moving my hair as the arm wrapped around my middle begins to drift down. "I'll take that as a yes."

"Alexei..." my father says cautiously as he straightens in front of us.

His tears are gone as he squares his shoulders. The faint tracks down his cheeks the only proof that they ever existed.

I sense Alexei moving his head, and then his damn hand is forcing me to move the gun.

Forcing me to lift it up to aim it at my father's head.

I close my eyes and open them, hoping that what is playing out in front of me will change.

"Ah, yes. Your father was about to tell you who killed your mother before I so rudely interrupted... Well, go on, Brady, tell her," Alexei says with a hint of laughter.

My father looks from me to Alexei and then his forehead creases with worry. "You said you wouldn't hurt her. That was our deal."

"And I won't... even though our deal was broken."

My father stiffens and narrows his eyes at the gun pointed at him. "Hurt comes in many forms."

Alexei sighs and his grip on my hand forces me to wave the gun at my father. "Just answer the fucking question."

My father's eyes meet mine once more, full of shame and apology. And I know the answer before it even passes his lips. "Alexei killed your mother."

A sob escapes my throat and my knees threaten to give out.

Alexei killed my mother and my father tried to marry me to him...

My father flinches at the look I give him.

Before I can even muster up the strength to ask *how could you*, my father explains, "He killed her when I refused his offer of alliance. Then threatened to kill you if I refused again."

"Yes," Alexei says with absolutely no shame or remorse. "I'm so glad you came to your senses, for Meghan's sake."

My father shoots Alexei a glare full of murder and his hands squeeze into fists. "Since accepting his alliance, he's used us to do all his dirty work for him."

"Well, not *all* of my dirty work," Alexei snickers.

A look of pure disgust washes over my father's face before he tears his attention away from Alexei and looks to me again.

His eyes are begging me for forgiveness, a forgiveness I'm not sure I can give, as he says, "I'm sorry, Meghan. I tried to send you away. Tried to—"

A sharp pain shoots up my arm as Alexei forces his finger over mine and the gun goes off in my hand.

Just like back in the church, everything seems to slow down.

My father jerks back and his open mouth goes slack. His eyes suddenly dim as if the lights inside them blew out.

A hole. A dark hole appears on his forehead.

Behind him there's this blast, an explosion of blood and gore that splatters against the Audi's window.

With nothing holding him up, he slumps down the car like a marionette whose strings were just cut, making this horrible squelching noise while leaving a slick trail of blood and brain matter behind him.

Horror. Unbearable horror floods through me, and everything inside me just falls *out*.

Then a scream pierces the air.

A scream full of shock and pain.

A scream that's coming from me.

"He should have never tried to keep you from me," I hear Alexei say as my lungs drag in more air to scream again.

The death grip around my hand loosens, and then the gun is pried from my aching fingers.

I start to fight the arm wrapped around my middle, fight to reach my father.

"Stop that now," Alexei grunts, tightening his arm around me so hard I feel it bending my ribs.

But I don't care. I don't care what happens to me now. There's just this unbearable need to reach my father.

To take back what I just did.

Another scream flows from my throat and it's not enough, not enough to expel this pain inside me. Not enough to ease it even a fraction.

I start to claw at Alexei's arm, start to fight him with this primal, feral need to hurt him, to escape him.

"Goddammit, I said *stop*," Alexei snarls.

And then something cracks against my head so hard everything goes black.

19

GABRIEL

What the fuck is Meghan thinking? Why the fuck would she run to them? I thought we had all this fucking shit figured out?

"Fucking hell!" Simon yells into my ear. "What the fuck is going on?"

Bullets rip into the trunk of the Lexus as I start trying to go after Meghan. God-fucking-dammit!

Hunkering down, I look behind me and watch as the state police officers raise their weapons at me.

Well fuck.

I don't drop my rifle, but this shit isn't looking fun,

"Simon, we're all going to need a quick extraction," I say into the comms, and try turning toward the Audis that are now revving their engines.

Fuck it. I gotta do something or she's going to get away.

Standing up from the Lexus, I try to get a peek at the Audis. My view is mostly obscured by some big motherfucker holding onto Meghan.

I see Meghan's father fall to the ground and I can feel my stomach drop with him.

"Chief is down, Brady is down. We've got two state highway patrols screaming at us," Johnathan says into the comms.

"Damn them all to hell!" Simon yells. "I'm currently trying to get them under control. Do not shoot them. Respond to their commands."

"Put your weapon down!" an officer behind me yells at my back as I watch Meghan being shoved into the back of one of the Audis.

"Simon, they're taking Meghan," I growl into the comms.

"Understood," Lucifer says in a cool, quiet drawl. "Follow the officer's orders."

"Fuck that!" I shout and start to raise my rifle at the Audi.

"Don't do it!" a shout comes from behind me and I can hear a quiver in the voice over all the shit that's going on around us.

That quiver tells me that the officer is going to put a couple of rounds in me the moment my rifle raises enough to be a threat.

Fuck.

If I shoot now, I won't have a clear shot of getting the driver and fucking Alexei. Too many variables could go wrong if I try anything. I could be shot in the back before I have a chance to hit one of the car's wheels. I could also a get shot in the back of the head. That wouldn't do anyone good.

Dropping the rifle, I slowly stand up from behind the Lexus. Motherfuckers. I swore I'd never raise my hands again in submission to fucking pigs.

"Kick the rifle away!" the officer screams at my back.

The black Audis slam into reverse, trying to run over Andrew as he stands in place, pointing the gun in his hand at the back of the Audi closest to him. Diving out of the way of the car, he's as helpless as I am.

None of us can take a shot without risking hitting Meghan or the police opening up fire on us.

"God-fucking-dammit. For fucking shit's sake, get this shit straightened," I shout into my comms mic.

"I'm working on it right now. Do as they say for now," Simon hisses.

"Chief's dead, confirming it now. Same with Brady. Both have fatal shots to the head," Andrew says over the comms.

I can see him from my view, but not what's on the ground as the Audis tear away from us. Both heading away at a breakneck speed. One of the patrol officers the mic, but neither of them try to take off after the fleeing pricks.

Fucking hell, this is just getting worse.

I can't hear what one of the officers is shouting into his radio, but I do understand what the other one is saying when he tells me to kneel down on the asphalt.

My back may be to him, but he knows better than to have me turn around on them. I'm a big guy, there's no way of knowing if I've got a gun in my waistband up front or if I'd smash their fucking heads in.

"Get the fuck down on the ground," the pig yells at me.

Shouting over my shoulder at him, I say, "The fuck I will, asshole. Go after the guys who started shooting people!"

That quiver in the officer's voice is gone now that he saw me drop the rifle.

"Kneel on the fucking ground and put your hands behind your head, asshole! I'm going to fucking taze you if you don't do it now."

Turning my head to the side so I can get a good look at him, I say loud enough for him to hear, "You taze me, boy, and it's the last thing you'll ever do."

"Kneel down and take the cuffs, Gabriel," Lucifer says into the comms.

"Fuck you," I growl back at him.

"Take the fucking cuffs now! They'll be told to release you soon," Lucifer orders.

"I told you I'm not going back to a cell, Matthew," I say quietly.

For the first time in my life, Lucifer sounds worried. "I've already promised you won't."

Simon breaks through before I have a chance to respond. "The Highway Patrol have a car close to the Audis, for now they are in pursuit. But it's only one car at the moment."

"Good," Lucifer says through our earbuds.

The officer not giving me orders is taking a wide berth as he draws his gun, aiming at both Johnathan and Andrew. Both men are already lowering their pistols to the ground as the original officer from Garden City starts yelling at them to kneel down on the ground.

"They got us, boss. We could shoot our way out, but I'm not sure if we'd could get away without taking a loss," Andrew spits into the mic of our comms.

Fuck.

Slowly dropping to my knees, I say over the comms, "Do what they say. We'll go after the Russians as soon as Simon can get us out of this."

"I'm putting a call into the Governor's office right now. Give me a few minutes. They'll have to have extra cars and men there before they can haul you away. We'll have enough time to get you free," Simon says.

"I'm about a minute away from the scene. There isn't a lot of traffic right now, but you guys will be causing a backup soon enough," James says over the comms.

"Do not stop. We need to get someone after the Russians," Lucifer says.

"What about the Chief? Who the fuck killed him?" James asks, and I can hear a hint of something but I don't know what in his voice.

"Not our immediate concern. All we know is that it was one of the Russians," Simon says.

The officer who's been shouting at me the whole fucking time strides up behind me. I can feel the barrel of his gun not quite touching the back of my head. It's got my hackles raising pretty damn fast. He's damn lucky I don't turn around and snatch that gun from his hands and beat him with it.

"Lace your fingers behind your head, dickhead," the officer spits out at me.

I slowly raise my hands behind my head as I look over my shoulder and say, "I bet you you'll be taking these cuffs off me within the next five minutes."

He grabs my right arm and slaps a cuff as tight as he can around my thick wrist.

Pulling my left wrist down, he says, "Shut the fuck up before I shove my gun down your throat."

"I seem to remember shoving my dick down your wife's throat last night," I grunt as he pushes both my arms down so he can cuff me fully.

The metal handle of his gun slams into the back of my skull and for a brief moment I think I see stars.

"Stop resisting arrest, asshole," he shouts at me before the toe of his boot slams into my back, right where my kidneys are.

Hunching forward, I give a shout of pain. "Jesus, little dick, it's not my fault she wanted to go ass to mouth."

"Real funny, smart-ass, but remember you're the one in cuffs," he says before he kicks me in the back hard enough that I fall forward, slamming the side of my face into the Lexus.

"Stop baiting him, Gabriel," Simon snickers through the comms piece in my ear.

"Would if I could," I grumble as I slide down the car to land on my side.

Two long minutes go by with me lying here on the side of the road, my head *accidentally* kicked more than once by the power-hungry douchebag. I'm pretty sure he got pissed when I started with the innuendos about his mother and a goat. Fucking asshole is gonna die sometime soon.

Don't give a shit what kind of problems that causes.

My head is fuzzy from the kicks, but it's not so fucking fuzzy that I don't think of Meghan and how she fucking ran around the Lexus toward the very fucking men who want to kill her.

What the fuck was she thinking? She said she'd by

my fucking side. Thick and thin, we're supposed to be fucking together. Motherfucker. I'm going to punish her ass so fucking badly when I get her back.

Spankings... biting... I'll even fuck her in it until she screams her submission.

Fucking hell, I'll lock a damn chain collar around her neck. Chain her to the fucking house. She's going to be on fucking lockdown when I get her ass in my hands again.

Gonna have to spank her ass for being so fucking stupid. Spank her right after I grab a handful of that hair of hers and kiss her so goddamn hard it bruises her lips.

My stomach dropped watching her being so fucking stupid, running away from me.

Fucking hell.

"Hey asshole, your dad ever tell you about the time I fucked your mom in the ass in front of him?" I shout out at the officer.

"I swear to god I'm going—" he shouts at me before the other officer yanks him away from me.

"Stop, dumbass! Lieutenant is trying to get a hold of us," the other officer says to his jackass partner.

"So what? Where's our damn backup?" Jackass asks.

Looking up at the pair, I start to fucking chuckle. "Bet ya the Lieutenant is going to tell you to let us go."

"You'll be in prison so fucking long you'll rot," the asshole says to me before he spits at my head.

The nice one looks over to his partner, his eyes wide as can be. "We have to uncuff them."

"What?!" Asshole screeches.

"Official orders. We have to release them immediately. If we don't, we'll be subject to arrest for impeding an ongoing investigation," the calmer one says, and from the look on his face I bet he's just been told his career could be in jeopardy, if not more.

Now, if I was smart, I wouldn't want to be the one who uncuffs my pissed-off ass. I've already been pulling my wrists apart so damn hard that I can feel the chain beginning to groan.

All those kicks to the head have pissed me the fuck off.

"Sit up, you fucking criminal," the asshole cop sneers at me.

Rolling as quickly as I can, I growl, "Told you."

"Fuck you," he says, extremely pissed off about having to let us go.

Pushing my back up against the Lexus, I slowly slide my way up to my feet.

Standing up to my full height, I grin down at him before turning around to show my cuffs. "Remove 'em, pig."

∼

JOHNATHAN PATS Andrew on the shoulder and jogs past the cops to catch up to me as I climb into the Lexus.

Opening the door, he drops down into the seat. "Head to Bethlehem. They'll be there somewhere, running to get underground."

Nodding my head, I roll down my window and extend my arm to the officer who kicked me.

Raising my middle finger to him, I say, "See you soon, fuckboy."

"Goddammit," Simon all but screams over the comms.

His voice is so loud, Johnathan and I both wince.

Lucifer talks over Simon's yelling. "The Russians slowed down long enough for the Highway Patrol officer to get close to them. Then they opened up with automatic rifle fire, killing him. We've lost them in the ensuing traffic panic ahead and behind them."

"You what?" I ask in disbelief.

How the fuck could everything be going so fucking wrong?

"James, what's your location?" I snarl out into our comms.

How the fuck could we lose them so fucking easily?

"In traffic. I could jerk off and the line will probably have not moved. We're at a standstill," James grumbles.

"Fuck!" I shout as I pound my hands on the steering wheel.

"Everyone get off the next exit possible. We'll guide you through the backroads to Bethlehem," Simon says.

"They're going to ditch the cars. Those Audis are going to be way too hot to travel in right now," Johnathan says from my side.

"I know," I growl, and punch the steering wheel again.

He's fucking right, too. Alexei will dump the cars as soon as they possibly can. Those fuckers have cop killer written all over them.

Fuck. I have no clue how we can get back to locating them if they get rid of the cars.

"I want that pig who pulled them over early. We need to talk to him. Fucker needs to give me the reason he went outside of what he was told to do," I spit out.

"We'll make sure to bring him in. I'm trying to figure out why he would do it when the chief of police was in pursuit as well," Simon says.

"Is it possible he's with the Russians?" James asks.

"I doubt it," Simon says.

"Put the word out to all our contacts that we're on the lookout for Alexei's dumped vehicles. Also, we're looking for any Russian or Irish thug we can find," Lucifer says.

"Already on it. I'll have their faces on fucking milk cartons by the end of the hour," Simon says.

"Make sure you put on Alexei's that he likes things shoved up his butt," James says with a laugh. "Also, that

Meghan could be considered a midget next to her husband."

"You're—" I start.

"We're going to need all hands on this," Lucifer says through the comms.

"We have Thaddeus arriving from Ohio in three days. Having Jude here now helps, as well. I also have a line on a new guy coming in. He'll be good for us," Simon says.

"Would that be Eric?" Lucifer asks.

"Yes," Simon says.

The line goes quiet as we all begin to navigate the back roads toward Bethlehem. It's not a tremendous distance from Garden City, but having to avoid the interstate certainly adds time we don't have.

Fuck, if Meghan could have just fucking played this smart instead of running the fuck away from me...

Slamming my fist into the wheel again, I mutter, "What the fuck was she thinking?"

"What do you mean?" Johnathan asks me.

Looking over, I say, "She fucking ran to those moth-erfuckers. We had a fucking..."

I stop talking for a moment. My rage is threatening to erupt, and I can just feel it in my bones how badly I want to hurt someone.

Raising his hands in a settle down motion, Johnathan says, "I ain't saying you don't have a right to be fucking pissed as hell, but you might have been at a disadvantage in seeing what went down."

Rolling my shoulders, I try to settle my shit before I ask, "What do you mean?"

"Well, let me preface this with the conversation we had right before we all got to the scene," he says.

"Fine. Get to the point, fucker," I grunt

"She just heard that dear old dad wasn't right about who blew her mom to bits," he says.

"Yeah, don't mean she needed to run to that fucker the moment she had a chance," I say.

Chuckling at me, I can see he's getting ready to tell me something I missed. I just wish the fucker would get to the fucking shit I need to know before I snap his neck.

"She had her gun out and pointing at dear old dad's forehead. She had that motherfucker dead to rights. I couldn't hear all the words she spoke, but it looked like she was pretty damn pissed. Then Alexei snapped her up and pulled the trigger on her father with her. He forced her to shoot her own dad," he says.

My stomach fucking drops out from me as I think on what I just heard. Fuck me with a broomstick. Both of those little facts are a huge fucking revelation.

She was still stupid as fuck to run away from my fucking protection, but she did it for answers. I probably would have done the same thing.

"Fucking cock-sucking, tiny-dicked fuck," I growl.

Johnathan leans back in his seat as he pulls his gun out and does a quick check to make sure it's loaded. "Yep."

"WE HAVE A POSSIBLE LOCATION FOR ALEXEI," Simon says over the communications channel all of our guys are currently using.

"Where, and how reliable is the source?" I ask quickly.

So far none of us have had any luck driving through Bethlehem. The Audis were found ditched and lit on fire. They did it under an overpass as soon as they got away from the highway. The cops were actually the first to spot the burning cars.

"Warehouse district on the north side of the city. The source is coming from one of the Heralds of Hell. Apparently a probationary was out on a task and spotted them dragging Meghan toward a warehouse," Simon says.

"Probably out there checking for new spots to hide a body," Andrew says.

"With them? I'd think they're smarter than that," Johnathan responds.

"That's neither here nor there. The probationary wasn't able to say which one of the two warehouses they're at just yet. But he is in a spot that he can remain in in case they leave," Simon says.

"Are the HoH willing to provide us a security perimeter?" I ask as I aim the car toward the north side of the city.

"Perimeter security only, at the moment. They don't have enough of a lockdown on the city, and are already spread thin with their war going on with the cartels trying to get a foothold," Simon says.

"Offer a very large cash incentive and a favor from us," Lucifer says through the line. "I don't want these pests getting away from us."

"That could be costly. They're in a large bind right now with members and infighting," Johnathan says.

"I don't give a fucking shit about cost. I'll do anything they need me to do if they help," I say.

The line goes silent as we head toward the warehouse districts. My head is fucking racing a mile a minute as I try to figure out an angle that will work. I can't risk another fucking minute of Meghan getting hurt.

"I'm sending the latest updates on the warehouses they're suspected to be in to your phones. James, you're closest. Get a position up high and see if you can spot heat signatures with any of the gear you have," Simon says.

"Roger that, but I need to leave here as soon as this shit's over. I've got something I need to take care of."

"What do you have that's more pressing?" Simon snarls out.

"He's cleared it with me and I'm in full agreement. James needs to do another job. Right now, we have a small group of outsiders tailing the police chief's daughter. We need one of us watching her now. We still don't know why they took out the chief," Lucifer says.

"Fine, but we all need to have a meeting soon. We're becoming stretched too thin. We need more men in here," Simon snaps.

The suspected warehouses are only fifteen minutes away, but it feels like fifteen hundred fucking miles.

Five minutes out, a panting James comes back on the line. "Got into a nice little hidey-hole. Saw the probationary for HoH, he didn't see me though."

"Do you have heat signatures in the buildings?" Simon asks.

"Confirming right now. First building is as empty as your testicles, Simon," James says with a chuckle.

"You little fucking shit—" Simon starts to snarl at him.

"Hush, young man, I'm working here," James retorts. "Everyone hold about a minute out. I'm getting heat signatures and I need to get placements."

"Can you confirm any of the Russians?" Lucifer asks after a minute. "We don't need to break up a meat packing plant."

"Nah, we won't be doing that," James says, then goes on. "Got 'em. Eleven bodies. One is laying down on what is probably a table, but shows no cold spots. Gonna say from the sizing it's Gabriel's little munchkin. She's got two men with her. One is going to be Alexei, I bet."

"Good," Lucifer says. "Meet up and swarm."

20

MEGHAN

Pain. So much pain pumps through me, tearing through my head, my heart, *my very being*, I sink into the oblivion to escape it.

I welcome the darkness. I welcome the relief it gives.

I don't want to remember; I just want to forget.

But words drift into my dreams. Words that tickle at my mind and threaten to pull me back to my horrible reality.

Words that don't make any sense.

"I should have blown you up with that mother of yours... or sold you to the fucking Saudis. You've been nothing but a pain in my ass since the moment I laid eyes on you."

The pounding behind my eyes increases. It's so

terrible, I fight off consciousness. Fight off having to face it.

Someone sighs heavily.

"But alas, you've fucking bewitched me..."

Blissful silence wraps around me, the annoying voice quieting, and I begin to drift away...

Only to be yanked back again.

"If only you weren't so beautiful... so perfect..."

Something touches my head and I whimper, trying to move away from it.

Just go away and leave me in peace, I want to yell, but it would take too much effort to do so.

"Are you hurting, *zaika?*"

I groan and squeeze my eyes tight, wishing the words would just stop. Not only do they cut through my head, they're also a hook and line, reeling me out of my darkness.

"Good," the voice practically purrs, and then there's a sharp tug on my scalp. "You deserve the pain and so much more for what you've put me through."

Inside I'm screaming in agony as my head is forced up.

"Do you know how much I've worried about you?"

Someone's cool breath hits my face.

"Do you know how much I've suffered not knowing what those *pizdas* were doing to you?"

I don't care. I don't care. It's nothing to me.

The voice grows sharper, angrier, as if it's in tune

with my pain, finding its beat. "You're mine... mine to break and tame and mold as I please."

Fighting the grip on my hair only causes a spike of intense agony to slam into my brain.

"Tell me... Answer me honestly and I'll give you something for the pain. Did he fuck you? Did he use what belongs to me?"

A tightness wraps around my throat, but the discomfort is insignificant compared to what I'm already experiencing.

"This is your one and only chance to be honest with me."

Even in my nearly delirious state, I understand the significance of the question and fear answering it.

A fleeting thought whispers beneath the pain.

I'm not the only one in danger here.

Suddenly the tugging on my scalp eases, but the constriction around my neck increases.

As the seconds tick by, it becomes harder and harder to breathe.

True darkness rises up inside me, cold and black and ready to swallow me.

This darkness isn't like the other, though, and it frightens me.

"Tell me!" the voice demands.

I'm shaken, and pure, sheer agony courses through me.

"Tell me!"

Seeking only to get the voice to stop so I can be left in peace, I manage to push out a choked whisper. "Yes."

The grip around my throat goes slack for a moment, long enough for me to pull in some much-needed air, and then it suddenly tightens until it's crushing the life out of me.

Pressure. There's so much pressure.

My eyes pop open from the power of it.

Alexei's snarling face stares down at me.

"I'll fucking kill him."

His face begins to blur, that darkness creeping back in until it completely swallows me up.

"I'll kill them all!"

SOMETHING hard and cold slides inside of me.

Unlike earlier, the feeling is so jarring, so disturbing and violating, I immediately stir to full consciousness.

What the hell is going on?

It felt like it does when I go to the...

Oh god.

Immediately, I take stock of my body. Strangely, I'm no longer in any pain, but I can't seem to move my limbs.

And there's this a pressure... an uncomfortable pressure below my waist.

"Ah, yes..." a foreign, unfamiliar voice says from somewhere below me. "She was used."

I begin to open my eyes only to stop when I hear Alexei's voice.

"Used?" he clenches out.

I don't know why, but instead of trying to fight, I stiffen, petrified of moving. It's as if I've suddenly turned to stone.

"Yes, most definitely used," the unfamiliar voice says in a detached way. "And from the micro-tearing I'm observing, she was used roughly."

Alexei mutters a bunch of Russian words I don't understand, and I nearly jump out of my skin when there's a loud thud.

The terror holding me hostage tightens its grip.

"Remember, I'm Armenian, not Russian. Speak English," the stranger grumbles.

Alexei mutters some more in Russian before taking a deep, calming breath. Then he asks, "Was she forced?"

There's a pause.

Then the stranger answers, "You'll have to ask her."

Alexei's voice is instantly cold, all the heat evaporating from his voice as he snaps, "I'm asking you, Dr. Petrosyan."

The doctor hums under his breath and then says reluctantly, "It's possible."

Alexei returns to growling in Russian again.

As if suppressing a laugh, the doctor says, "If it makes you feel better, know that she is not permanently damaged, and I doubt it's causing her any discomfort. She should be, as they say, as good as new in a few days."

"That's reassuring, for her sake," Alexei says with so much malice all the little hairs all over my body stand on end.

A chuckle slips out of the doctor. "Indeed. However, we'll need to take a few steps to ensure there's not an unwanted pregnancy."

Wait... what? There's no way I'm pregnant...

"Unwanted pregnancy?" Alexei hisses.

"Yes. There's evidence that whoever used her didn't use protection. Given that it's been a few days since we've removed her contraceptive device, there is a slim, very slim, chance she could be pregnant."

My knee-jerk reaction is disbelief.

The doctor must be confused, because I still have an IUD...

A strange numbness suddenly tingles across my flesh.

He said they removed my contraceptive device a few days ago...

Oh god... Oh fuck.

That sick fucker must have done it when they sedated me before the wedding.

As all the implications hit me and my mind struggles to come to grips with the sick revelation, Alexei is ominously silent.

At first, I'm not even aware of it, but as time passes, it becomes more obvious, and an overwhelming sense of dread forms in the pit of my stomach.

I could be pregnant... There might be a child inside me. Gabriel's child. And I'm stuck in this place, completely at Alexei's mercy.

My heart begins to race and the need to escape, to get away, to protect myself and my possible unborn baby, grows with every passing second.

Just as I try to move my arms again and find them still restrained, the stranger breaks the tense silence.

"That is, if you think she's worth the effort of salvaging."

I freeze as I sense someone moving closer to me. Cracking my eyes open just enough to peek out of them, I see Alexei's dark form stalking toward me through my lashes.

The look on his face is so icy, so foreboding, I squeeze my eyes shut again.

"Ah... that's what I'm not sure of," Alexei admits. "Is she worth the effort?"

I can't see him, but I can sense his presence looming over me, nearly smothering me with the weight of it.

"Only you can decide that," the doctor says quietly.

A hand touches my head and brushes my hair back. And it's everything I can do not to squirm or give-away that I'm conscious and aware of what's happening.

"Explain the process and the odds of success," Alexei says.

"Well, there are a few options," the stranger says thoughtfully. "We could use medication to terminate any possible chance of pregnancy, but it might not take."

Alexei sighs. "So what do you suggest?"

"A preventive termination via menstrual extraction."

The words bang around inside my head, not making any sense.

"And, pray tell, what is that?" Alexei asks with a hint of irritation.

"A simple suction procedure that will remove anything unwanted in her womb."

Fuck me. This guy wants to vacuum out my insides? Are you shitting me?

Sounding almost bored now, Alexei asks, "And the chance of success?"

His hand continues to stroke my hair back, and I pray to God I don't start to break out in a cold sweat.

The doctor sounds overly cocky as he says, "In my hands, I can assure you one hundred percent."

One hundred percent... One hundred percent chance that if Gabriel's baby is inside me, this fucking butcher of a doctor will kill it.

Alexei's hand stills against my hair as he asks with more interest, "And she'll be able to have more children after the procedure?"

"Of course," the doctor says almost cheerfully. "If you like, you can begin to breed her immediately."

Breed me?

Breed me?!

"Oh? There's no recovery time?"

The doctor snickers. "None is needed. The procedure itself might be long and painful, but once it's completed her body will be ready to be impregnated."

God help me. Is there no end to this fucking madness?

"How soon can you perform the procedure?" Alexei asks, sounding eager now.

Bile rises up in my throat and I fear I might be sick. Once again, I attempt to move my arms and legs, but there's absolutely no give.

"Immediately. Thanks to our current operation, we already have all the equipment on hand."

"Excellent," Alexei says, and he moves away, taking the unwanted touch of his hand with him.

Hinges creak as a door swings open, and I peek open my eyes once again.

This time Alexei's eyes meet mine, glittering with dark amusement.

He smiles at me and then looks to the man seated between my spread legs.

"I'll leave you to it, Doctor. Inform me when the procedure is completed."

21

GABRIEL

Racing into the warehouse parking lot, I slam on the breaks as hard as I can before yanking the gearshift of the truck into park. It's going to kill the fucking transmission treating it like this, but I don't have any other choice.

Every second Meghan isn't in my protection is a second that fucker could be hurting her.

The truck swings sideways as we come to a screeching halt.

We've got luck on our side to the extent that the entrance to the warehouse and parking lot looks like a giant upside-down L. Trees and small buildings hide our approach, giving us the opportunity to get the jump on these dick-sticks.

Johnathan and I slide out of the driver's side of the Lexus so we can get a good angle on the building and the two guards in front of it. Both guards stand at the office portion of the warehouse, guarding the door. So far, these are the only ones dumb enough to stand outside where we can get to them this fucking easily.

Both guards go down quickly as Johnathan and I bring our M4's up to our shoulders and let out two suppressed shots. Blood, skull, and brain matter splat against the wall behind them before they drop to the hard asphalt.

The office portion of the building is entirely made up of bricks, with one steel-framed door for its entry. The rest of the warehouse is made of sheet metal. We knew this fucking door would be the biggest issue for us getting in.

Big issues mean big ideas. Our big idea is a shit ton of plastic explosive.

Johnathan sprints up to the door before us, his hands already moving to place the plastic explosive to take out the door frame and hopefully fuck with whoever's in the room behind the door.

"Breach, breach, breach," Johnathan growls out into the communication wrap that's fitted snugly around his throat.

With those words instantly entering our ears, we all turn away from the blast zone and count down from three in our heads.

There's a loud boom as the charges blow the door completely off the hinges, sending shrapnel flying into the room. I'm supposed to be the first guy into the building, but we have a strict protocol we follow.

So I toss a flashbang grenade into the room first. Then Andrew tosses a shrapnel grenade after mine goes off.

Disorientation and collateral damage are the keys to fucking these bastards up.

Shock and maximum carnage.

We didn't have time to fully plot anything beyond our tactical squad order and just the roughest outlines of how the building is laid out. There simply isn't any way to plan an operation like this without risking something bad going down with Meghan.

I can't fucking allow that. Meghan is the one spot in my world that I base my sanity on. Without her by my side, I'm not sure I'll be able to function. I fucking hate that I've put such a dependency on her.

But that's what happened.

Somewhere between her pulling the trigger on me in the church and when she got shoved in the car by Alexei, I've grown to need this woman with my very fucking being.

She's mine. Mind, body, heart, and fucking soul.

Loving her makes me feel human again.

Knowing that Alexei has dared laid a hand on my fucking woman, on my fucking *salvation*, has my damn mind shutting down to a narrow fucking focus.

"In on three... two... one..." I say as I quickly move

through the door with my M4 raised up to my shoulder and my finger already on the trigger.

"Following," Johnathan says quickly behind me.

"Targets moving through the building," James comes over the comms as I quickly aim my rifle at a staggering man.

"Hostile One down," I say after a burst of three shots from my rifle.

"Hostile Two and Three already down on the floor from the explosives," Johnathan reports.

Andrew grumbles into the comms as he follows us in, "Couple of shots for good measure."

Six suppressed shots snap loudly in the room as he puts a hole in the heads and hearts of each downed target.

Nasty business that, but it ensures that we won't have any sneaky fuckers getting up and shooting us in the back.

"Front office clear," I say, and quickly move to the door that has a stairwell exit next to it. "Entering stairwell. Flashbang only."

Pulling a second flashbang grenade off my vest, I wait for Johnathan to open the door before I toss the grenade inside. Pushing the door closed, we wait outside for the bang and ultrabright flash before yanking the doors open.

Finally hearing it go off, I look in and up to see if I can spot anyone. Empty.

"Stairwell empty," I report.

"Got two guys coming up on the roof. Looking to see what they're up to before—Holy tits!" I hear him shout before there's a loud bang and the front of the office implodes on us.

Brick and metal shrapnel explode all around us as we rush into the stairwell for cover.

"What the fuck was that?" I yell into the comms strap around my neck.

Fuck me, I can feel a large chunk of something lodged in the back of my right shoulder. Lodged and fucking burning a damn hole in me. Pressing myself up against the wall, I pant for a moment, trying to center my mind away from the wound.

"RPG took out your car, Gabriel," James says before I hear him start to snicker loudly in his mic. "Both targets down. Shot one in the pecker first, though, before I got a good headshot on him."

"Oh, for fuck's sake," I hear Simon grumble into the comms chip in my ear.

"Get extraction vehicles out here if you can, Simon," Johnathan says into his mic.

"Already on their way," Simon says.

"Michael and I are fifteen minutes out," Lucifer says into the mic.

Well, fuck me. Big man's getting involved.

"Yay! Lily let you come out to play with the rowdy kids!" James cheers into the mic like a fucking kid.

"Shut up, James," Lucifer says with laugh.

James isn't as old as most of us, only a couple of years younger, so I'm guessing the fucker gets to be the fucking baby of the family. Lucifer treats the immature shit as if he's another one of his sons anyway, from what Johnathan and Andrew say.

"I'm telling mom," James taunts before his voice snaps into business mode. "They've got another guy coming up on the roof. Shooting in one... two... three. Target down. Searching the building for heat signatures."

"We need to fucking move," I growl into the mic.

I don't have my brother's fucking eloquent words or fucking analytical mind. I'm the brute fucking force. I smash through the fucking walls. I don't sit behind and fucking work on a fucking keyboard. I'm the fucking hellhound. I'm not paid to think. I'm paid to fucking move and hurt.

All this shit's going on and all I can do is grind my teeth at the slow fucking pace we have to keep. I want to charge in and murder every fucking soul in this damn building.

Sliding along the wall, I move toward the stairs. If they haven't decided to move toward us in the stairwell yet, they will soon. I don't want to be a fucking fish in the barrel. I hate stairwell fights, topside always has the advantage.

"Moving up," I say as I start sliding my body

around the outside of the stairwell, trying to get the best view I can of what's above me.

"Hold up," Andrew says. "Fucking hell, you're trailing blood."

Looking back to the wall, I growl. I don't have time to be injured. But there it is, a trail of my blood smearing against the wall as I move.

"No time to patch me up," I grunt as he shoves his hand against the wound.

"You got a fucking chunk of metal in your shoulder, I need to get this fixed up," Andrew says.

"After," I say, before I feel him ripping at my shirt. "What the fuck are you doing?"

"Putting a temporary bandage on there to keep you from bleeding out like an asshole," Andrew grumbles before I feel him pushing something against my shoulder.

Pushing around the wound, he says, "It's a compress with blood clotting shit in it. I'm going to need to remove that chunk of metal as soon as we can, though."

"Thanks, Doc," I mutter and wait for him to finish up.

"Looks like he stuck a maxi pad on you," Johnathan says with a chortle.

"It's not," Andrew says with a small laugh himself. "But I've used 'em before when I had to stop someone from dying on me."

Moving forward, we quick-step up to the second floor of the building. It's a three-story building, but James has seen all activity on the second floor through the heat signature scope he's been using. I'm guessing the guys that got onto the roof used the stairwell at the opposite end of the building.

My hands start to jitter. Not good. I have to remain calm. I have to remain in perfect fucking control of my body. I can't fucking wait for this shit to be over and done with. I need Meghan fucking safe. This waiting shit is for the birds.

"Taking target down," James says into the comms. "They don't seem to understand that windows are bad places to hide in front of."

"Exiting stairwell on three," I say into our comms before quickly kneeling on the floor.

Johnathan quickly pulls the door open and I lean around the edge to look out.

Bullets hit where a man's chest would be above me.

Spotting the two shooters standing behind a desk of some sort, I blast a hole through the throat of one guy and the forehead of the second.

Andrew moves into the long room as I stand up from where I've been kneeling.

Standing up though, I can feel a warm fresh pulse of blood seep out of my wound. Andrew was right about me needing to get this fixed up, but now's not the time. If we don't get moving, we're going to lose the advantage.

Jogging in the lead of our trio, I stop when I come to a door leading down a long hallway.

"Anything on the heat scope?"

"One coming out of the office on my side. Your right," James says quickly.

Kneeling again, I wait for them to poke around the corner. Lining up my sights on the M4, I shoot the guy in the knee while Andrew blasts a bullet through the head of our target.

"Fucker. We've got a big heat signature rushing back to the suspected room with Meghan. You need to move. I don't see any more discernible targets," James says in a rush.

"Moving," I shout into my comms and start off at a quick pace.

Each pounding stomp of my foot brings a jolt of pain through my body. That piece of metal isn't the best thing to have hitchhiking inside me right now.

With each step, though, I can feel the anger in my blood boiling. Boiling so fucking full of hate and rage. My eyes want to glaze over in a berserker-induced blackout, but I can't allow myself to do it. Not with Meghan in so much danger right now.

"I've got a shot. It's going to be through the wall, but I've got one I feel I can take without endangering Meghan," James says

"Any idea who it is?" Andrew asks.

"No, but taking it now," James says.

I hear Meghan's high-pitched scream coming from up ahead of me.

"Target One down. Second is ducking behind Meghan and the dead body that collapsed on her," James says.

"Fuck," I spit out.

"Distance to the office?" I ask quickly.

"Fifteen feet," James says. "Ten... seven... four... You should be close to the entrance now."

"Put two more rounds through the walls. Close enough to scare the shit out of them, but not hit them," I say.

"Doing so now."

A bullet round slams through the outer wall of the office wall and Meghan screams again. Fuck, I don't want her to ever have this kind of fear. I can't stand it. It's fucking murdering my fucking brain to hear her screams.

The second bullet tearing through the wall gives me a damn good idea of who's alive inside of the room with her, though.

Alexei's bitch voice shouts, "Goddammit! Pick up your fucking radios!"

Shouting into the room, I say, "They're all dead, motherfucker!"

"I'll kill you all and then this fucking whore!"

Alexei yells back at me before he starts shooting through the walls at us.

Good thing I'm not close enough for him to hit me.

"He's only got a gun and he just shot six times!" Meghan screams out to me.

"Holy fuck!" Johnathan bellows with a rough, tumbling laugh. "Chick's got some fucking balls on her!"

"Shut your whore mouth!" I hear Alexei scream followed by a heavy slap of skin.

"Fuck you, tiny dick!" Meghan yells back.

Alexei roars in anger.

Racing around the corner, I flip my M4 around in my hands. Instead of holding it like a rifle, I wield the motherfucker like a baseball bat.

Taking a monstrous swing, I cover the ground between Alexei and me with an almost inhuman speed. I don't know why time has slowed down so much for me, but I thank every fucking devil I can name that it does as the stock of the rifle connects with the Alexei's hand.

His eyes go wide as fuck as his pistol goes flying across the room.

Alexei's a big fucking man like me, but I can see in his fucking eyes he isn't a warrior. He's pumped some weights to give himself a look, he didn't spend those hours in the gym to build muscles to hurt. He spent them to look good in fucking suits. He may be good with a pistol, and has probably been in a couple scrapes before, but he isn't a brawler like me.

Squaring up on him, I raise my hands as I give him a smile. It's probably not what he was expecting when I bum-rushed his ass, but I'm going to give him a chance to fight me.

He'll fucking die here one way or the other, but I don't want it to be quick and painless.

"I'll fucking kill you all," he snarls at me.

"Doubt it," Andrew says from behind my back.

And then I hear Johnathan laughing. "I want a piece of him, if anything's left after you're done."

Slowly circling to Alexei's right, I wait to see if he's going to try to make a play for Meghan or me.

"I'm taking my wife home with me. We're also going to be waking your dear old dad up, too." I grin.

Eyes wide, Alexei seems momentarily stunned by my words. And I don't think it's me taking Meghan home that has him looking like he's seen a ghost. We've got a lot of questions for his father. Questions that will be pulled out of him at *our* warehouse, where we can take all the time in the world.

"Possibly pregnant wife," Meghan slurs.

Glancing over at her, I see that her lip is busted and a trickle of blood is running down it.

My eyes swing between Alexei and her.

My brain is processing too much shit. Her hurting and exposed. Him fucking living and breathing.

She's strapped down on a fucking medical table, her legs up in fucking stirrups. And I have no clue who the fuck the dead man slumped on top of her is, the way his face is mangled from the exit wound of the bullet makes it impossible to tell.

"You hit her. You fucking touched her," are the only words I can get out before I finally allow the red haze of lustful rage filter my sight.

There's a loud roaring sound that reverberates around the room as I charge at Alexei, and from the wide-eyed look the bastard gives me, I get the feeling it's me who's doing the roaring.

I thought it was the fucking blood rushing in my veins, pounding in my ears, but it's not. It's me, and I'm finally allowing myself to be the fucking Hellhound I've always been.

There's nothing fancy in the way I'm going to hurt him. I just want to get my hands on him and beat his body to a bloody fucking pulp. I don't need weapons or instruments of torture. Those wouldn't work for what I want to do.

I need to get my fucking hands on his fucking body and cause pain.

I throw a huge fucking haymaker at his jaw, but he's smart enough to see how much I'm telegraphing that punch. While he's ducking low to steer clear of my overswing, I change the direction of my punch to land the arm around his shoulder.

Wrapping him up, I slam into the desk that's been pushed over into a corner of the office.

He screams at me in Russian as he wrenches an arm around my neck, trying to get a hold of me.

Nothing he does though is going to work. My mind has had too many fucking ups and downs. Too many gains and losses over the last couple of weeks.

The final straw that breaks the chains of my inner fucking beast is Meghan's blood. Blood that's my fault. Blood that I should have been able to prevent from being spilt.

He keeps going for the choke, but he can't get the grip he so desperately needs around my neck. Growling out, I get both arms under him before I rip him off my neck. Tossing him across the office, I watch as he slams into the wall.

His body leaves a good fucking sized dent. He's only crumpled down for a moment before he starts to stand up.

I've shaken his ass and rattled that big fucking head of his.

Stalking over to him, I grab him by the collar of his shirt. He's a prissy-dressed fuck in his suit and tie. But that about figures, all fucking dressed up like a bitch. Probably never truly had a hard day's work in his life.

Slamming my fist into his face makes me feel so much better as I wrangle him to stand up in front of me.

"Didn't your cunt of a mother ever tell you not to hit a lady?" I ask him, slamming him into the wall.

"Fuck you!" he screams at me as he punches me in the stomach.

He's got a good jab, but it's not hard enough to make me release him.

Slamming my forehead into his nose is so fucking cathartic I do it two more times. Each time, I hear a crunch of bone breaking.

Blood is all over my face when I finally pull back from him. It's all his, though.

Eyes glazed, he continues to shout a litany of broken English and Russian.

I have no clue what the fuck he's saying right now, and I really don't care.

Moving my hand down to his waistband, I lock onto it with a firm grip, then I latch onto his hair with my other hand.

I want to see how far I can toss this motherfucker.

Twirling around once, I lift his body into the air and send him flying across the office to slam into the opposite wall.

"Fuck me! He tossed him at least ten feet!" Johnathan says with a laugh.

Stomping over to Alexei, I can feel my hands squeezing. They ache with a need to hurt him right now, to cause more damage.

Dragging Alexei up by his hair, I lean back and finally let the full force of my pent-up rage out.

The first couple of hits are to the side of his jaw. It might be more than a couple, though, because soon enough I feel something shatter in his jaw.

Teeth spit out of his mouth as he tries to desperately get my hands to release the grip I have on his head.

"Useless motherfucker," I snarl into his face as I rain blows into his ribs.

Him being on the floor isn't good enough for me right now so I stand him up like a fucking punching bag.

How he stands there wobbly as a motherfucker, I don't know, but I want to see if I can keep him from falling with just my fists.

Each hit lifts him up enough to keep him from dropping between blows of my fists. I know there's ribs cracking and breaking beneath my fists.

Five or fifty blows go by and I can't recall which number I'm closer to. All I know is that he stopped screaming somewhere in the middle of my punches.

Pulling back from him, I watch as his body crumples to the floor.

"Fucking anticlimactic motherfucking pussy!" I bellow at his unconscious lump of a fucking shit body. "You're supposed to be some big bad! Some motherfucker who can put some damage on me! Fucking waste of breath!"

Rearing back, I kick his kidneys with my fucking boots. Kick 'em until I know I've caused serious internal bleeding.

"You made me this fucking mad and you can't even fucking put up a real fight!" I scream at him.

Kneeling beside him, I raise my arm to start working on the side of his head when something pierces my brain like a bullet.

"Gabriel," a soft, feminine voice calls to me.

I drop a fist to the side of his head with the intention of seeing if I can cave in his motherfucking skull.

"Gabriel, stop it! I'm fucking naked under this sheet! Help me. Please," she calls to me again, and that the red haze finally fades away as the colors of the real world seep back into my vision.

"Fucking bitch," I spit out on the body that's barely breathing.

Standing up, I look over to Johnathan who's watching me with a bored look on his face. "You done?"

Glancing around the room, I notice the blood splattered all over. All Alexei's.

Fucking feels damn good.

Andrew's not around though, so I'm guessing he's outside securing the perimeter.

"Almost," I growl out.

"Andrew's right, though. You're going to need to be stitched up. You're bleeding from your shoulder pretty good," Johnathan says, then I hear his boots walking away from the room.

Turning back to Meghan, I walk over to her, and the feelings of murderous rage start to slowly fill me again as I take in her small body bound to the medical table.

I want so badly to go back to beating Alexei, but having a dead body slumped over her chest is enough of a deterrent to hold me back for the moment.

"You okay, baby?" I ask as I shove the corpse away from her with one hand and push the sweaty hair away from her eyes.

"If you untie me, I will be," she tells me in a matter-of-fact tone.

"Sorry. Kinda got carried away over there," I say as I begin to unfasten all the straps holding her down.

"I can't believe you killed him with your bare hands like that," she whispers to me, her eyes widening with the realization of what she watched me do to a man.

Her eyes need to see what I'll do to any man that dares to touch her.

"He's not dead," I say with a shrug. "I figured I'd give you the choice of ending that piece of shit's life."

22

MEGHAN

Once Gabriel has unfastened all the leather straps holding me down, he lifts me up into his arms. The bloody sheet covering me begins to slip down my legs as his massive biceps wrap around me in a crushing hug.

But I don't care.

After everything that's happened, after watching what he did to Alexei, the need to be held by him, to feel him, to know he's real, is all that matters right now.

Sitting down on the edge of the medical bed, he pulls me onto his lap, and I press myself against his chest while something inside me cracks. The strength I've been holding onto crumbles away at his touch.

If I could somehow burrow myself inside him and hide for the rest of eternity, I would.

"It's alright. Everything is fine now, baby girl," he

murmurs as I start to shake uncontrollably. "I've got you."

I toss my head back and forth in disagreement, tears bursting from my eyes. It's not alright, and everything isn't fine now.

Cocooned in Gabriel's warmth, the shock, the adrenaline rush, the focus on survival is gone, and all that's left is the devastation of what's been done.

I almost lost everything.

My life...

The possibility of a life growing inside me...

My father... oh god, my father.

Gabriel kisses the top of my head, and I just can't stop crying. I don't think I've ever cried this hard before in my life. But there's so much pain inside me, so much pain and anger, I can't keep it locked inside.

It's not until I start to squeeze Gabriel back and sense him stiffening, that I can get the slightest grip on my emotions.

"You're hurt," I say accusingly, and force myself to pull away.

"It's just a scratch," Gabriel says gruffly and tries to squeeze me back into the hug.

Bullshit, I think as I wiggle out of his grasp.

If he's showing any sign of being in pain, it must be bad.

"It's nothing," Gabriel frowns down at me as I

begin to run my hands all over him, searching for the injury.

I ignore him, finding purpose in taking care of him. My tears dry up as I explore his chest, sliding my palms over his tactical vest. Finding nothing, I cover every inch of his arms. His knuckles are a bit busted up from punching the shit out of Alexei, but otherwise he seems okay.

Once I reach his shoulders, however, I catch him sucking in a sharp breath.

Scowling, I position myself until I'm kneeling on his lap so I can see what the hell is going on with his shoulders.

"Holy fuck," I growl and yank my fingers back when they run over something sharp. "You have a chunk of metal stuck in your shoulder!"

Being more careful this time, I gently probe at the big chunk of metal embedded in Gabriel's flesh just on the edge of his tactical vest.

"Doesn't hurt at all," Gabriel says with a slow smile curving along his mouth. "In fact, I feel better already."

"What?" I blink up at him in confusion, then I follow his gaze downward.

"Oh my god, are you seriously checking me out right now?" I ask as he stares with absolutely no shame at my naked chest.

Gabriel's smile only grows wider.

I'd hit him, but knowing him, he'd probably like it,

so I just cross my arms over my breasts. "You need to get that looked at."

"Yeah, yeah," Gabriel grumbles and once again tries to pull me back in for a hug, but I shrug him off.

Narrowing my tired eyes at him, I say firmly, "I'm serious."

Smile fading, he sighs. "I'm sure Andrew will be around soon."

As if saying his name summoned him, Andrew begins to stroll into the room, saying, "You rang?"

But then he takes one look at me and stops dead in his tracks. "Oh shit."

His eyes immediately drop to the ground and he starts to back out of the room.

"Fuck off," Gabriel growls, yanking me into his hold and turning to shield me from the door.

"What seems to be the problem..." I hear another voice drawl out as my face is shoved into Gabriel's neck. "Oh, I see."

I try to push away from Gabriel to see what's going on, but his arms are so tight with tension it's impossible to break his hold.

"Here Gabriel, this should cover your wife."

Gabriel grunts as he twists back around only enough to grab whatever was offered to him. Twisting back around, he drapes a dark suit jacket over my shoulders and then clutches the front tight against my chest.

"May we enter now?" the smooth voice drawls out again, and my brain finally makes the connection of who it belongs to.

Gabriel's boss, Lucifer.

"Yeah," Gabriel says reluctantly, as if he'd rather they not.

"Ah... I see you've made quite the mess of Alexei," Lucifer says as he strolls into the room, his eyes taking in the scene with a keen interest.

"He deserves worse," Gabriel spits out and his arm tenses around me.

"Agreed," Lucifer smirks.

Something about that smirk of his puts me on edge, and I watch him warily as he walks up to Alexei's prone body.

The man is just too beautiful, too surreal, and it fucks with my head. He looks completely out of place in this gory mess, and yet at the same time, somehow he seems to fit right in...

It doesn't make any fucking sense.

Lucifer nudges Alexei's side with the toe of his expensive leather shoe. "Pity, though, that you couldn't keep him alive long enough for us to get some information out of him."

Gabriel grins that maniacal grin of his. "He's not dead yet."

Lucifer glances back at him in surprise.

I curl up against Gabriel, wishing that Alexei was dead and all this shit was over with.

"He's Meghan's," Gabriel says firmly, and my hands clutch at his shirt.

"Well, I guess the poor bastard couldn't give us anything useful given the state of his jaw, or rather the lack thereof, anyway," Lucifer says, inclining his head.

Then he turns back to Alexei and gives him another, though harder, nudge with his toe.

Alexei lets out a weak, bubbling moan and Lucifer snickers.

"Can I enter now?" Andrew asks from the hallway as I bury my face into Gabriel's chest.

"Yes, Andrew, please do," Lucifer answers.

I sense someone approaching, and after the ordeal I've gone through, my body immediately stiffens with apprehension.

A bag drops on the table and I nearly jump out of Gabriel's lap.

Gabriel lets out a warning growl. "Watch it."

"Sorry," Andrew says, sounding sincere, and I force myself to relax a bit.

My anxiety only seems to be putting Gabriel on edge.

"Let's see what we have here..." Andrew murmurs thoughtfully.

Gabriel grunts in pain and I decide to finally lean back to see what's going on.

"It's not as bad as I thought," Andrew says as he examines Gabriel's right shoulder, "though it's nasty enough that I'll have to stitch you up right here."

"How long do you think it will take?" Lucifer asks.

Bending down and rummaging through his bag, Andrew answers, "Only a few minutes."

"Good," Lucifer says. "Simon has given us a fifteen-minute window to depart."

"I should be done in time," Andrew says in acknowledgement, and straightens with a pair of pliers in his hand.

My stomach clenches at the sight of the pliers and I look away, only for my gaze to fall once again on Alexei's mangled and broken body.

Fifteen minutes... Sometime within the next fifteen minutes Gabriel is going to expect me to kill him.

And I seriously don't know how I feel about it. I can't even begin to figure it out with Gabriel hurting.

"This is probably going to fucking hurt," Andrew warns Gabriel.

"Just get it fucking over with," Gabriel says impatiently through clenched teeth.

"Alright then," Andrew chuckles.

Gabriel's hand finds mine, his fingers squeezing gently around my fingers. I squeeze back, offering him some comfort, though I doubt he needs it.

"Has anyone ever told you you're a big motherfucker?" Andrew asks casually, as if he's trying to make small talk.

"Yeah, a time or two..." Gabriel starts to chuckle, but then the chuckle turns into a groan.

Alarmed, I tear my gaze away from Alexei to look at him.

There's this strange expression on his face, a weird mixture of pain and euphoria.

"Shit," Andrew grunts and then he goes stumbling back as he yanks the chunk of metal free from Gabriel's shoulder.

"Fuck yeah," Gabriel nearly roars.

There's a moment of quiet following the roar, and I think we're all rather stunned by Gabriel's reaction.

Then Lucifer begins to chuckle.

"You're a weird fucker," Andrew mutters and shakes his head.

With the chunk of bloody metal still clenched between the pliers, Andrew pulls a plastic baggy out of his medical bag and drops it in.

"That felt fucking good," Gabriel groans and rolls his shoulders. "Like a fucking rotten tooth getting pulled out."

"I'll have to take your word for it," Andrew says as he drops the baggy into his bag and wipes off the pliers.

"Simon is now impatiently informing me that we only have thirteen minutes," Lucifer says.

"Yeah, yeah," Gabriel grumbles, his good mood vanishing. "Tell that fucker we'll be out of here before he can get it up for his wife."

"I'd rather not," Lucifer chuckles.

"It will only take me a couple of minutes to staple Gabriel up," Andrew says and pulls a plastic device and spray bottle from his medical bag.

Gabriel frowns and glances over at Andrew. "Staples? What the fuck? I thought you said you were stitching me up."

"Yeah, well, the wound is bigger than I originally thought, and this will get us out of here quicker," Andrew says with a shrug.

"Fuck, let's just get this over with," Gabriel says with resignation and then he looks down at Alexei with a look of disgust. "Every second that cocksucker gets to take a breath is a second he doesn't deserve."

"Oh, I'm sure he's suffering plenty," Lucifer says with a hint of amusement.

And I find myself saying, "He'll never suffer enough."

The room goes quiet for a moment.

And then the amusement fades from Lucifer's face and he nods his head at me. "Indeed."

Gabriel takes one look at me, at my face, and says, "Fuck this shit, let's get this done."

"You can't stop now, you'll fucking bleed out,"

Andrew protests as Gabriel stands up from the medical bed, holding me in his arms.

"Just slap another fucking maxi pad on it," Gabriel growls as he gently sets me down on my feet.

Cursing and muttering under his breath, Andrew drops the bottle and plastic device in his bag then pulls out a white bandage.

"Here you go," Andrew says as he literally slaps the bandage over Gabriel's wound. "But if you bleed out, it's your own damn fault, you big dumb fuck."

"Fucking noted," Gabriel smirks and then he starts to tug me over to where Alexei is laying.

Tugging on his hand, I look up at him with concern. "Gabriel…"

The thought of him dying because he'd rather help me with this is just too terrible to fathom.

"It's fine, baby," he says, and gives my hand a reassuring squeeze.

I glance over my shoulder at Andrew.

Seeing my worry, Andrew nods. "He won't die. That bandage gives him a couple of hours."

Deciding to trust Andrew, I sigh and turn my attention back to the man that's caused me so much heartache and pain. The man who killed my mother…

The man who forced me to play a part in killing my father.

I start to stumble, nearly tripping and falling, as

flashes of my father's brains hitting the car pulse through my head.

The sound he made as he slid down the side of the car still rings in my ears.

Grip tightening around my hand, Gabriel keeps me upright, but it reminds me too much of when Alexei forced me to pull that trigger.

Even now my fingers throb with the ache.

Lucifer steps out of the way respectfully, and I glance down, taking in the full carnage of what Gabriel did.

For once, Alexei's outside matches his inside. He's so ugly and mangled, so fucked up and broken, I don't even know how he's still breathing.

"How do you want to do this?" Gabriel asks.

Hysterical laughter wants to bubble up in my throat, but I swallow it back down.

"What are my options?" I ask him instead, and to anyone on the outside looking in, it might look like we're casually discussing something, like what to have for dinner, instead of how we should kill this piece of shit.

Gabriel's lips quirk with amusement. "We've got guns and explosives."

I nod my head, figuring as much.

Such a death seems too easy for him, though. At this point, it would simply be a mercy.

There's only one way to go that's fitting for this asshole, I realize.

My throat tries to close up as I ask, "What about fire?"

Gabriel's eyes gleam and that quirk of his lips stretches into a full grin. "We can do fire."

As Gabriel turns to Andrew and starts barking orders for the things we need, I remember the reports I read about my mother's death. My father tried to keep them from me, but I had to know what happened.

According to witnesses, she didn't die immediately. The explosive itself didn't cause her death.

It was the fire.

Good Samaritans heard her screams and attempted to help her, but the car was encased in flames and no one could reach her.

She suffered a terrible, agonizing death.

And Alexei deserves no less.

My need for justice will accept no less.

I can't walk away from this, I can't go on, until I know he's paid a portion of the penance for all the shit he's done.

"Ten minutes," Lucifer says. "And if we're going to be burning him alive, Simon wants us to remove his thumbs first."

"Fuck... what's up with the thumbs, man?" James asks as he strolls into the room with a rifle slung over his shoulder.

"Someone hand me a knife," Gabriel demands.

Lucifer chuckles. "Simon has his reasons."

"Probably wants to stick them up his ass," Gabriel smirks as Andrew walks over with a knife and a big bottle of liquid.

Andrew snaps open the black tactical knife he's holding and hands it over to Gabriel.

Wasting no time, Gabriel drops down and grabs Alexei's hand.

Alexei releases a weak, gurgling groan, but otherwise doesn't put up a fight as Gabriel works at sawing off his thumb.

I scowl down at him, not liking his lack of reaction. I want him to feel what's happening to him, and I want it to fucking hurt.

I want him to experience a moment of my agony.

"Here's one, thumb boy," Gabriel says and tosses the thumb he just sawed off to James.

"Fuck!" James shouts, fumbling to grab the slippery thumb as it hits him square in the chest.

Dropping Alexei's right arm, Gabriel grabs up the left one and gets to work.

Alexei doesn't even release a groan this time, he remains perfectly still.

"Is he dead?" I ask, wondering if I've missed my opportunity to make him pay.

Gabriel pauses halfway through the thumb he's working on to give Alexei a hard slap on the cheek.

When Alexei's eyelids flutter and he moans, Gabriel says, "Nah, but he's fucking close."

Shit.

I'm probably grasping for straws, but I ask regardless. "Is there any way to wake him up? Make him more aware?"

If there's not, we're probably just wasting our time.

Gabriel snaps off Alexei's left thumb and tosses it to James before he looks to Andrew. "You got any of that cocktail stuff Simon mixed up in your bag?"

Andrew tosses the bottle he's holding to Gabriel and grins. "Yeah. I got the recipe off him after seeing what you did with it back at the warehouse."

"Why do I always get stuck with the fucking thumbs?" James grumbles as Andrew walks back over to his bag.

Straightening from his crouch, Gabriel shakes his head at James and then gives the bottle he's holding a squeeze, squirting liquid all over Alexei's body.

I take a few steps back, giving Gabriel room to work.

Once he's completely doused Alexei's body, he makes a trail of liquid leading to the doorway.

Tossing the empty bottle away, Gabriel looks at James. "Why don't you be useful, thumb boy, and find me a light."

James opens his mouth, but Lucifer cuts him off.

Looking to me, his eyes piercing right through me, he says, "There's a zippo in the right pocket.

It takes me a second to figure out why he's telling me that, then I realize it's his suit jacket I'm wearing.

Reaching my hand down into the right pocket, I find the zippo and pull it out.

"Tell me when," Andrew says, walking back over with a syringe.

Gabriel nods to me. "On Meghan's go."

All the guys look to me, and I have no clue what the fuck is about to happen, but I can't put this off any longer.

Lifting my chin and stiffening my spine in preparation, I tell Andrew to, "Do it."

Andrew gives me a quick, sharp nod, then he crouches down and sticks the syringe in the side of Alexei's neck. Pushing in the stopper, he yanks the needle out and stands back up.

As if the drug is a breath of life, Alexei sucks in air and his eyes snap open.

Andrew takes a step back, but I find myself taking a step forward.

And another.

And another.

I walk up to Alexei until I can look him in the eyes.

At first, he doesn't look at me, and isn't aware of me staring at him.

His eyes stare up at the ceiling.

Groaning, he struggles to get up from lying prone, his arms and legs giving out on him until he finally manages to get his body into a kneeling position.

"If he goes after her, put a fucking bullet through his head," Gabriel says.

Hearing Gabriel's voice, Alexei's head lifts. He looks to him, then his gaze finds me.

I stare into the black abyss of his swollen eyes. Stare into the darkness that stole so much from me.

My mother...

My father.

Not only did he steal all the years I would have had with them, he created a rift between my father and I that will never be mended now. There's no hope of reconciliation.

I can't get any of it back. Killing him won't bring them back.

They're lost to me forever.

And it hurts. It hurts so fucking bad I can barely breathe.

Pain slices through my chest, tears push at my eyes, and hatred boils up inside me. A hatred as thick, black, and endless as the emptiness in his fucking gaze.

He's hurt me... he's hurt me more than I can bear, more than I can fucking process right now. Hurt me so bad, he almost broke me.

But I'm not his only victim.

There are countless others out there. Countless

other lives he's ruined and destroyed without care, with pure malice in his heart, and I'm not only doing this for myself.

I'm doing it for them.

Flipping open the lighter, I spin the wheel that lights the wick.

"Meghan, baby..." Gabriel calls out behind me, and I almost ignore him for trying to ruin my moment.

I want...

No, I *need* to watch this motherfucker burn for his sins.

"If you're going to light that fucker on fire now, come back here and do it."

I feel a tug on my sleeve.

"Here, let me escort you," Lucifer says.

As my feet carry me backward, my focus remains locked on Alexei. I keep staring in his eyes, hoping to see... something.

Anything.

It's not until I reach the safety of the doorway that he tries to work his mangled jaw. A garbled word comes out of him. A word that sounds Russian.

A word he used against me.

Then his mouth mangles my name as he reaches a hand out to me. "Meghan."

"You should be safe now," I hear Lucifer say beside me.

And that's all the push I need.

Tossing the zippo forward, I hold my breath as it moves through the air.

When it lands, it catches the trail of liquid that Gabriel left on fire.

A line of flames blazes up to Alexei.

Giving up on standing, he falls to his hands just as the flames reach him.

The heat and pain must not register at first. As the flames climb up him, he begins to crawl forward.

Then he suddenly stops and rears back, screaming.

His agony is a beautiful lullaby, soothing the dark, vengeful monster that's awakened inside me.

I watch, mesmerized, as the flames lick, flicker, and dance across his body.

His suffering, his screams, cleansing me.

His desperate attempts to put the fire out, and failing, filling me with a sick joy.

I hope to god, he's experiencing the worst pain a person can feel right now. I hope it's a taste of what he'll feel in the bowels of hell.

I don't know how long I watch him, my eyes literally burning from the light and smoke, before someone finally speaks.

"Damn, I almost forgot what a burning body smells like," Andrew grumbles.

"Pussy," Gabriel chuckles.

But now that Andrew has mentioned it, I'm starting to smell it too...

Searing the image of Alexei thrashing around, trying to put his flames out, one last time into my brain for those long nights when I'm missing my parents, I turn my back on him.

"Damn, I knew you would do it right," Johnathan grins at Gabriel, walking up to us from the end of the hallway. "I can't wait to tell Beth."

Chest puffing up with pride, Gabriel jerks his chin toward me. "Wasn't me."

Johnathan's eyes cut to me and then fill up with appreciation.

"I don't mean to rush things along," Lucifer says apologetically, "but Simon has just informed me that we're about to go outside our window. Shall we be on our way, gentlemen?"

"You ready to go?" Gabriel asks me, and once again I feel all eyes on me.

Voice raw, I nod my head and say, "Yeah, it's starting to get a little smoky in here."

Gabriel chuckles and wraps his arm around me. I lean into his side as we walk down the hall.

"I can't fucking wait to get home," he says as we step outside, and takes a deep breath of fresh air.

"Don't even think about it, asshole, "Andrew says, coming through the doorway. "You still need to get stapled up."

Gabriel mutters, "Fuck."

Andrew nods his head. "Yeah." Then he looks at

me, staring at my head like it's somehow personally offended him. "That's a nasty looking knot you've got on your forehead…"

I reach up and wince when my fingers find the knot on my forehead.

Gabriel snarls. "Alexei cracked her with a gun."

"Yeah, I can tell," Andrew says. "And I don't like those bruises around your neck…. You'll both need a thorough look over."

Funny, I didn't notice any pain until Andrew pointed out the knot to me, but now I'm aware of nearly every little ache in my body.

I hurt all fucking over.

"We can do it at the compound," Lucifer says, coming up to join us. He smiles at me. "Lily has been worried sick about you, Meghan. And I have it on good authority that Evelyn and Abigail have been baking up a storm, preparing for your return."

His words floor me, and I can only gape at him.

People were worried about me? People besides Gabriel?

"Yeah, Beth will probably want to give you a hug too for taking care of that bastard," Johnathan says. "If you're up for it."

Looking at the faces of the men surrounding me, it suddenly hits me. Almost every one of them has a wife and kids waiting on them.

And they put themselves in danger. They risked their lives to save me.

Choking up, I push out a smile for Johnathan and try not to burst into tears as I tell him, "I think I'm up for it."

"Excellent," Lucifer says and then motions to a dark car. "You can ride with Michael and me."

Tucking me back into his side, Gabriel leads me over to the car.

Voice dropping down to nearly a whisper, he frowns and asks, "You okay?"

No, I'm not quite okay with everything that just happened. It will take some time to process and deal with it all.

But looking up at him, at the man I love, at the man who saved me, I know, "I will be."

Because despite all the shit that I've gone through. Despite everything I've lost...

I've gained Gabriel and a family that cares about me.

And I fucking love them.

EPILOGUE

Gabriel

Pulling up to Lucifer's warehouse, I'm ready to start figuring out what the fuck Alexei was doing with his old man.

We've got a lot of questions for the old fucking pile of shit, but we might not get any answers. We have no clue what shape he was in when he went into the coma, he could have fucking Alzheimer's for all we know.

Only Simon's car is out front, so that means the body hasn't arrived yet.

Andrew and a trusted medical friend of the family were charged with waking the old fucker up from his coma and assessing if he's even worth talking to. That started yesterday, and there were good signs that we'll be able to get something out of him, but how much is the question.

Like Lucifer said, he could have a mushy fucking brain and we don't get shit.

"Where the fuck is everyone?" I ask Simon as I walk into the backroom of the warehouse.

Fucking place looks a bit different than normal, filled with all the medical equipment that's been brought in for this shit show.

"Lucifer is on his way now. Johnathan and Andrew are bringing the man here. He's still under a light sedation in case he gets volatile during the transport," Simon says as he waves his hand toward the medical equipment. "James is off on whatever the hell Lucifer gave him permission for, and Thad is on his way home."

"What about Jude?" I ask as I start to remove my phone, wallet, and keys from my pockets.

Looking up from the laptop he's typing shit out on, Simon says, "Flying to Ukraine. He's going to be visiting an old friend of ours to see if he can find out more about Alexei's father."

"Sounds good," I say as I drop all my shit on a cleared desk.

When we got home last night, Meghan worried like a mother hen over my shoulder. She was worried that Andrew didn't really know what he was doing, and it took a lot of explaining to get her to understand that I was fine.

I had to grit my fucking teeth when he did a quick exam of her body. Thankfully they both agreed that she didn't need to be inspected like Alexei's doctor inspected her. With all my heart, I wish I was the fucking one who killed that motherfucker.

Fucking Armenian bastard.

I'm surprised how easily we both fell asleep last night, though. No sex, of course. I wasn't willing to risk hurting her on top of what she's already been through.

I did tell her though that she needs to find out which doctors the wives use for themselves and their kids. We need to get shit in order. No reason not to make sure she is completely taken care of.

Fuck, no sex last night is fucking killing me right now. Even if there's a chance I might have already knocked her up, I want to pound her ass so fucking hard there's no way she's not pregnant.

Those sexy fucking hips of hers are going to look so good when she's walking around with my kid inside her. Fuck, there might even be two, given that the chances of a twin having twins is higher than normal.

"What the hell are you doing?" Simon grits out at me as I pull my gun off my hip.

"How long till they all get here?" I ask.

"Twenty minutes," he says, and then realization flares across his face as he figures out what I'm up to.

"Twenty should be enough time, right?" I ask as I watch him stand up from the laptop.

"Yes, just enough." Simon grins at me with that little twinkle of violence in his eye.

Yeah, this motherfucker's been wanting to do this as much as I have.

"Meghan thinks I knocked her up," I say with a laugh, and deep down inside I'm pretty damn sure I did.

I've fucked the hell out of her since I've met her. Fucked her hard enough and long enough that there's no doubt in my mind that she isn't.

"Is that so?" Simon asks as he removes his suit jacket and then begins to quickly remove his tie.

"Yeah, she's got the idea in her head that if she's knocked up, then that means you'll be an uncle. She wants to get to know you and your wife," I say while I yank my shirt up and over my head.

I wince slightly because of the wound on my shoulder. I keep forgetting I need to be more careful with how I move for now.

"I'm going to be an uncle?" Simon asks, and for the first time in a long time I see something I didn't think was still there inside of him.

He's got a smile on his face.

"Sure, just like you're going to be a father."

"That's not too surprising given our family has a very healthy reproductive ability." He chuckles.

"Although, that also means Coss will be a grandfather."

Both of us still at that thought.

"Will Lucifer give us the go ahead to kill him?" I ask.

"I don't honestly know," Simon responds.

"It's easier to beg for forgiveness than ask for permission," I say without a hint of remorse in my voice.

"How very true," Simon says before he continues to remove his dress shirt, followed by his undershirt.

"It needs to be done before your wife gives birth," I say while I start to get the blood pumping through my body.

"Agreed," Simon says before dropping his shirt onto his suit jacket.

Following behind me, Simon and I make our way over to a clear area of the warehouse.

"Same rules as always," Simon states.

"Of course."

No nut shots, no eye gouges, and no throat jabs.

Everything else is legal.

Simon's not slow about starting it.

Ducking down to avoid a high arching kick he aims at my temple, I rush in to strike at his chin. As his head snaps to the side, the best feeling I've had since fucking Meghan floods through me.

Both of us pull back from the first flurry, warily eyeing each other.

"I want to fucking kill the old man for everything he's ever done to us, but I'll say this... He did teach us how to fight." I grin before I rush in again to swing a massive haymaker at his face.

Ducking quickly under my arm, Simon slams his fist into my ribs and gives me a good taste of the medicine I just gave him.

Wrapping my arms around his torso, I try to wrangle him in while I slam my foot on the top of his foot.

Need to slow his ass down so I can hurt him some more. He's always had speed on me, but I've always had brute strength.

Squeezing my arms tight, I can see the pain I'm causing him from those still cracked ribs. He probably should have waited to fight me... But fuck it. We both need this shit to happen.

Slamming his head into my nose, I momentarily see stars and drop him back down.

"Yes, he did do that." Simon snickers.

Taking a couple steps back, I reach up and wipe away the blood that drips down from my nose. He didn't break it, but there's some busted capillaries up there.

Fuck, it feels good to be fighting this prick again.

It's been too fucking long since we've gone a couple of rounds.

It's not exactly like I hate the man who stands across from me. But I can't love him, either. We've been through too much, seen too much to ever be able to come to terms with who and what we've become.

Coss made sure of that, knowingly and willingly. The death of my twin fucked him up too, I guess. Coss got twisted up in a bad mental way, Simon became the germaphobe neat freak, and I became the black sheep. Mom... Well, mom drank herself to death, so fuck her and the gun she used to finally end her suffering.

Fucking stupid waste.

Slowly wading into closer range, I snap my fist out twice before I kick hard at the side of his knee.

Taking the blow to his knee, Simon delivers a quick uppercut to my chin that knocks my head back.

Pulling away again, I shake my head to clear it.

The fucker starts limping toward me and I grin at him. "Missed you too, big brother."

"WELL..." Lucifer grins at both Simon and I as we sit on a desk beside each other, addressing our bloodied noses.

"We had to talk some shit out," I say as I remove my shirt from the desk and pull it over my head.

"Yes. Gabriel and I decided to go over the finer points of the conversation we'll be having with Mr. Rastov when he arrives," Simon says as he begins to retie his tie. "He should be arriving at any moment."

Sliding off the desk, Simon nods his head in my direction.

Nodding back to him, I know he understands this was only round one.

"Meghan doing okay with Lily?" I ask Lucifer.

"Oh, they're happily house shopping as we speak." Lucifer grins at me and I know that he knows what kind of a fucking punch in the face that is for me.

Fuck.

House shopping...

Meghan's going to try to domesticate me.

Fuck.

Before I can think of a way to keep it from happening, I hear voices coming from the entrance of the warehouse.

I stand up from the desk as Andrew pushes a gurney past us and into the opening we've created for this special moment.

Almost as one, we all walk over and surround the bed.

Lucifer looks down smugly at the drowsy man.

Andrew pulls a needle from his black medical bag and looks over to Lucifer. "Ready to get this shit started?"

"Of course." Lucifer grins.

Shaking his head with a chuckle, Andrew pushes the needle into the IV that's connected to the old man's hand.

"He should come to pretty quickly. I'm using one of Simon's wakeup cocktails. Not good for the heart, but it's not like that matters much," Andrew says.

Watching as the old man slowly begins to blink his eyes, we all wait for that moment of lucidness that will let us know if he's here with us or not.

The old man's eyes suddenly widen as he takes in everyone around him. He must realize we sure as shit are not the ones he was expecting.

Lucifer offers him a sly grin. "It's so good of you to join us, Andrey. We've been waiting a long time to speak with you..."

The End

PLAYLISTS

Gabriel's Playlist

Available on Spotify - https://spoti.fi/2VAtci5

Brand New Numb - Motionless In White
Through Hell - Palisades
Cry Little Sister - Marilyn Manson
EXXXIT - 3TEETH
The Hand That Feeds - Nine Inch Nails
Time Again - Combichrist
THE GUILTY PARTY - While She Sleeps
Doomsday - Architects
King of Diamonds - Upon A Burning Body
Soft - Motionless In White

Meghan's Playlist

Available on Spotify - https://spoti.fi/2Hp5ouS

Land of Confusion - Epic Trailer Version - Hidden
Citizens

Sweet Dreams (Are Made of This) - Emily Browning

Luci - ZAND

Survivor - 2WEI

I Take What I Want - Unions

Jungle - X Ambassadors

Personal Jesus (feat. Coleen McMahon) - J2

Slipping - Hidden Citizens

New Religion - Migrant Motel

Dissolved Girl - Massive Attack

Bad Moon Rising (feat. Candace Devine) - Palestra

Dark Nights - Dorothy

Stand By Me (VIP Remix) - Ki:Theory

Roots - In This Moment

SEAN'S ACKNOWLEDGEMENTS

First, a huge thank you to the Toledo Police Department for your help with research for this book. LPRs are fascinating!

I also have to give a huge thank you to Angi Clingan for offering her medical expertise. Anything medically wrong is all my fault!

~ Sean

IZZY'S ACKNOWLEDGEMENTS

Miranda, you are my heart and soul. You know it. In another life, we're totally married and I had your babies.

I seriously don't know what I would do without you. You were there with me every step of the way. It's hard being a 'tortured writer', and I feel a little guilty for putting you through it, but kind of not.

We got this awesome book out of it.

Nic, thank you so much for your help with this book, and for being the first person to ever read it. Your input, encouragement, and help mean the world to me. I tend to really freak out when we're getting close to publishing, as you've seen, and having you there is a huge relief. Such a huge relief, I think you'll have to Beta read everything I write from now on!

~ Izzy

STALK US

Seriously, stalk us and be our Simon.

Join our Facebook reader group where we talk about our books, give exclusive sneak peeks, offer random fan appreciation giveaways, access to ARCs, and live chats where you can ask us anything.

Facebook reader group: Izzy's Sweeties and Sean's Side Chicks:
https://www.facebook.com/groups/IzzysSweeties

Our Instagram:
https://www.instagram.com/seanandizzy/

Never miss our next release.
Follow us on Facebook:
https://www.facebook.com/authorizzysweet/
https://www.facebook.com/authorseanmoriarty/

Follow us on Amazon: amazon.com/author/izzysweet
amazon.com/author/seanmoriarty

Follow us on Bookbub:
https://www.bookbub.com/authors/izzy-sweet

Join our no-spam mailing list. No spam ever, promise.
Only get emailed when we have a new release or sale:
https://dl.bookfunnel.com/bbfg23ehl8

Check out our website: www.dirtynothings.com

ABOUT US

Izzy Sweet & Sara Page – The one and same brain.

Sean Moriarty — The real life alpha bad boy that Izzy tamed.

Residing in Cincinnati, Ohio, Izzy and Sean are high school sweethearts that just celebrated their 11th wedding anniversary, though they've been together since they were teenagers – over fifteen years.

Both avid and voracious readers, they share a great love and appreciation for a great story, and attribute their early role-playing days as the fledgling beginnings of their joint writing career.

You can see more of our works at our website - www.dirtynothings.com

Gettin' Dirty

Star Joined Series

Craving Maul

Taming Ryock

By Izzy Sweet

Letting Him In

Stepbrother Catfish

PREVIEW: KEEPING LILY (DISCIPLES 1)

My husband traded me away to save his own life...

And now I belong to the devil.

One night and everything in my life changed. Two words and my world turned dark.

"Take her."

Owing the most ruthless crime lord in Garden City five million dollars, my husband chose to trade me and my children away to save himself.

I was on the cusp of freedom, so close to divorcing that scumbag I was married to.

Now I'm enslaved to a man who is obsessed with me. A man so wicked and beautiful they call him Lucifer.

So alluring, he makes the angels weep with envy. He's so powerful, I can't stop myself from bending to his will.

He's determined to master me, and he won't rest until I give him all.

He wants my light, and he wants my dark.

He wants my body, and he wants my heart.

But most of all, he wants the one thing I can't give him. The one thing I can't bear to part with...

My soul.

Chapter One

Lucifer

"Motherfucker!" Comes out of my mouth in a growl as I shake my hand.

The punch to this piece of shit's jaw sent tingling sensations up my arm.

Mickey Dalton sputters gibberish out of his busted lips. "I... I... Swear I will pay... just gotta..."

I'm tempted to keep this up, but fuck it. I have bigger fish to fry than this small time fucking gambler.

Looking over the man's shoulder, I nod to Andrew. "Ensure he fully understands how much he owes. Remove his pinky."

"Yes, sir." Andrew nods.

"Wha... No!" Mickey shouts as Andrew heads to the table where he keeps a black bag stowed.

Turning around, I look at Simon, my right-hand man. "Where are we at with the other three files?"

"Two have been collected on, the last I was waiting on your judgment."

"Marshall Dawson."

"He has flat out refused to cooperate with any of our attempts to collect. He believes his status is untouchable. He will give us no answer on where he was or what has happened to our money."

"Is he finally home?" I ask.

"Arrived earlier tonight."

A metallic snip rings out into the room followed by a high-pitched scream. I turn to see Andrew wiping the blood on the guy's t-shirt.

Andrew raises his voice only slightly as he grabs the man by the throat. "Stop fucking squealing, asshole. Lucifer doesn't like hearing pigs fucking about."

Walking out through the door and into the hall, I look to Simon. "How are the spreadsheets with Bart coming along?"

"Clean, with everything accounted for..."

"Yet, you still have doubts?" I ask him as we walk.

"I do. I just can't explain why."

"Keep an eye on him then."

Simon holds an umbrella over my head as we walk out of the abandoned hotel. The shattered glass door slams shut behind us as he ushers me into the sleek black Mercedes SUV.

Getting comfortable in the backseat, I reach over and pull the file left on the other seat for me. The name Marshall Dawson is neatly typed on the tab.

I let out a quiet sigh to myself. I knew this one was going to come back as a thorn in my side.

Marshall Dawson is a waste of breathable air. The man used the connections he had with my father and another city boss to secure a loan from us. Five million in *cash*.

Five fucking million dollars with nothing to show for it.

Five fucking million dollars down the drain.

I took this on as a favor to Sean O'Riley. A favor to a now dead and buried man.

Shit like that doesn't sit well with me. But when I went to the top to seek retribution, I was stonewalled. I was told the man who killed Sean, and all the surrounding issues, have been dealt with.

Fuck that. I want my pound of flesh.

Shaking my head, I open the file. It's no use going down that train of thought right now. I can pursue it another time if I need to.

I slowly flip through the pages we have on Marshall.

It's funny how we can put a file together on a person where he is reduced to twenty or so pages. I can see every payment he has made on his mortgage to how many times he has been in the overdraft with his bank.

I look at his legal outstanding debts, and I look at the five-million-dollar debt he now owes to me personally. Anger is slowly creeping through my veins.

Flipping through the pages, I look at his family life. Since he borrowed the money I have had one of my men keeping close tabs on his family. He is married to Lilith Merriweather, aged twenty-seven, and has two children, a boy and a girl. Both children under the age of seven.

I look at the picture of Marshall for a long time as we drive through the late-night rain. The man is closer to my father's age than mine. How did he marry a woman so young? Money and his slimy charm must have played a large part of it.

I look through the pictures of his family quickly. The children are pretty in a child way. Blonde hair and blue eyes, they must take after their mother. Marshall must have married way out of his league.

My fingers stop as the picture of his wife comes up. Emerald green eyes, sensuous pink lips, high cheekbones, pale flawless skin and long blonde hair. All of those parts on their own would make her remarkable. Even if her face was overall plain just one of her features would stun a person. But together they make something otherworldly.

She is beauty incarnate.

Fingers tracing the lines of her lips, I frown. How the hell did that man marry a woman like this? I flip further through the pictures of her. There aren't many, but what I do see shows me that she is unlike any other woman I have ever laid eyes on.

She is perfection.

There is a rather candid photo of her putting groceries in the back of her red Volvo station wagon. Her hair is all over the place. Her slender legs are encased in yoga pants, feet in Uggs. Her daughter looks like she is giving her problems as she tries to watch her and still put groceries in the back.

Even this... domesticity calls to me.

There is a glamour shot of some type mixed in and

I can see just how haunting those eyes are. They are calling to me, pulling me in to get forever lost. I can feel my hands curling into themselves. She is pulling me from where I sit in the SUV.

"Take me to Marshall's, James," I say to my driver.

Looking back at me from the front seat, Simon says, "Now? You don't want to wait until tomorrow?"

"No. We're going there *now*."

The car makes a few turns as we pull off the freeway and then back on again.

My eyes drift out the window for a moment to look at the rain that has been pelting down on the city all week.

Looking back to the picture, though, I see something I haven't seen before—a light. Inside I feel an ember flaring to life.

My muscles are going taut with expectation.

I need to see this woman; I need to see if what the pictures show me is true.

Lily

MY HUSBAND, MARSHALL, is sleeping beside me, snoring loudly, and I have the strongest urge to smack him.

I want to scream in his pale, pudgy face. I want to tell him to wake the fuck up. I want to ask him why he's back in my bed.

But I just lay beside him and stare up at the ceiling instead.

It's time to accept reality.

Our marriage is done.

Dead.

Today was the final nail in the coffin.

First thing in the morning, after I get the kids off to school, I'm going to meet with a divorce attorney. I can't go on like this. This is no way to live, this is just...existing.

And I'm sick of it.

After growing up dirt poor, I married Marshall thinking I would finally have financial security. I would always have a roof over my head. I would never go hungry again.

Foolishly, I believed his lust for me would turn to love. That like an arranged marriage, our feelings for each other would grow after time. If we had children, we could make a real go of it.

But this, the lack of love, the lack of care, isn't worth it. I rather starve than stay in this loveless marriage.

Marshall has been gone for weeks, *traveling on business*. He's gone more than he's home. Ever since our first child, Adam, was born six years ago, he's been finding more and more reasons to leave us.

There's always some client on the other coast that needs his help. Or some corporation up north that has to have his expertise or they're going to lose millions on... something...

It's funny, even after almost eight years of marriage I still don't know exactly what his job title or true profession is. Whenever I ask him about it he just brushes me off, doesn't have time to explain it, or says I wouldn't understand.

Like I'm some kind of idiot.

If I was an idiot I wouldn't know about all the women he's been hooking up with. I know that's one of the reasons he's always leaving us. He has a girlfriend in every city.

Yet, he won't even touch me when I throw myself at him.

I sigh, looking down at the red nightie I bought from Victoria's Secret and pull the blanket up to cover my breasts.

He won't even touch me when I've taken great pains to dress up for him.

Suddenly my eyes feel swollen and my nose stings. I have to blink back my tears and take a deep breath. Rolling my eyes back up, I focus on the ceiling.

This shouldn't hurt, dammit. This isn't a bad thing, this is good.

This is... *freedom*.

I no longer have to pretend this is a real marriage. No more keeping up appearances on Facebook. No more making excuses for him with my family and friends.

No more trying to explain to the children that daddy is sorry but he had to miss their birthday —again.

This is a fresh start, a new beginning.

I've been doing everything on my own for years now. Losing him won't make much of a difference.

Marshall suddenly grunts loudly and rolls over.

The air turns sour and I resist the urge to gag.

Gah, he is such a pig.

Chapter Two

Lily

I'm not sure what wakes me up. It could have been the light turning on.

Marshall's loud, "What the fuck?"

Or the soft, menacing voice that says, "Hello, Marshall. I'm not interrupting anything, am I?"

Even under my warm blanket, that voice sends a chill down my spine and I peel my eyes open, shivering.

At first, the light is too harsh on my eyes and I have to blink several times before the strange man standing in our bedroom comes into focus.

This must be a dream, I convince myself and squeeze my eyes shut. I open them again but I still just can't believe it.

There's no way that man is real.

Standing in the center of my bedroom, the man is illuminated by a halo of light coming from the lamp. The light seems to love him, clinging to him. He's glowing and so alluring, he looks almost angelic.

"What the fuck are you doing in my house? You can't just come walking in here..." Marshall sputters. His fat fists grab the blanket, yanking it away from me as he pulls it up his hairy chest.

I gasp as the cool air hits my breasts and the sound draws the attention of the angelic stranger. He turns his icy blue gaze on me and I'm utterly stunned as our eyes meet.

With just a look I feel held by him.

Trapped.

Frozen.

Helpless.

He's so beautiful it *hurts* to look upon him. The kind of beauty that's so strong, so deeply felt, it's like experiencing a piece of music that *moves* you and staring into the sun at the same time.

Tears prick my eyes and my skin tingles as I break out in gooseflesh.

His face is a composition of features so perfect that

now that I've glimpsed them I fear all other men will be forever compared to him.

Chiseled cheeks, full, pink lips. A strong jaw and straight nose. Blonde hair so pale it's nearly snow white and brushed back from his forehead.

It feels like an eternity passes as we stare at each other across my bedroom and then his eyes break away only to slide down, warming as they lock on the pale swells of my breasts.

A flush creeps up my chest. I'm not naked but in this little lacy nightie, I feel like I am.

I grab the blanket and Marshall cries out as I yank it back. He shoots me a dirty look but I give him my coldest glare and practically dare him to try and take it back.

Screw him, no one cares about his hairy man-chest.

The stranger watches our little tug of war, his lips curving with a hint of amusement.

Marshall finally gives up on trying to wrestle the blanket away from me and decides to steal my pillow instead. Covering his chest with my pillow, he hugs it tightly and puffs up as he says, "If you leave now, Lucifer, I'll forget this incident ever happened."

Lucifer? Is that the stranger's name? How strange and morbid. Yet, I swear I've heard that name before, on the news or in the paper...

The stranger's eyes flash and the amusement disappears from his lips. Two dark shadows shimmer behind him and I swallow back a gasp as I realize those two shadows are two other men.

What the hell is going on? Who are these men and why are they in my bedroom? I turn to Marshall and watch him squirm uneasily.

What did Marshall do?

"You'll forget this ever happened?" Lucifer says coolly and his eyes narrow with menace. "Just like you forgot to pay me back the five million dollars you owe me?"

All the color drains instantly from Marshall's face and his eyes dart from side to side as if he's trying to figure out an escape plan. "I already paid that back. You'll have to talk to Sean if you want your money."

"Sean's dead."

I watch Marshall's mouth open then close, then open again. He sputters and gasps like a fish out of water, his face starting to turn blue from the lack of oxygen.

I can't believe Marshall borrowed five million dollars. What would he need with so much money? I know I haven't seen a penny of it.

"I paid Sean the money," Marshall finally gets out, and then rushes on to say, "I don't have five million to pay you..."

Lucifer takes a step towards our bed. "That's too bad."

"Wait!" Marshall cries out in panic, the grip of his

fingers tearing at the pillow he holds to his chest. "Maybe we can work something out? I could—"

"I've had a look at your assets. You have no means to pay me back," Lucifer says dismissively and takes another step toward the bed.

I look between Lucifer and Marshall and now I'm starting to feel panicked. Lucifer has only taken two steps towards our bed but there's clear menace in the way he's moving.

What is he going to do? Are they going to hurt Marshall?

Are they going to hurt me?

Lucifer takes another step and Marshall whimpers. He *whimpers.*

The sound has my hackles rising and I wonder if there's something I could do. I glance towards my phone on my nightstand. The moment I don't think they're looking at me I'm going to make a grab for it.

But it might be too late for Marshall by then...

I could start screaming, but the only good that will probably do is wake the children.

Marshall is pushing back against the headboard like he believes he could escape through the wall if he tries hard enough. Then he shoots a pleading look towards me.

As if I could help him...

Marshall's eyes widen suddenly as if he's had a revelation.

"You want my life as payment?" he squeaks out.

Lucifer lifts an eyebrow and inclines his head. "Yes. That's how these things usually go, isn't it?"

Marshall licks his lips nervously, looks to me then back to Lucifer. "Would you accept another life as payment?"

He's not about to say what I think he is, is he? No, he wouldn't. No decent human being...

Lucifer's upper lip curls with disdain but his voice sounds interested. "What are you proposing?"

Marshall is too cowardly to stop hugging his pillow so he nods his head to me instead. "Take her. Take my wife in my place."

I'm so shocked, so floored, I suck in a sharp breath that never ends.

"You want me to kill your wife?" Lucifer asks and it feels like all the warmth was just sucked out of the room.

"No, of course not..." Marshall recoils at the murderous look on Lucifer's face. "Just hold her as a deposit, an insurance, while I get you the five million."

"You mean a ransom?" Lucifer clarifies.

Marshall nods his head up and down. "Yes, yes, that's it. A ransom."

My lungs full of air, I expel it all in a loud, "How could you!" and make a lunge for Marshall.

I'm not an object he owns. He can't just trade me

away to some creepy, beautiful stranger to save his own neck.

Marshall squeaks and scrambles away from me. I end up chasing him until he falls out of bed, landing on his ass.

I grip the edge of the mattress, panting with anger as I watch him scuttle backward until he bumps into Lucifer's legs.

"As much as I would love to accept your offer," Lucifer says as he pushes Marshall away with the toe of his shoe. "I'm afraid your wife is not worth the five million you owe me."

Damn. I blink up at Lucifer, feeling utterly conflicted. On one hand, I don't want to be given away, but on the other, it stings the ego a bit to hear I'm not worth five million dollars.

I snort though as Marshall goes to his hands and knees, kneeling in front of Lucifer to beg for mercy.

"Please," Marshall begs, reaching out and grabbing Lucifer's leg.

I'd pity him and try to help the poor bastard if he didn't just try to trade me away in his place.

"There has to be something else I can give you..." Marshall sobs.

Lucifer makes a face of disgust and looks down at Marshall like he's a bug he'd like to step on.

"Anything," Marshall wails as Lucifer kicks at him. "Anything."

I sit back on my heels and watch Marshall beg while taking the kick, wondering how all of this happened.

Lucifer's head lifts and his eyes lock on me. His features are still, utterly calm, but there's something dark stirring in the depths of his icy irises.

"Anything?" Lucifer queries.

"Yes, anything!" Marshall nods his head with sudden enthusiasm.

"I'll accept your offer," Lucifer grins at me. "If you give her to me permanently, and throw in your children."

"No, no! You can't!" I scream and I'm off the bed in an instant.

Marshall yelps and scuttles back until he's hiding behind Lucifer's legs.

Lucifer between us, blocking me, my hands clench into fists and I pant, trying to control the rush of rage that has flooded my head. I swear if Marshall offers this... this... inhuman monster my children, I'll strangle him with my bare hands.

Lucifer smirks down at me as if he finds all of this amusing. I bristle under that smirk but suddenly feel self-conscious standing so close to him. He's tall, with at least a foot on me, and I feel puny now standing in front of him.

"Well? Do we have a deal, Marshall?"

Marshall continues to use Lucifer as a shield like

the coward he is. He pokes his head out only long enough to peek at me. "Yes!"

"No!" I screech and lunge forward, reaching around Lucifer to grab Marshall.

Marshall squeaks and stumbles backward, just out of my reach.

Lucifer grabs me by the arms, stopping my forward lunge and hauls me back. Chuckling, he pins my arms to my sides and I screech and struggle, trying to escape his grasp.

"We're done here, Marshall. I suggest you leave now before I change my mind..."

"Leave? Why do I have to leave? This is my house!" Marshall protests.

Head tipping back, I glare up at Lucifer and continue to struggle. Damn, he's stronger than he looks, though it is hard to tell just how built he is under that suit he's wearing.

Once again Lucifer looks me directly in the eyes, staring into me as if he can *see* inside me. "Not tonight."

"But... but..." Marshall starts to sputter.

Lucifer's face hardens, his features as cold and harsh as the blizzard swirling in his irises. "Simon, remove him."

"No. No! I'll go!" Marshall says, panicked, and though I can't see what's going on due to the huge body blocking my view, I can hear a great deal of shuffling going on behind Lucifer.

Marshall grunts loudly and then there's a thump. "Hey! I'm going, I'm going!"

The bedroom door opens and then slams shut.

I jerk in Lucifer's arms in surprise but then feel all the fight go out of me. No matter how much I squirm, no matter how much I try to free myself from his grasp, I can't escape him. If anything, I feel like all my struggles have only tightened the grip he has on me.

Head dropping forward, I quiet my panting so I can listen to Marshall stomping and continue to throw a tantrum about being removed from his own home.

After a minute, Lucifer sighs and I feel his grip loosen a little. "James, assist Simon. If Marshall wakes the children, feel free to make him regret it."

"Yes, boss," the second shadow answers and I don't even hear him as he walks out. I only know he's gone by the sound of the closing door.

A moment later there's some muffled arguing coming from the hallway then all goes quiet.

The seconds tick by. My panting slows as I catch my breath.

All at once I am suddenly aware that I'm alone with this strange man.

The air thickens.

Slowly, I lift my head and peer up at him. He's looking down at me so intensely I gasp.

My gasp seems to amuse him, and a slow smile spreads across his lips.

I stare at him in disbelief, my mind racing a mile a minute, trying to process everything that just happened. My mouth feels dry and my stomach is twisted. I want to believe this is a nightmare, that I'm still sleeping in my bed.

My husband didn't just trade me and our children away to save his own neck. He couldn't... He wouldn't...

Yet the fingers tightening around my arms remind me that he did.

I can't let this happen. I can't accept this. I have to protect my children. He cannot have them! I won't let him hurt them.

Gathering up every ounce of courage I have inside me, I lift my chin and say, "You can't have us. We're not objects you can own or trade away at whim. I am a *person*, a person with rights, and I will not stand for this!"

Lucifer's eyes twinkle at me and it's so condescending I just want to spit in his face.

My anger only seems to amuse him even more. Head tipping back, he chuckles with mirth and just as I start to struggle again, he lifts me up.

It only takes him two long strides and then he throws me.

I go flying through the air and land on my bed with a grunt.

He's not far behind me, and quickly I get to my hands and knees, scooting back as he approaches.

Long, strong fingers going to the bottom of his suit jacket, he begins to unbutton it as he asks me, "Who's going to stop me?"

Buy on Amazon: Keeping Lily (Disciples 1)

Printed in the USA
CPSIA information can be obtained
at www.ICGtesting.com
LVHW051035280324
775740LV00017B/111